# THE AVENGER

There was nothing, no one, left between Mama and Sissy and the raider pack. "Mama, Mama!" Sissy cried.

As she called out, the raiders heard another voice. It carried to them shrill and high, the single outraged word, "No!" And they hesitated.

Bubba stood dark against the outer light, daubed on the worn threshold of the door like some small avenging angel of death.

In the boy's hand was a gun.

A very large old gun.

It was The Redeemer...

Avon Books are available at special quantity discounts for bulk
purchases for sales promotions, premiums, fund raising or educa-
tional use. Special books, or book excerpts, can also be created to
fit specific needs.

For details write or telephone the office of the Director of Special
Markets, Avon Books, Dept. FP, 105 Madison Avenue, New
York, New York 10016, 212-481-5653.

# WILL HENRY

## SUMMER OF THE GUN

AVON BOOKS ◈ NEW YORK

FOR VALERIE
*dearest daughter*
*ever true friend*

AVON BOOKS
A division of
The Hearst Corporation
105 Madison Avenue
New York, New York 10016

Copyright © 1978 by Will Henry
Published by arrangement with the author
Library of Congress Catalog Card Number: 88-91527
ISBN: 0-380-70594-X

First Avon Books Printing: September 1988

AVON TRADEMARK REG. U.S. PAT. OFF. AND IN OTHER COUNTRIES, MARCA
REGISTRADA, HECHO EN U.S.A.

Printed in the U.S.A.

K-R 10 9 8 7 6 5 4 3 2 1

## Author's Note

This account is based upon a frontier legend. The legend of a fabled 1847 Walker Colt revolver. An ancient, rusted, giant relic of a gun. A vast, four-pound, fifteen-inch, .44-calibre, six-shot behemoth of a Texas Ranger fighting pistol called THE REDEEMER.

# PROLOGUE

•

There are no more of their kind left alive. All of them are long ago under the buffalo grass. They sleep out yonder where the night wind sings sweet-lonesome through the prairie draw, and the coyote cries them down his last good-byes from the rimrock above the creek. They left a story, though, before their string was run, this Texas family that would not quit. That would not give in. That would not, ever, say the word *surrender*.

The war tried to kill them off.

The Comanche had a crack at it.

The town did its best to humble and break them apart.

The dust, the drouth, the blizzard, the twister, the rustler, the sodbuster, the banker—all worked what hell they might to see them beaten and brought down.

They stood their ground and held it.

Even the law reached out its left hand instead of its right to help them when they needed help, the way it did for poor folks mostly.

It was no different: the family would not fall.

The strength drew from the father, who taught them that if folks were not free they were not anything. That was why he brought them to live out in the buffalo grass, the Comanche country. It was the only place where people would not be pushing at them all the while to be like they were. People did not like it when other folks were different from themselves, the father warned. And he was surely right. The kindest thing they ever heard said of themselves in the settlements was that the McCalisters were crazy.

Maybe they were, a little bit. It was true they ran wild

1

out on the Paint Creek homeplace. But their father always told them they could not be tame and stay free.

Their mother finally understood this by the time the Comanche killed their father. It was why she herself would not then give up and go into the town to live, and why she told the children they were going to stay out there and make their father's dream for them come true: that they would be their own people, truckling to no one, yet not trampling on anyone, either.

It worked for the family through the years of bad grass and good until the fearful day the raiders came.

These dread guerrillas were the scum of Confederate deserters washed west from the war, then in its fiercest hour. They drove across Texas seeking the sanctuary of the New Mexico and Arizona territories. The more desperate of them struck even beyond for the promised land of California. In any of these havens it was understood their past crimes would not pursue them. They had but to get out of Texas and hit for the territories, riding hard on sound horses. After that, no ranger's rifleball or sheriff's hanging rope would likely reach to bring them back.

Texans still do not like to remember the sins of these Confederate renegades. Yet nothing can turn on a man meaner than his own dog. And there is no enemy a man will ever face as dangerous as his brothers from a lost cause. Or a cause they know is in the losing and which they want frantically to get from beneath before it falls upon them.

Such were the soldiers of ominous cavalry who came riding to the McCalister homeplace on Paint Creek, out in the Comanche buffalo pasture, that long-ago summer of 1863.

The Summer of the Gun.

# 1

The McCalister place was west of nowhere, Junior thought.

It was the last one "out" of the white ranches in West Texas. It was, by horseback reckoning, twenty-nine miles out in what was called the "Comanche grass."

The nearest settlement was a day's pony ride east. By wagon, it was a jolting nine-mile trek over broken prairie just to reach the Overland Mail Road that led to Red Hawk. This was the north branch of that famous old road, the route Captain Marcy had pioneered for the California gold rushers in '49. It ran from Emigrant Crossing of the Pecos to Fort Belknap and the Brazos. By Junior's time, it had fallen into poor repair and evil reputation, but you used it if you wanted to reach the town of Red Hawk. Which town, after it *was* reached, had always seemed to sixteen-year-old Junior McCalister hardly worth the struggle to get there. But that was before today.

Today changed everything for him and brother Lon.

It might just be the greatest day any two young Texans ever spent in Red Hawk. Not only had the stage from Fort Belknap brought their Chicago mail-order present for mama's anniversary but also the most exciting copy of the Fort Worth newspapers ever to reach Red Hawk.

Oh, those grand black headlines!

## THE WAR IS ON!
## CONFEDERATES FIRE ON SUMTER!
## UNION COMMANDER SURRENDERS!

Then, in the littler print but still mighty stirring:

3

Well, if the newspapers said a thing, you had to believe it. Newspapers never lied. You could bet that war was on, all right. The only worry was that it would last long enough for the Texas brave boys to get there in time to fight for what was right and noble.

Junior McCalister cut loose at lung-top when he saw the Forth Worth papers. Brother Lon turned dead serious and allowed in his quiet manner that he would be ready when it came to the fighting part. But, foremostly, he reminded Junior, they had to get the wagon loaded up and the wheels squealing for Paint Creek. Mama would surely want to wear her present on her anniversary next day. "We dassn't delay our start," the older brother insisted. "A present ain't no good a day late."

That's what Lon said, and Lon had been the one to say for the McCalisters for the last three years, ever since papa had not come home from chasing the Yamparika chief, Tabebekat—Sun Killer—the spring of '58.

Junior did not debate it but all the same let out a second war whoop and commenced tossing the cornmeal and bean sacks from the general store's boardwalk up into the McCalister wagon like they weighed ten pounds rather than a hundred. It didn't bother him that old Lon was so sober about it. He was like that, Lonnie was. He was more of a one to think inside his head, and he seldom yelled about anything. But coming to old Junior McCalister, well, he had papa's style. He was the sort, papa was, who made a laugh out of being alive. Not a joke of it, mind you. Just a grin, sly chuckle, or outright belly shaker that made him, as well as the folks about him, feel good. Especially when things were curding to clabber in a hurry and it appeared there wasn't anything funny to be found between Galveston and El Paso. That was when Jim Senior would open up with a shout or a shoulder clap or just a friendly bear hug to get things "elevated," as he saw it. That was one reason it had

4

seemed such hard doings when the good Lord had picked him to go under in the brush with Sun Killer's bunch.

Still, as Lon had said afterward, the Comanche were a part of the price to live "total free," as papa had always wanted, not alone for himself but for his children. That was why he had come so far out into the buffalo pasture to raise his family. Papa had reckoned it a worse gamble to stay back in the settlements and rear his kids there midst the bad things he said people always brought with them. He had rather a hundred times, he said, take his chances with a wild-tail Indian than with a Christian-tamed settlement sonofabitch.

No matter for that, Junior knew, and Lon knew, and Bubba and Sissy and mama, they all knew how papa's gamble had turned out. Happy as he was, Junior had to frown between tossing the last sacks aboard the wagon, at that memory.

To begin with, a Texas Ranger band had come by chasing the Sun Killer Comanches and had needed a tracker to stay on their trail. They'd known papa when the family had lived in Bexar County and knew papa was the best to find and stay on an Indian trail of any white man west of Fort Worth. Naturally, papa had to go with them.

Well, old Sun Killer had lost a lot of men in the wild fight when papa had caught the rangers up to the red devils. Then the chief had doubled back to the McCalister ranch on his run home to the Pecos. He'd had a breed interpreter with him and the breed told mama what had happened and that Sun Killer wanted to honor the wife of such a great tracker.

In fact, the chief's heart was so good for the McCalisters that he had brought mama a special gift from the battleground. At which words a huge Indian had ridden out of the bunch. He was toting a dirty old army grub sack. With a leery grunt and a Yamparika grin, he had dumped something out of the sack and onto the ground in front of mama. It was papa's blood-dried head.

Mama almost went down but she didn't.

5

She was still standing proud when the chief told the breed to warn her he would be back one day to collect the rest of the debt she owed him, and owed the squaws of all of his warriors who were not riding back to the buffalo country with Tabebekat, the Killer of the Sun.

The Comanche had loped away then without a sound or a single look back. They had never been seen or heard from again near the McCalister place until just two days gone. Then a company of rangers had ridden into the ranch looking used up as buried dog bones. Sun Killer was heading toward Paint Creek. The rangers had come to escort the family into Red Hawk "for the duration."

Well, mama had not been entirely right since seeing papa's head, and got a scarey look on her face and told the ranger sergeant he would have to bind her over a spare pony to get her into town. She *wanted* to see the Yamparika chief again. Just once. Over the sights of papa's rifle, which the earlier rangers had brought back with his other things after the fatal brush of '58.

There was another rock in the road. Lon and Junior had already gone into Red Hawk in the wagon to fetch out the spring load of ranch supplies—food, gunpowder, clothes, mending materials, medicines, all of it—and wouldn't be back until next afternoon, earliest.

A deal was made with mama.

The rangers needed the rest and they agreed to stay at the McCalister place until the boys got back from Red Hawk. Meanwhile, a fresh horse would be saddled from the McCalister corral and ranger Kyle Shelby sent on the gallop into town to hurry up Lon and Junior. That ranger had hit the town limits about the time the Belknap stage got in and all the hell about the war news broke out. So he'd been of little use to the boys beyond bringing them the word of how things were at the ranch.

For reasons of his own, the ranger wanted to get away from town without any citizen help. So he told the town marshal about the Sun Killer scare and asked that the marshal give him a couple hours' head start of the concerned citizens of Red Hawk, which the marshal agreed to do. The rangers always wanted to work alone. They said people made them more damn trouble trying to help them than the Indians did trying to lift their hair. This one felt he and the McCalister boys could make it easy to Paint Creek by driving through the night; they would attract far less attention than with some damned cavalcade of Red Hawkers putting up a column of horse dust into daylight air, where a Comanche could spot it forty miles off. So that was the way it went.

Junior McCalister, bending to it, hurriedly tossed the last sack of milled flour into the wagon. Lon and ranger Shelby spoke a few words together. Lon swung up to the driver's box and unwrapped the lines. A friend or two of the town waved them good-bye. The marshal exchanged a nod and hand sign with the ranger, who nodded in his turn to Lonnie McCalister. Lon nodded back, ticked old Sam Houston with the popper of the whip, added a kind word for Sugarplum, the off-wheeler of the bony team, and the McCalister wagon creaked away from Hubbison's General Merchandise, Red Hawk, West Texas.

It was then a little after four o'colck in the afternoon.

For the first two hours, and six miles, out of town, things were quiet. With six o'clock and the sun sitting on the rim of the Pecos buffalo pasture, dead-slant into their eyes, a rider was sighted quartering in from the north and west.

## 2

Lonnie McCalister took the slack out of the reins and the team slowed. Kyle Shelby turned his pony and came back to the wagon. "Whoa up," he said to Lon, and the thin dark youngster halted Sam Houston and Sugarplum and let the wagon stand in the middle of the Overland Mail Road. Junior, asleep on the grain sacks in the wagon bed, awoke and sat up. He saw Lon and the ranger watching off to the left, squinting against the sun to make out what, or who, was riding in on them.

"It's no Injun," Lon decided after a moment.

"Nor it ain't much of a horse he's riding." The ranger scowled.

"Hell," Junior said. "We should have brang Bubba like I told you. That kid can see the sweat beads on a wild pig four hundred yards off."

"Yup," Lon agreed. "Little brother's a human wonder for eyesight. But even I can tell you that ain't no javelina pig yonder. Howsomever, I will guarantee you that, whoever it is, he's sweating."

"He's sweating that horse. Sure as bear sign smells bad, that's the truth." The ranger's glum look brightened a shade. "I'd guess he's white, or scairt white. But I cain't see nothing red chasing him."

Lon McCalister turned to Junior. "You see who it is yet?" he asked.

Junior, who next to little brother Bubba had the "farest" eyes in the family, looked surprised at the question. "Hell's fire, yes," he said. "Whyn't you ask me right off? I thought you and the peanut ranger was talking about the horse. Coming to that, I reckon I cain't help you, Lon. Horse is a stranger to me."

"Dammit, Junior," Lon said, "who is riding him?"

"Old Cap Marston," Junior answered quick enough. "You know, the mail rider. But that ain't his regular horse. It's a dark bay that goes stiff in front and stumbles a lot. He must have stole him off'n some squaw's pack string. I don't know when I've see'd a animal that gant and poor."

"For godsakes leave off," the ranger said. "We don't give a bull chip where he got the horse."

"Oh, I was just funning you, mister ranger," Junior explained carefully. "Old Cap, he wouldn't steal no horse off nobody. Not even a squaw. Old Cap, he—"

"Back off, Junior," Lon McCalister said.

"He had better," the ranger warned, "or I will back him off." The ranger hadn't cared for being called a peanut by Junior McCalister, who angled up into the air some six feet two or three inches. But Junior had love in his heart for most of mankind, and now just grinned.

"Leave me handle old Cap," he suggested. "Me and him are special friends. I will get it out of him in no time how come he is so lathered."

Older brother Lon reached and patted Junior's knee. "Sure," he said. "But first let me and the ranger talk to him. I'd like to save you for the finish."

"You bet, Lon. You go ahead and badger him."

"Thanks, Junior. We'll turn him over to you whens we cain't dig no more out of him."

The ranger gave them both the fishy eye. "You two," he said, "are as crazy as your old man was." He shook his head. "And you say you got another one coming along out there to the Paint Creek place?"

"Bubba," Lon said. "Didn't you see him?"

"No, he must of been off somewheres."

"Likely out scouting the Yamparika," Junior broke in. "I never see'd a kid so all-fired curious about Injuns. They cotton to him, too. Old Sun Killer took a shine to him. Lon heard him grunt to the breed interpreter that Bubba would be a good one to take along and rear up as a Comanche, he was that steady for so young. But the breed was edgy and talked the chief out of it. He understood that what they'd done to papa was more than enough. Wasn't no use adding to it by stealing Bubba. Besides, Bubba was already coming eight, too old to make a Yamparika out of him. But from then on, we've had it some tough keeping the kid convinced you cain't play Injun with Injuns. Not Sun Killer's kind you cain't."

"Jesus," the ranger said to Lon. "Is there no way to quieten him down?"

"Sure, he'll be still like I told him."

The ranger clearly doubted it, but the old mail rider was whipping his staggery horse up to them just at that moment and what the old man had to tell them soon enough put the talk onto where they all lived just then.

The Comanches had come back to Paint Creek.

They were out there now, surrounding the rangers and the family in the ranch house. Somebody had already died when old Cap had showed up, having sense enough to get down off his horse and back of the ridge east of the ranch, before being spotted by the Indians. The old man figured the deaths by the fact that, about a mile southwest of the house, buzzards were wheeling low and even dropping to feed. So it wasn't anything wounded out there in that southwest brush and gully land. It was dead.

"Maybe they run off and kilt some of the steers we had in the gathering corral," Lon said, talking low and short. "Maybe it was dead beef they was dropping on."

"Could have been," the old man said. "How many head you have in that corral?"

"Twelve."

"I counted twelve in a bunch wandering loose due south. No sir, it wasn't beef baiting them buzzards."

The ranger interrupted, his face hard with the dark possibility. "I can guess at it," he said. "Likely, a buck or three showed up ahead of the main pack and run off the stock like they was alone. Sergeant Coffey ought not to have bought that bluff, but you never know. He could have sent out a couple of the boys to—" He trailed it off, and Lon McCalister nodded.

"Cap," he said, "get in the wagon. Junior will take the horse. Tie him on the back, Junior. Hop it."

"No," old Cap objected. "Turn him loose. I had to borry him at a Mex shack halfways here. He ain't no good to anybody else. But I ain't never stole nobody's horse afore. He'll wander home. Turn him free."

"Do it," Lon ordered Junior. Then, to the ranger, "How many in your company?"

"Six counting me. Five left yonder with your mother and kid sister."

"Cap, how many Comanch'?"

The old man crawled shakily from his saddle over the sideboard of the wagon, collapsed on the sacks. "Must have been fifty. I could count them like flies on a piecrust in the window. They was mainly on the rimrock back of the corral. A handful was in each of them twin gully ruts you got flanking the house. Nobody could move out of the door, front or back, without he took riflefire. And these wasn't bow-and-arrow bucks. They had more rifles than the CSA Calvary, at Belknap."

"Damnation," Lon said softly. He shifted his glance to the ranger. "What do you think?" he said.

The ranger reviewed it gritty as dry-wash sand.

Suppose the worst. The Comanche had got one or two of his comrades. Say the other three were forted up in the ranch house with their mother and kid sister, the kid brother maybe with them, maybe missing. The mail rider had caught glimpses of "some" rangers moving in the house, and the mother and sister with them. He had not seen the kid. He might be the buzzard bait. It didn't matter now. What counted now was how best to serve, and if possible save, those that were left.

"What do *you* think?" the ranger countered to Lon, suspending his own dark guesses.

Lon McCalister, thin, dark complected, quiet, was no quick fighter, no instinctive frontiersman. But down inside him was a fire, and it was burning now.

Assume, he said, that two hours behind them now came the marshal of Red Hawk and a strong posse. They could wait where they were and join the posse when it came along. They could ride on for the ranch, right now, risking all to hold off the Comanche until the posse could get up to Paint Creek and drive them off.

"Sure," the ranger said grimly. "You know what I think of that?"

"Likely, just what I do," Lon answered.

"Sure," the ranger said again. "Let's go."

They drove the wagon into a dip of the Overland Mail Road and then up a sandy gully, parking it so that it was screened off from the road, and from cross-prairie view, by both the gully and a stand of small cottonwoods.

"Stay here and lay low and you got a better chance than we have," Lon told the old mail rider.

"The hell!" the old man cried out, faded eyes afire. He

slapped his bony thigh, whereon was strapped a giant old Walker Colt half an inch deep with rust and looking unfired since the Alamo or, at the best, San Jacinto. "You ain't leaving me here. Me and this here old Texas pistol put under our full share of the Comanch' whens you McCalister boys was still peeing your diapers!"

"Likely before that," Lon agreed. "But you're staying. You got a job to do, Cap. Happen you don't lay up here to guide in the posse, how they going to know to plan their ride from here? You and that old Walker Colt can make all the difference. You hold here."

"All right, Lon." Old Cap hitched at the Walker Colt and spat. "I see your point. I will hold the rear for you. Me and The Redeemer." He pulled the great four-pound revolver from its verdigrised sheath, cussed when he could not get the rust-frozen cylinder to turn, slid the storied weapon back into its leather. "Remember, now, they're on the west ridge and in both north and south gullies. You come in behind the east rise and you'll see what I say. Light out now."

Lon and Junior had by this time taken the team out of harness, save for bridles. Junior rode Sam Houston, Lon took Sugarplum. The ranger remounted his horse.

He looked at the two young Texans and made his decision. The quick nod went to seventeen-year-old Lon McCalister.

"You take the lead," he said.

Bubba McCalister was up with Big Red.

Big Red was the many-scarred and coyote-chased Rhode Island Red rooster who, like all McCalisters, was damned if the world was going to do him in. In Red's case, the damning extended to his three Mexican fighting chicken hens and maybe to young Bubba McCalister, of whom Red thought a great deal. Which fondness was returned by the eleven-year-old ranch boy, both as to Red and his trio of Mexican wives. They were Bubba's chickens. And he was damned, Bubba was, if he wasn't going to keep them alive at least until he got some chicks out of them.

So Bubba and Big Red had a deal.

If Bubba would get up and come out of the house when Red first chanticleered the West Texas sunrise, Red would agree to quit crowing on the boy's command. This was so mama could sleep. Mama and Sissy. Those were the two Bubba McCalister cared most about in the West Texas world. They were the ones he would do anything for. And right then, on that particular eerie-quiet dawn, Bubba had a feeling that mama and Sissy—yes, and Bubba, too—had uncommon need to be wary.

That was the reason the boy had not even waited in his tiny loft bunk for Big Red to call him out. The ancient cock bird had been only yawking and kicking dirt and getting *ready* to crow up the new day when Bubba snared him by his scrawny neck and advised that he be silent on pain of ending up Old Fricassee rather than Big Red.

Bubba talked only Spanish to Red, since the rooster had been Mexican reared. But the doughty Rhode Island cock never argued back in any tongue. Small as he was for his eleven years, Bubba McCalister had a way about him that let things around the place understand it wasn't safe to trifle with him. Little redheaded boys are like that, West Texas or anywhere. They will fight.

"*Callate*, Red!" the boy warned, easing off on his stranglehold. "*Cuidado, comprende?* I hearn something just now from up in the loft. Out toward the west rise, it were. Sounded like ponies snuffling to me."

Bubba paused, eying the five ranger horses in the "Comanche lean-to" alongside the house. This was a shelter where ranchfolk in that risky land could put their horse stock when the moon was big and friend Comanch' could be expected to come looking for whatever he could lift. And that "lift" went all the way from handy horseflesh to beef cows to human hair. Especially, long human hair, like hung down mama's back, and Sissy's. The Comanch' were hell on white women.

Bubba freed the rooster and looked at the ranger horses again. They were quiet. They hadn't heard any pony noise off west, that was evident enough. How about their masters? Bubba shot glances to the hay shed and rick. Three rangers were out there, the other two out front of the house bedded beneath the long-pole roof of the porch.

Bubba had checked the front porch pair on his way out of the house. One had been nodding with his hat over his face. The other was snoring loud enough to rustle the lizards out of the bear-grass thatch of the roof. Now, watching the shed and rick tensely, Bubba caught no sign of the trio posted there. Maybe one of them was awake, as he sure as hell ought to have been, but the boy doubted it. The snorer out front was the sergeant of the company himself! How was that for ranger work?

Bubba McCalister scowled.

He had little respect for Texas Rangers. As a very small boy might, he blamed them for his father's death and, naturally, through that, for the terrible, fearsome price that death had drawn out of mama. It did not occur to the boy that Sunny Jim McCalister had been the one to bring that tragedy on mama. Sure it was him, papa, that had moved the family out here in the buffalo grass. But mama had been like Ruth in the Bible, and she had gone whither papa went, and never a cross word, nor mean, to nick his hocks or bring him down from behind like so many women would have.

She'd been the one to teach Lonnie what Sunny Jim said—that it was part of the price they must pay, as McCalisters, to be their own people, this living out in Comanche land. And of course Lon, in his time, had passed the idea along to both Junior and Bubba. Junior hadn't really comprehended what it meant, nor given a "feeble hoot," as he put it, and it had come down to Bubba to try and separate out the idea for himself.

He was not able.

All he could make of it was that the rangers had come for papa, and papa had never come back.

Now the rangers were here again, all unwatching, waiting for Lon and Junior to get back, and Bubba McCalister had been aroused from his sleep by thinking to hear the snuffling of strange ponies "out west of the place."

Bubba knew he might just have been imagining he heard that sound. After all, the rangers had stopped there the night before in special order to warn the family that the Comanch' was out and that the McCalisters should "wagon up" and get on into Red Hawk under ranger escort and guard.

So of course he had been *thinking* of Indians up there in his loft bed under the roof pole. He understood that.

But Bubba understood something else, too.

He not only had the keenest eye in the family, but what Junior called the "cutest" ear, meaning the sharpest. Bubba was also known to have a nose better than a blue-tick hound.

Lon always said, "That cussed Bubba will spook you. He can see, hear, smell, and just plain feel out things like he was part varmint. He *thinks* funny, too."

To which Junior would surely respond, "Yep, gives a body the fantods, don't he? He ain't all human-kid, that kid ain't. Got something elst in him to boot."

Then old Lon would tie it off with, "What elst he's got in him is our mama. It's like papa didn't have nothing to do with making Bubba. He's all mama—different."

Bubba felt a heart tug thinking of Lon and big dumb Junior. He loved his older brothers. What lucky boy wouldn't? They could do anything between them. And both would be as fierce to defend mama or Sissy as ever Bubba himself. But Lon was right. Bubba wasn't like him and Junior. He *was* like Mary McCalister—different.

There was something more burning in Bubba than the fire in Lon's belly or the boistering fun in Junior's simple head. Bubba thought a lot about what it was.

Maybe it was that Bubba was the last of the McCalisters. Maybe it was that he was the littlest. Maybe it was that he favored mama and that, from that, the others all thought the more of him. But Bubba knew better. It wasn't those things. It was what he had heard the people in town say when they didn't know he was over behind the store counter, or catnapping back of the McCalister wagon seat waiting for the family to get done with their shopping in Red Hawk, and head home to Paint Creek.

"That Bubba kid is daft," he had heard them say. "He is stranger than a lost wolf whelp. Ever see that crazy look in his eye? Ever try to talk to him? He's touched and that's the truth. Pore Miz McCalister. She's bore a heap of hell out there. It's got to her. She plain dotes on that boy. Reckon she figures she's *got* to."

The look on the thin face of the redheaded boy was not happy there in the April dawning, but he shook his head and put his mind where it belonged. Something had told him there were Indians out there beyond west ridge. If he didn't want the sun, or the rangers, to cut him off from scouting the rise for the red devils, he had to move now and make no sound about it.

He went floating out away from the house running bent over and keeping the hay rick and shed between him and the ridge. There was a short dash across open ground to the cover of the home corral, then that carried him to the south gully. Diving into that, he raced up its channel toward the west rise. He had just reached the limestone outcrop up near the head of the gully when he *smelled* Indians. He didn't smell horse with them, nor hear any pony sounds. Jesus! they would be afoot. He was walking into them.

Like a rock squirrel, the slight figure twisted up out of the gully and into the upthrust of the outcrop. There, he lay flat, breath suspended, eyes fixed. He never heard the Comanche. They were just suddenly passing along the gully toward the ranch house, down rise, going like ghosts past where Bubba McCalister lay unbreathing in the breakup of the rimrock, five feet from the glittering dark eyes and war-painted faces of the Yamparika riflemen filing down south gully without a sound.

When they had gone, the boy found his feet and ran.

He made little more noise than had the red raiders and, using the broken limestone to fullest advantage of cover, he was able to reach a straggle of salt piñon that grew up to and created west ridge. Bubba waited not in the safer lower fringe of this haven, but went at once and swiftly upward through its gnarled camouflage until the ridge top lay beneath his panting belly and he could see the far side.

It was then he knew how right the rangers were.

# 4

"Mama," Sissy said, "what's the matter?"

Mary McCalister was sitting on the edge of her side of the double brass bed. She held a warning finger to her lips, pushed aside her long black hair. The ear so uncovered, she bent her head to its side and poised thus, motionlessly.

The girl got out of bed on her side, tiptoed around to stand by her mother, waiting.

She was frightened. But frontier reared, she did not ask further questions, just watched the slender dark woman who was the widow of Sunny Jim McCalister.

"I heard something," Mary McCalister said at last. "Go get Bubba up. He hears better than I do."

"Or anybody," nodded Sissy. She shook back the flood of tawny hair that cascaded about the startlingly beautiful young face. "Don't worry, mama," she said. "We got the rangers out yonder watching."

"Hurry on," the woman ordered. "That scoundrelly rooster will be crowing any minute."

Sissy went up the ladder to the loft, moving with

17

athletic ease. "Bubba!" she whispered. Then, eyes growing accustomed to the greater gloom of the underroof bunk space, "Mama! Bubba's gone. He's not here."

"Oh, my God." Mary McCalister did not say it hysterically, nor raise her voice above the whisper level they had been using. She simply stated what it meant in that time and place to have an eleven-year-old son out of bed and out of the house, with hostile and very likely vengeful Comanche horsemen reported riding for their ranch.

The girl was back at her side again. "Mama," she said, "Bubba is all right. You know him. He'd have to be out early to see that the rangers do their jobs right."

"No," Mary McCalister shook her head. "Bubba's gone."

"But where, mama? He's surely just outside. I'll go ask the rangers."

"No, wait. Button up your dress. I'll go out and talk to them. Fetch me Sunny Jim's gun and foller out."

Sissy got her father's old Sharps buffalo rifle from its place over the field-rock fireplace, hurried with it after her mother. Outside, it was still murky with night's lingering. The dawn gray was spreading but had not yet struck the flats. Up along the crest of west ridge, however, the gray was tinging with pink. It would be day in minutes.

"Mama!" the girl called into the shadowy yard.

"Over here," came the reply, softly from the direction of the hay rick and shed, past the saddle-stock lean-to.

Sissy came up having trouble keeping the Sharps's heavy barrel raised. She found her mother in low-voiced, angry talk with the rangers. One of the three men, noting the lowering rifle barrel, reached for the Sharps. "Here," he said. "Leave me have that, fores you shoot your foot off."

Mary McCalister shot out a lean, strong hand, took the Sharps from Sissy.

"That's mine," was all she said to the ranger.

What her mother and the men were arguing about, Sissy found, was what translation to put on the disappearance of Bubba. The men just didn't believe that the boy was out there in the utter stillness of that graying day nor, if he might be, that he was up for deeper reason than relieving himself. "You know, Miz McCalister, ma'am," one of them grumbled, "everybody gets nervouser when there's Injuns about. They riles the human bladder."

"And you rile my human patience, mister ranger," the ranchwoman advised. "My boy isn't wetting his pants because of Comanche, nor is he out in this early muck to make water. He heard something, and he's gone to find out what he heard, and I know what it was."

"Well, what was it, ma'am?"

"It was the Comanch'. I heard them myself."

"Oh? You and your boy used to hearing things, are you, ma'am?" the third ranger asked. He said it in a way to make it clear he thought he was being clever but Mary McCalister didn't smile nor bend to him.

"We are," she answered flatly. "And you rangers better listen, too!" she flashed at them. "And hard."

One of the men chuckled. Another hawked and spit to clear the night-gather from his throat. The third man muttered something mean about women and just said to Mary McCalister, "Well, ma'am, you put on some coffee and give us a chanct to perform our duties and we will think about listening for whatever it is that has got your wind up." He softened the last of it a mite, knowing the dread the Comanche put into isolated people like these. "You understand, Miz McCalister, that we ain't funning you flat out. We been and see'd a few Injuns of our own, you know. Go on along now and make us a pot of java. That'll be the best medicine for us old Injun fighters. That right, boys?"

The other two agreed, still making light of things, and Mary McCalister said to all of them, softly, "Damn you for fools, the three of you. The Comanch' is out there and you won't even listen to hear where he is!"

There was only the sparest of silences following her curse, and then far, far up on west ridge, thin with the distance, a rooster crowed.

The three rangers came rolling to their feet. They

froze in listening crouches. Big Red, the McCalister flock master, flew up onto the cross-timber of the corral gate and gave shrill answer to the crow from afar.

"Good God," the first ranger said. "What was that?"

"That," said Mary McCalister, stony faced, "was my son Bubba. He's found the Comanch' for you."

The ranger leader whirled about and fired three signal shots into the air. He was answered by a "Yo!" and three return shots from the rangers in front of the ranch house. Next instant, all five rangers were firing at north and south gullies, trying to stem the Yamparika attack, which, but for Bubba's warning rooster crow, would have taken them all under.

As it was, the rangers did break back the first wild rush of Sun Killer's warriors, gaining the time to get into the house and fort up there. But they had paid a mortal price. Ranger Bob Jacks and ranger Charley Holt were missing. They had gone down in the cross fire, and the Indians had carried them off. What the rangers had bought at the McCalister ranch was two lives less than a Mexican standoff.

They found that out when the sun got up and they could see the turkey buzzards beginning to circle off to the south.

# 5

Thirteen-year-old Sissy McCalister was a rangy child just giving promise of the lovely woman she would be. Her thick blond hair and cornflower-blue eyes would all too soon be thumping hearts and arousing rivalries 'mongst the swains of the llano. But for that day in April, 1861, she was a slender pixie of a tomboy, more prairie urchin than nubile womanchild.

The two older boys adored her in that special warm way of older brothers with little sisters. They found her funny, outrageous, flirtatious, devious, pesty, and pert by chameleon turn. They tolerated her in their loving. Not so, young Bubba.

To Bubba McCalister, Sissy was the world next to mama. Bubba loved his only sister with a passion and devotion that surpassed any other loyalty in his life, again excepting mama. The reason was—at least Sissy always figured it was the reason for Bubba's steadfast fealty to her—that Bubba had a very hard time getting things out of himself and said the way he wanted to say them. On the other hand, Sissy was as outgoing as an orphan colt. She was old Bubba's interpreter. He could tell her things he couldn't tell anybody else, and she would be able to pass them on for him to the others of the family, and so keep baby brother from falling farther behind all the while.

Sissy also tutored Bubba. Not even mama could do so good a job of getting Bubba through *McGuffey's Reader* and, after that, the older books that mama had brought along with her—an entire trunkful of them—when she came to marry papa and the family moved out of Bexar County to the buffalo grass.

Because she was his principal teacher, Sissy also knew more than the others ever would of how quick Bubba was in his mind. It was just that he looked at things from a different view than most, that gave the feeling that he was slow or in some other way held back from being—well, right.

So Sissy and Bubba had a very special friendship and it was for this reason that Sissy found that day of the fort up at Paint Creek ranch the longest stretcher of a day that she had ever endured.

She continued to hope that Bubba would show up by some miracle, even after the rangers had decided that he would not. By high noontime, Sergeant Hayes Coffey was showing the first signs of real uneasiness. He was confiding to Mary McCalister that he was then certain it was his two missing men the turkey buzzards had found down to the south and that not even a lizard could slide in through the Indian lines, let alone an eleven-year-old boy.

"I will say one thing, though, ma'am," the ranger concluded. "That kid of yours has either got more innards than a cornered bobcat or he is not quite bright. Him crowing like he done is all that saved any of us. Without he done that, we'd all of us be with Holt and Jacks." He caught the ranchwoman's eye, lowered his voice. "We may be with them anyway, ma'am," he said. "Happen ranger Shelby and your two older boys don't get back from Red Hawk sometime tonight, we will be. We won't have ammunition enough to hold them off tomorrow." Again, the ranger lowered his voice. "Excepting, that is, for the two rounds that'll be saved back for you and missy, yonder."

Mary McCalister nodded, dark eyes burning in the gloom of the shuttered ranch house. "I will take care of my little girl and me," she told the ranger. "You can use your two bullets on yourselves. I don't mean to die in here. Do you understand that?"

She was still clutching the Sharps rifle of her late husband. By the light in her eyes when she warned him, Sergeant Coffey understood at least part of what she was saying to him; if he moved to bring mercy to either her or her daughter, Mary McCalister would blow him open with her husband's Big Fifty Sharps buffalo gun. Sergeant Coffey had seen the holes made by such huge-calibre weapons and had little stomach to see another, under the circumstances.

"Ma'am, Miz McCalister," he answered her at length, "I truly do understand. Rest easy. Your boys and ranger Shelby will get here."

"Maybe," said Mary McCalister, gripping the Sharps more fiercely still. "But I know who is already here. Out there." She pointed toward the now silent Indian rifle lines. "He's the one I mean to see. Whether by tonight, or this afternoon, or anytime that I can," she finished ominously.

The ranger sergeant did understand now what Sunny Jim McCalister's widow intended to do. "Sun Killer?" he asked her softly. She nodded almost imperceptibly, not looking at him but out toward where the Comanche lay waiting. And Sergeant Coffey left her there and went and told his men, when he thought Mary McCalister wasn't watching him, or listening, what it was they must do. "She means to get outside and shoot the damned chief," he said. "We got to get the gun away from her and keep it away. She's touched, boys. Watch her."

But over across the room, Mary McCalister called out to Sissy, and said, "Come and sit here with me, honey. If the rangers move to come close, yell out. They want papa's gun. They're going to try to get it away from us, Sissy. We must see they don't."

The girl patted her mother's arm and drew up a crude stool and sat beside her and commenced to stare at the rangers unblinkingly.

"By God," one of the men muttered to Sergeant Coffey. "She heard you. How you figure that?"

"I don't." The sergeant scowled.

"I do," the third man said. "She's witched, like you said, sarge. That's where that spooky-strange kid of hers get it from."

"That's right, sarge," the first ranger agreed uneasily. "You ever hear of a eleven-year-old kid rooster-crowing up on a ridge full of hostile Comanch' Injuns? Not before, you ain't," the man answered his own question. "And now look at the girl blank-eying us. I tell you, boys, these people are off upstairs."

Sergeant Hayes Coffey shook his weary head. "No, they ain't," he said. "They've just been out here too long and took too much. You've heard the story. You blame any of them?"

The two men agreed they did not. One of them called over to Mary McCalister, apologizing, but the dark-haired woman did not reply, nor look their way.

"Mama's resting," said Sissy McCalister. "Please leave her be."

The three men looked at Sissy and saw a very brave but frightened and tired young girl. They were sorry for their thoughts of cracked minds for this family but said no more of it, nor of apology.

"Sure, little sister." Hayes Coffey nodded. "We could

all use the rest. Miz McCalister, be easy. Jepson," he said to one of the men, "get up in the loft lookout. Werner will relieve you in a hour. You awake enough?"

Jepson grunted. "If I ain't, it's the first time I had any falling eyelid trouble in the middle of fifty Yamparika Comanch'."

He went up the ladder to Bubba's loft room, where there was a false dovecote built astraddle the ridgepole that gave full-circle view of the prairie, all ways from the Paint Creek drainage. Jepson put eye to the slit.

"Quiet out yonder," he called back down to Sergeant Hayes Coffey. "Siesta time, even for red-gut Injuns."

Coffey didn't answer him. Nor did the other ranger.

The stillness of noontime deepened. In the narrow quarters of the McCalister ranch house the only sound was that of the flies buzzing, the only smell that of human fear. Had the Comanche come then, it would have been over. But noon was not to be the hour of the Yamparika attack. Nor did sundown prove to be that hour. Nor the darkness even of the night that followed.

So it would be at daybreak, then.

The final silent rush of Sun Killer's avenging war party would come with the misting pink of first dawn.

A Comanche sunrise.

And the very last day for all of them there in the gray-board ranch house.

It was three o'clock in the morning, black as the snout of a coal scuttle. The three horsemen putting their mounts up the long slope of the rise just east of the McCalister place on Paint Creek drew in together and slowed their pace.

"There's a spring just ahead," Lon McCalister said. "We'd best tie up our horses there and go to the top on foot. We will leave Junior with the horses."

"Like hell you will, Lon."

"Junior, we got to have somebody to our rear. The Comanch' know that spring's there, well as we do."

"That's so, Lon."

"All right, here we are." Lon swung down from his mount. Junior and the ranger did likewise, Junior gathering the reins of all three horses.

"I'll just hold them," the big youth told Lon. "I mightn't be give the time to untie them, if the Comanch' drops in on me."

"Sure." Ranger Kyle Shelby grimaced. "That way you can grab your pony and get the hell out of here, and me and your brother can whistle for ours. Lon, this boy's not bright. I better stay back with the horses."

The response to that came not from Lon or Junior but from another brother.

"Hell's fire!" the thin voice piped from the inky blackness of the jack oak scrub nearby. "They don't none of you need to hang back here. I'll tend the damn horses."

There was a common indrawing of breaths by Lon and Junior, and Lon let his out first.

"Bubba! you little sonofabitch. What you doing out here without your mama?"

"Goddammit, kid," big Junior sobbed. "Come on the hell out here and leave me hug you, bear-paw style. I reckon we all figured you was did for."

There was a rustle of brush and the small shadow of Bubba McCalister drifted up to the startled horsemen.

"Lon," the boy apologized, "I done my best to get past the Comanch' early today, so's I could cut you off the quicker. But I was lucky to get this far. I had to hide up all daylight in a coyote burrow up under the ridge. God a'mighty but it stank in there!"

"Oh," Junior said soberly. "Is that what it is? I thought you had soiled your drawers from the pure joy of finding your long-lost two brothers."

"Cut it," Lon ordered Junior. "Bubba, is mama and Sissy safe?"

"I don't know. I couldn't see nothing from the ridge excepting Injuns. Lord God, Lon, there must be half a hundred of them just around the ranch. But that ain't all. I got up on the west ridge just as the sun hit the tips, and down the far side, hid from the ranch, there was nothing but Yamps and horses and all them little Injun fires that smoke about as much as a cheap cigar, each. Must be a full hundred Injuns, all told."

Lon nodded quickly. "So you left the ridge come dark and been all this while getting to the spring here, eh?"

"That's so. I figured you would come up this draw."

"You cain't tell us nothing else?"

"You asked about mama and Sissy. You want to know something about the Comanch'?"

"All you know."

"Well, I come down along the back of north gully. I could hear them talking only when I got way down near the house. I take that to mean there was only a sentry bunch watching the place. Rest of them likely went back over the ridge, to the camp, for the night."

The ranger interrupted, looking at Lon. "You figure that would mean the same thing for the south wash?" he asked. "Just a picket or three for the night watch of the house?"

"Likely," Lon answered. "You got the same idea I have, Shelby?"

"Let me guess," Shelby said. "You're thinking could we cut off both heads of this here Comanch' snake, mebbe we could get in close enough on the main body to stomp it dead."

"You mean in the dark?" Junior said, alarmed.

"There ain't no superiorly time three white men and a runt-ass redheaded kid could pick to try stomping out a hundred Yamparika Comanch'," Shelby replied acridly.

"Hold on," Lon said. "If we can get those pickets in both gullies and do it without making any noise, we can gather up whoever's left at the house and ride out for Red Hawk in what's left of the night. I wasn't hardly thinking of jumping the Comanch' camp, Shelby. Jesus."

"I'm downright relieved," the ranger said. "Neither was I."

26

There was some more tense talk about it, whether to try for the house first, or get the pickets killed first. It was voted to go for the north gully group, then worry from there. Bubba could lead them squarely to where the north bunch were. They had to commence with them. Any other way and they would risk getting shot either by the Comanche in the south gully or their own people in the house. The north gully it was.

Junior McCalister reached out in the dark and gathered up Bubba and clinched him to his chest in a bear hug, and said, "Bubba, goddamn you, you little squirt. Come here and let old Junior crunch a rib for you. Boy, you done wonderful work today."

"You ain't heard it all," the boy said, trying to get his breath past Junior's huge arms. "I ain't told the whole of it. There's a chanct mama and Sissy and even some of the rangers is safe in the house."

"What do you mean some of them?" Shelby demanded.

"I think the Injuns got a couple of your friends, mister," the youth answered. "I seen them with two bodies slang over a packpony. They wasn't Injun bodies. They tooken them down past south gully somewheres. I seen buzzards circling in after a spell."

"So we heard," Lon told him, and gave him the story of old Cap, the mail rider, and what he had seen of the Comanche surround.

It was Bubba's turn then, after Junior finally set him back down, and asked him, puzzled, "Hey, Bubba, how come you think the Comanch' didn't get mama and Sissy and all of the rangers in the first rush? You ain't explained that."

The boy quickly told them of his rooster crowing from west ridge. "I got it off before any of the Injuns came out of the gullies. I know mama knows my rooster crow, and I know they had to hear it because old Red answered me back, and he's least halfways deef." He paused, bobbing his shaggy red mop. "I reckon it give them just about that time to look out sharp."

Lon McCalister picked the skinny boy up and held him

out at arms' length. "Dammit, Bubba, you're all right," he said. And put Bubba back down and said low and quick to him, "Lead on out, I'll be right behind you. Make a sound and I'll—"

"We know what you'll do," Junior put in. "You'll pee your pants."

The hulking youth finished helping ranger Shelby tie the horses. The ranger then said to Lon, "All right, go ahead. Let out your tracker. Let's see if he can run a line as good as his daddy could."

The remembering of Sunny Jim McCalister made them all quiet for a moment, then Lonnie said to Bubba, "Go ahead on, boy. Tread light and watch for loose rock."

"Yeah." Junior scowled, giving Bubba a starting push. "And don't break no wind upbreeze of them Injuns, you hear? Did you know a Injun could smell a white man's gas separate from his own? You betcha. You got to watch out how you break wind around Injuns."

"Christ," ranger Shelby muttered. "There's nothing in the world worse nor a educated idiot. Lonnie, shut him up."

"Shut up, Junior," Lon said. "Bubba's got enough coyote stink to him from that burrow hole up on the ridge to make all of us Comanche-safe."

"That's so," Junior agreed ponderously. "Coyote is a safe smell to a Injun. Iffen they wind old Bubba when we get over yonder to the gully, they won't even give us a look. We can walk right in on them. Coyote smell is just the best there is to fool a Yamparika with. Yes, sir."

They went on through the night, moving swiftly, silently, none of them answering Junior.

Lon stopped his followers fifty paces out from the mouth of north gully. Here, Bubba was to drop out and lie in the brush to see what happened in the gully. If it went right, and they got the Comanche without noise, he would rejoin them for the sneak to south gully. If it went wrong, Bubba was to make for the house and get into it by a way he knew that would not get him ranger-shot. Then he was to tell the rangers what had happened, and for them to hang on, even so, for the people from Red Hawk were on their ways and old Cap would bring up the McCalister wagon with enough gun fodder and other supplies in it to hold off the whole Comanche nation.

Everyone already understood his role and now Bubba picked a saltbush clump and sank down behind it and brother Lon reached in the dark and found Bubba's small hand and gave it a hard squeeze. Then he was gone with Junior and the ranger.

Bubba lay thinking of them and what waited for them. Lon and the ranger had Jim Bowie knives and Junior had his hand axe, which he wore in a sheath, just like a big Bowie blade. Bubba knew that axe. Junior had taught him to throw it and to hand-spar with it against a knife and Bubba figured, lying there in the now windy darkness, that he would about three times over face both Lon and the pinty-sized ranger with both their Bowie blades than one old Junior with that damned Yamparika belt axe.

In the moment of that thought, the boy heard a single grunted "Unhhh!" over in the gully, silenced instantly by a splitting, sodden sound that the boy knew had to be Junior's axe blade. There followed two more shorter grunts, the way a pig will grunt when it is stuck for butchering, then about thirty seconds of utter nothing, and then Lon and Junior and the ranger moved in out of the blackness and Lonnie said to Bubba, "All right, baby brother, there is three good ones down yonder and you was right again. They was where you said they was, not five foot off. Let's go south!"

They had the same plan agreed for the south wash and the only difference was that Bubba did not stay put in his brush-clump lay-up this time. The reason he didn't was a Yamparika Comanche Indian. A big one. One that all the McCalisters had burning cause to remember. And one who came walking out of the night and, all unknowing of any white men or boys being outside the four walls of the Paint Creek ranch house, went right past where Bubba lay to guard the rear of his brothers and the ranger.

It was Tabebekat.

Bubba could smell him, feel him, sense him. He knew it was the Yamparika chief who had killed his father.

Yet he could not see recognizable detail beyond throwing distance of lasso rope, and the big Indian was no more than a darker blot in the blackness of the early morning. But Bubba knew it was him. He guessed, too, why he was down here off the west ridge. A war chief did not grow as old as Sun Killer by letting others do his work for him. The chief was down there checking on his guards. Thank God and also the Comanche great spirit Kadih that Sun Killer had chosen to visit the south gully first. It gave Bubba time to think of what to do to warn Lon and Junior that trouble was walking up on them.

It wasn't much but it was the best a boy could do. He would have to use his coyote yelp imitation, then hope it worked as good as the rooster crow had with the rangers that morning.

Bubba threw back his head and let loose his howl.

It burst so near to Sun Killer, as a matter of south gully fact, that the chief believed he had stepped on the very coyote that gave the wild-crying alarm. But the unwary Sun Killer was only getting started getting startled. Next instant, a fierce-warning Yamparika shout rose from the gully, a shout throttled off in mid-utterance.

The Comanche chief went sideways and up into the night air in one leap. Circling to his right, away from the strangled sound, he slid into the gully. The last Bubba heard was the thud of rapidly running moccasined feet fading away up the gully, toward west ridge.

As for those Comanche in the gully, they were still there long after Sun Killer had fled. Lon so informed Bubba moments after his coyote yell had almost ruined their attack on the guard party there. "Four more," a relieved Lon said. "But who the hell was that galloping off up the gully? Damn, that'll rouse them. You see him?"

"The chief," Bubba answered simply enough. "The one that killed papa and made mama strange. It was him."

"The hell!" said ranger Shelby. "You knowed him in this pitch dark?"

Big Junior McCalister shouldered up to the ranger. "If Bubba says it was him, bet your last peseta on it," he growled. "Little brother can feel them."

"And he's the one says mama's strange, eh?" said Shelby cynically. "Well, where does this leave us?"

"Running for the ranch house," answered Lonnie McCalister. "Like this." And, suiting action to his own advice, brother Lon lit out for home. His only other instruction went on the run to Junior, laboring by his side. "Tune up, Junior!" he yelled. "Best let them know we're coming in."

Junior threw back his head and gave issue to a longhorn bull's bellow of greeting to those within the silent Paint Creek building. "Yo, the house!" he thundered. "It's us. Open up!"

Seconds later, the four were inside with Mary and Sissy McCalister and the three other Texas Rangers. One stub of candle was lit for five minutes, while the family hugged and kissed and the boys gasped out their story of the brush with Sun Killer just outside, after their clearing of the twin gullies of Comanche pickets. At the same time and on the same short candle, ranger Kyle Shelby gave his report to Sergeant Hayes Coffey. It was when the last minute ticked off and Junior was telling for the third time how special Bubba was, that Lon McCalister looked suddenly around in the shadowed light, and his dark eyes narrowed.

"Wait a minute," he said, "where's mama?"

Sissy had the only answer that mattered. "She's gone," the girl said. She looked across the smoky, low-ceilinged room, voice rising. "Lonnie! She's tooken papa's big buffler gun with her. It ain't where the rangers put it no more."

They all looked where the white-faced girl pointed, the corner beyond the fireplace where the heavy weapon had been placed under ranger guard. The corner was as empty as Mary McCalister's chair.

Sergeant Hayes Coffey looked at his men and then at Lonnie McCalister. "She said she would go after that Injun," he told Lon. "We watched her as close as we could. Got the gun away from her late this afternoon, when she and the little girl both fell asleep. I'm damn sorry, son. She must have grabbed it when we was welcoming you just now."

"She always said it, Lon," big Junior remembered suddenly. "She'd get him with papa's gun. Ain't that so?"

"Yeah, Junior, it's so." Lon nodded. He looked twenty years older in the guttering candlelight. "All the same, we got to go after her. Stop her iffen we can."

"Not in this morning black," Sergeant Coffey said. "You'd find only your own death, lad. Wait for the light."

Ranger Kyle Shelby, over by the rear window shutter, interrupted in a low voice. "You won't need to wait," he said. "There's a light yonder right now."

They came quickly then and peered through the crack of the shutters and all saw it going up south gully—a lone figure with a lantern walking slowly and singing in a high unsteady voice a song no one of them had ever heard. "It's mama," whispered Sissy. "Oh God, mama!"

Lon McCalister straightened from the shutters.

"Mr. Coffey," he called. "You got your field glass?"

The ranger brought him the glass and Lon focused it out the opened crack in the shutters. "She's stopped," he said. "Somebody's with her. A Injun, a big one. It's him. Lantern's setting on the ground. He's saying something. Moving his arms and talking. Mama is waiting. Oh, Christ—"

They all heard the booming explosion of the Big Fifty Sharps echo and reecho across the long flat rise of west ridge.

"Mama's still standing there," Lon said. "She still has the gun. I cain't see the Injun no more. No, wait. There's a whole passel of them showed up just now. They come from up-gully. Must be a dozen of them. All just standing there looking at mama. Oh, God, mama, mama!"

Sergeant Coffey moved in, took the glass from Lon.

"Move aside," he said, and raised the glass and focused it through the crack and upward to the far gully. "Hold on," he muttered. "Your Injuns are pulling out. Your mama is all right. They're leaving her standing there. They aren't even taking the gun. Christ Jesus."

He put the glass down.

Lon closed tight the shutter, rebarred it.

"I'm going up there," he said.

Lon found mama up in south gully standing with the old rifle, unmoving. The Indians were as gone as Sergeant Coffey had reported them. All except one of them. At mama's feet, sprawled with his face and half his head blown off by the point-blank discharge of the old Sharps, lay the Yamparika chief Tabebekat, the Killer of the Sun.

For a moment Lon could not understand why the Comanche had not removed the body. They never left wounded or dead behind if they could remove them. Well, almost never.

Lon looked up at mama from where he had crouched to make sure of the disfigured face of the dead Indian, and then he knew why they had not harmed her, and why, from that, they had left Sun Killer with her. Mama's mind was gone. She still crooned the senseless song they had heard her singing going up the gully to her strange appointment with the Comanche chief. She still looked off into the night as though for someone not there. She paid no heed to either Lon or the body of Sun Killer. The coal oil lantern she had taken from its outside hook beside the kitchen door yet burned upon the ground beside her. It shed its pale light up both walls of the gully and along its upward-climbing bed. It made monstrous shapes of both mama and the dead Yamparika. Lon shivered and bobbed his head, knowing then why the Comanche had not harmed his mother.

Crazy people were revered by them, made taboo, untouchable. They said of the demented that they were like children. And to the fierce Yamparika, most feared of all the Comanche, children were sacred.

These tribesmen of Sun Killer's had come quickly

down the gully from their camp beyond west ridge when they heard mama singing. Evidently, Sun Killer had still been on this side of the ridge, and seen mama's lantern and heard her eerie song, before the others got over the ridge. It seemed he must have gone back down the gully to meet her, knowing that any white woman in this Paint Creek drainage had to be the one he had promised to return and take vengeance on. And probably he had hesitated when he saw her up close and realized her condition.

In that hesitation must have lain his death.

For mama had shot him at a range of not over six inches. She had to have simply raised the Sharps and fired it into his face all in one crazed swiftness.

Then had come the chief's warriors, following down the gully to the shot within seconds. They had seen what Lonnie saw now; and by their silent withdrawal evidently had believed that mama's untouchableness extended somehow to include Sun Killer and even the great buffalo rifle within its *puha*—its magic power of personal medicine. So they had left the chief with the crazy white woman and the gun that had killed him. It was never explained better to Lon McCalister, and he believed it never would be.

For that terrible moment in south gully, however, the Paint Creek ranch youth was not thinking such distant thoughts. What he saw was his mother, a bright, brave, wonderful frontier woman who did not know where she was, or who, and likely never would again.

Lonnie reached for the lantern and took Mary McCalister's arm and said to her softly, "Come on, mama. We're going home now."

And Mary McCalister smiled and nodded and went away down south gully with her eldest son, humming the mindless song, nodding and smiling, nodding and smiling.

# 7

There was no sleep the rest of that night.

Sergeant Coffey wanted everything ready to either run or fight with daybreak. If the feared Comanche attack did not come at that time, he considered it a better gamble to strike out and meet the Red Hawk posse early along its way out to Paint Creek than to stay on at the ranch and risk second thoughts by the Comanche.

This decision was enhanced when, just at sunup's first streak, Cap rumbled down off the east rise with the McCalister wagon. The old fellow reported that the Red Hawkers had indeed come along the mail road and found him waiting for them. They had likewise loaned him their two packhorses to pull the wagon, and he, Cap, had "lit out to lead them the way," naturally expecting them to "foller faithful."

But "hell's fire!"—everybody knew those tinhorns.

Somehow, Cap and the damn posse had got separated in the night and evidently the tomfools had missed the turnoff to the Paint Creek ranch.

"As it be," the old mail rider concluded, "I reckon we will just about meet up with them coming back to see where they overrun the turn in the dark. The marshal surely knows the way by day, and so do six, eight others of them." He looked about at the sorry company gathered in the wan light of the ranch yard and waved cheerfully. "Meanwhiles, here's the wagon for Sissy and Miz McCalister to ride in, and here's ammo in the toolbox enough to fight off half the Yamp Nation, and even those damn crow-bait town ponies ain't too used up to pull good." Again the wave and the wrinkled grin. "All aboard for Red Hawk, Texas, folks! This here stage won't wait forever."

Sergeant Hayes Coffey and Lon McCalister agreeing, they departed forthwith.

They did not see the Red Hawk posse anywhere on

35

the road, nor any sign of the Yamparika Comanche off to either side of it. They came into the settlement right at dusk and were greeted by the townsfolk with great shows of concern and relief.

Mama and Sissy were taken in by the widow Niendorff, whose husband had been the blacksmith down in Live Oak, Texas, and who now ran the boarding-house and stage station at Red Hawk. Lon and Junior, with Bubba insisting on being included, spent the night in bivouac with the Texas Rangers outside town. The McCalister boys, all three, did their turns at guard. The night passed in quiet. The only disturbance came when old Cap showed up full of red-eye bourbon whiskey along about midnight. His story—that the town marshal's Red Hawk posse had turned tail and snuck back home after agreeing to follow old Cap—was a good enough one to call for all hands to help him finish off the spare bottle he was toting pinned under his left arm.

The rangers never reported the posse's cowardice nor mentioned it in the town.

They saddled up with daylight to go back out to Paint Creek to bury their ranger dead and to collect what things of brave Bob Jacks and Charley Holt the Indians might have left them. Among the things they didn't find out there were the scalps of the two men, and their manhood parts. Also, they didn't find the Indians Lon's party had killed in both gullies. The Comanches had returned for these, as by their custom. Strangely, they had still left the body of their chief, building for it a burial scaffold on the spot, high in south gully, where it had fallen. There, beneath his war shield, for many years a curiosity site, the body of Tabebekat, Killer of the Sun, awaited eternity.

· But for the older McCalister boys, it was farewell to the Texas Rangers that morning of the Red Hawk bivouac.

Sergeant Hayes Coffey came to Lon and told him that he was sorry about his mother's condition but that he, Coffey, had seen similar cases and he would have to tell the boys that they'd best not count on her good recovery.

"She may go along like this for years," he said. "And she may start talking again tomorrow morning. But it's no use to wait on her. I knew your daddy a long time. I don't believe he would want you to hang back from your own lives hoping your mother would come around. I know if you was my boys, I would want you to travel on."

He paused, singling out the doubt he saw in Lon's eyes.

"Listen, son, leave your mama to your sister and to the folks here in Red Hawk. The widder Niendorff is a good sort and won't expect pay from you boys for their keep until you're able to make it."

Lon nodded. He was thinking hard now about something scarce out of his mind since two days before here in Red Hawk. With mama "lost" the way she was, and Sissy and Bubba to wait on her, they were all three in the best and safest place they could be. When he and Junior got back, they would take the family and start again out on Paint Creek. Until they did get back, though, there was no white family that could dare to live out there in the Comanche grass without menfolk to fend off the Indians. Meanwhile, having the light of papa's dream for the ranch still lit while they were away was a warm, good thing. It would lead them home again. And it would give Bubba and Sissy, who were both just little kids, really, something to sort of hang on to in the idea that they hadn't lost their true home, only had to give it up a little while. One day, Lonnie and Junior would come back and they would all be together again out on Paint Creek.

Lon had been silent a long time with the thoughts of leaving, but Sergeant Coffey waited him out, understanding the pain of it for the taciturn youth. Lonnie McCalister was barely seventeen, Junior just over sixteen. Hayes Coffey couldn't even remember when he had been that young.

"I'm beholden to you, Sergeant Coffey," Lon said at last. "You know what I and Junior aim to do, I suspect."

"Yes. Just what I would do—what I did do at your age— only my war was the one for Texas independence. I reckon this one will be a sight more hell. Good luck, son. Tell your brother good-bye for me." The ranger started for his horse, being held nearby by the already mounted men of his band. Swinging to saddle, he turned a last time to Lon, and said, "Tell that little redhead sonofabitch that if he don't mind what his big sister tells him to do, Sergeant Coffey will come back and tan his butt the color of schoolhouse paint."

"I'll tell him." Lon waved, with a rare if fleeting smile. "But he won't listen."

The ranger didn't hear the last of it, nor had Lon McCalister intended that he should. He was just talking to himself, knowing he had much more than that to say to Bubba McCalister, and soon.

That morning, he and Junior made all the preparations they could for mama and Sissy and Bubba. The widow Niendorff was a little doubtful of the arrangement but agreed to it, "at least till winter." Since Lon and Junior did not expect to be gone anything like that long, the deal was struck. Down payment for the family's keep in Red Hawk was made with the McCalister wagon and all it had carried back into town from Paint Creek. With it went the team, Sam Houston and Sugarplum, to be sold at first, best opportunity to settle mama's board, and the kids'.

Having lost all the ranch riding stock to the Comanche raid, along with the beef cattle and even the old milk cow, Tinkle-bell, leaving only Big Red and his three Mexican wives to survive the Indians to cluck and scratch in the widow Niendorff's garden, Lon and Junior had to sell their saddles for stage tickets to Red River. After they reached there, Lon said, they would trust to luck. They knew that good folks everywhere along the line would be glad to help brave Texas boys get to where the war was going on.

So it was that at high noon they climbed on the eastbound Overland Mail stage, rolling for Fort Belknap, Montague, Gainesville, Sherman, and Texarkana. The last they saw of the family was the three of them, mama and Sissy and Bubba, watching after their coach from the stage stop in front of the widow Niendorff's boarding-house in Red Hawk.

Bubba was standing at attention, stiff and braced-back as a toy tin soldier.

Sissy was waving and crying and waving again.

Mama was just nodding and smiling.

She didn't wave.

Just nodded, just smiled.

# 8

For Bubba McCalister, life in Red Hawk was about all an eleven-year-old boy could manage.

He hated the sniffle-nosed town kids. He hated the school and the teacher. He was getting to hate old lady Niendorff, and he for sure could not stand all the pious catering-to that the townsfolk heaped on him and mama and big sister. Most of all, he could not tolerate any kowtowing from those Red Hawker menfolk who had been with that damned cowardly posse. Even though Sissy explained it to him every day, it wouldn't wash for Bubba. She could tell him till she was twenty years old, or a hundred, whichever came first, that the possemen were just trying to make it up to themselves for being such chicken-livered bastards. Bubba would never believe it. If one more of them said to him or Sissy, "Well, how's our little Injun orphans today?" or, "Hope your poor mother's better soon," he, Bubba, was going to belt him in his cajones and run like hell.

As those first months in Red Hawk dragged on with no word from Lon and Junior, it became increasingly difficult for Bubba to behave in school and be even gritty-polite to the townspeople. He wanted to leave, to run away, to go find his brothers in the war. What held him back was the fact Sissy was there and working so hard and long each day to care for mama and to protect her from all the nosey women wanting to come in and just look at her so they could say they had "been and see'd the Paint Creek crazy woman."

But Bubba stayed with it, waiting for that first letter from Lonnie and Jim Junior.

It came that winter of 1862, just as the money to pay the widow Niendorff her board bill ran out, and when the family had been expecting "at the most latest" to see Lon and Junior come home from the war.

It wasn't much of a letter for showing around. Just like Lon, it didn't talk much. But it hit home somehow, and it hit Bubba hardest of the three of them. That is, except for Sissy when she showed mama the letter and mama only nodded and smiled and went back to looking out the window toward the west, and Paint Creek. Right there, Sissy had almost cried, and she had said, "Oh, God, mama, ain't you never going to do nothing but bob your head and grin foolish?! This here's a letter from the boys. Your boys, mama! They're all right. And they're knocking the tar out of the Yankees. Mama, don't you hear?"

But mama did not hear and Sissy had fled out of the room, dropping the letter behind her.

Bubba picked it up and went over to the light of the window to read it by:

Dear Mama,

Vicksburg
Barracks

We had a good journey and no trouble finding the fighting. Just across Red River from Texarkana, we was took and swore into some Missouri Confederate foot troops, no matter we was looking all the while to find Gen. Hood and the Texas Brigade horse calvary.

We spent all summer with this here Missouri outfit and it was what they call gerilla fighting, and mighty mean.

We was up in north Tennessee come late fall, which is where I got hit.

It was at the Fort Henry fight, and hard-down winter

*by then, that old Junior was so bad injured. It's
Feberary now and brutal cold and we are back down
futher south. We was sent to Vicksburg to get well,
not being able either on us to walk.*

*We both are all right now. Junior can walk and I
can too, with help.*

*The surgeon tells us we can go back to the fighting
soon. And good news, mama! John Bell Hood's calvary
is coming through here gathering men. We will be
with him!*

*Junior says hellow to everybody and I say be good
to all of you, and God bless the family.*

*We will surely see you in the spring.*

*Yr. Lvng. Son*

*Lonsford.*

Bubba stared at the letter a minute after reading it
through. He was about to put it on the table where mama
sat in her rocker all day, when he noticed something.
Down in the corner where the paper was folded over and
where some dark brown stains had nigh covered it was
another small patch of Lon's writing.

Bubba's eye caught at the added lines because he saw
his name in them. Squinting and lip-reading, he made out
what Lonnie had put onto the end of it:

*Hello Bubba.*

*Are you taking good care of mama and Charlotte
May? Remember our handshake on you being the man
of the family whiles me and Junior are away. Junior
says howdy to you and don't get caught spying on the
girls' outhouse at the school.*

*Yours,*

*Brother Lon.*

Bubba had to grin both at what Junior said and at Lon
reminding him of Sissy's real name. But he quit grinning
when that made him think of his own baptized name,
which was Randolph Barnes McCalister, after old Captain
Randolph B. Marcy, who had laid out the stage road
running past Paint Creek.

41

There was a darker reason the smile flickered out.

It was the memory of his shaking hands with brother Lon and being told, "You're the man now, Bubba," the day Lonnie and Junior had gone away from Red Hawk.

That trust from old Lon was *really* what had held Bubba to his mark all the lonesome months since. He could never go back on brother Lon. Not ever.

For now, the ranch boy put the letter on mama's table and patted mama on the cheek and leaned over and kissed her, and went on out into the bite of the wintry day.

The next letter came in the spring. Again it was from brother Lon. The late May day that it arrived Bubba was out back in Mrs. Niendorff's garden chasing Big Red and his harem, Juanita, Chiquita, and One-Eyed Juarez Sally. The problem was that the Paint Creek chickens were scratching up the widow's three rows of sweet corn kernels faster than the old lady could get them into the ground. The ultimatum had been issued that either the chickens went or the McCalisters did. Bubba had wanted to take her up on that offer but Sissy, who was getting almost sweeter and more noble than Bubba could stomach, even though it was because mama was getting worse, had talked him into corraling Big Red and his Mexican hens.

He couldn't well refuse big sister's wish, since their only real friend in Red Hawk, Cap, the ancient mail rider of the Overland Road, had carpentered up a coop of sorts out of some packing-crate boards that had reached Red Hawk wrapped around a harpsichord ordered for the preacher's wife all the way from Galveston.

The harpsichord had arrived in a hell of a shape, but the lumber of the crate was just fine, and Cap had done a prime job with it. The coop did look like a Comanche tipi more than a hen house, but it would do. It would, providing Bubba could catch the damned chickens to pen them up in it. Which pursuit, as indicated, is what kept him from getting Lon's second letter before Sissy got her Nosey Parker snoot into it.

42

By the time Bubba got the letter, Sissy had cried over it and run some of the ink, but Bubba had waded through it lip-whispering each syllable and bobbing his shaggy head to every sentence start and period. The parts that stayed in his mind were those about the war. Brother Lon got into it, after addressing the letter to Sissy:

> The last I writ you, we was in Vicksburg pretty sick. Sinct then it has been a little hard but we are in the fighting yet.
>
> Old Jim Junior is the pet of our company. Gives everything he's got of food or warm coat to the other boys, does turn for the sickest ones at guard or work duty, and they all love him for it. And him so hurt still that he scarcely can walk. It is his leg which he got at Fort Henry. My own trouble plagues me as well. It is my arm whicht is stiff and kept me out of the calvary of Gen. Hood. As Junior wouldn't go without me, we got throwed into a infantry outfit and shipped on the railroad cars. They was cattle cars, slat-open sides, and mercey the rain and cold did blow in on the way up to Corinth, in Mississippi. But that wasn't nothing of the hell that waited.
>
> North of Corinth was fit the blackest struggle of the war. It was at a place called Shiloh Church, jest acrost the line inter Tennessee. We was in it, me and Junior. Us with our little company of brave and loyal Texas boys. We was forty going into it on the night of April Six, and thirteen coming out of it sundown of April Seven, when we had to fall back to Corinth.
>
> Our officers toldt us it was a great victory for the South but twenty-three of our troop's boys didn't think so, surely.
>
> You must not take alarm, Charlotte May, nor worry mama on this. But I and Jim Junior are in a old building here called Tishamingo Hotel, and it is a field hospital for them as simply just can't make it no futher. There is talk about Junior's bad leg and what must be done with it that I don't like to hear. The surgeons also been looking at my stiff arm, where the bone of it shows through in one place. But me and "little brother" ain't going to lay around here and wait for any more of

*that kind of talk. We have bribed a orderly to take us out of here tonight. He will put us in the wagons with the soldiers that can still walk, and so are yet of some use and by that took better care of than the poor boys in Tishamingo Hotel.*

*These disabled wounded is being wagoned down to Vicksburg to be put into the work troops of Gen. Pemberton, who holds that great city, and rest your hearts, you and mama, that me and Junior will be amongst their chose number when they unload down yonder.*

*So it will be all right for us, as you can surely see.*

*Back down to Vicksburg we will be only nearer to home when the muster-out is made, whicht we are told won't be much longer off.*

*However, it ain't so easy to believe that a'laying here in Tishamingo Hospital, which our troops, gallant lads though grim, call The Slaughterhouse Hotel.*

*Every night here I have thanked God that me and Junior have heldt together all this way. And He has answered me. Tonight we will be free of here. I know we will make it safe away in the wagons, and know we will make it on home the same way.*

*I have to close and seal this right now, Charlotte May. I must hurry. I see the orderly we give the money to stepping over the wounded on the floor to come for us. We have been told to play dead, and I can see the sheets over his arm which he will use to cover us with. Past him, I see the "meat wagon," a baggage handtruck from the R.R. depot, waiting in the hall outside. It is waiting for us. There is already some bodies stacked on it. Lord, Jesus, Junior whispers to me, don't a war get fearsome wrong and turrible sometimes.*

There was more of it past this part that stayed in Bubba McCalister's memory, but the boy didn't need the rest of it. He knew only that brother Lon and big old dumb Junior were mighty sick from the war. And even if he, Bubba, had got to be twelve years old since they went away, it made him deep uneasy about being the man of the family. He understood why that was, too.

All along, he and big sister Charlotte May had just

known that Lon and Junior would come home safe. Now, reading the letter from Tishamingo Hotel hospital, in far-off Mississippi, Bubba didn't *just know* any such thing anymore. It might be that they would never see their big brothers again, or ever get a third letter from the war.

Sissy said they mustn't show this letter to mama and Bubba agreed to that. Later that night, Sissy crept into Bubba's room after the house lamps were turned down and old lady Niendorff was flat-back snoring.

"Bubba," she whispered, "it's me, Sissy. I think we better pray."

Bubba sat up in bed, frightened.

"I ain't never been no good at it," he said. "You know I ain't."

"I got mama's Bible here," Sissy told him. "Something will come to us."

Bubba got out of bed and kneeled down in the dark on the cold squeaky floorboards. His hand found big sister's on mama's tattered book and Sissy started the words by herself.

"Our dear Lord Jesus whicht is up there in heaven, please shepherd safe home to us brother Lonnie and Jim Junior, and bring mama back to us, and the whole family together again at the homeplace—Amen."

There was an odd pause after that, perhaps three heartbeats long, then Bubba McCalister spoke for the first time of the prayer, and for himself.

"Me too, Jesus," he said. "Honest to Christ."

Then he put his hands up to his face and rocked back on his bare heels alongside the bed and commenced to shake. Sissy got him by the shoulders and said, "Bubba, don't do that," and sat with him there on the board floor until the shaking passed. When it had, she got him back into his bed, leaned over and kissed him even though he pulled away from it like little brothers did, and said to him in her soft voice, "I love you, Bubba. Don't be sad," and went back to where she slept in mama's room.

In a little while Bubba slipped out of the bed and

45

went to the attic window of his tiny room. It was a west window, like the one in the parlor downstairs. The one mama looked out of. And Bubba looked out of his window through the blaze of the full May moon and wondered if the Comanches were riding tonight out there, and what the moon was seeing where Paint Creek ran and the McCalister homeplace stood silent on the slope of west ridge. And, oh!, what stories the spring wind was rustling in the buffalo grass. Those stories that only Bubba knew, secret even from Sissy, and mama too, before her eyes went empty.

But now, Bubba wondered, *now* what was mama seeing when she looked out her west window? What stories was she hearing on the wind and in the rustle of the grass?

Was she thinking of Lon, and Junior, and papa, and the homeplace? And her heart feeling sad within her, like Bubba's was, to think of Paint Creek and all the old days before papa went away with the rangers, and Lonnie and Jim Junior to the war, and mama to wherever she had gone away to?

Bubba rubbed the back of a stubborn fist, first to one eye, then to the other, swallowing hard.

Dogged, but it was lonely in the night.

# 9

The year 1863 struck Bubba that it would never come.

All through the year before he had watched daily for the third letter that would tell that Lon and Junior were finally coming home. The letter had not come, no letter had come, and the second winter had set in.

January, February, March, April, and going into May of the new year, the days struggled by in an agony of endless hopes and following despairs. Then, magically, it was Junetime again and summer busting out from every hillrise, thicket, clear-water branch, live-oak savannah, and open sweep of Comanche grass. Given six weeks, it was two years almost to the hour that Lon and Junior had gone away.

Sissy and Bubba, standing out front of the widow's New Travelers Rest lodging house and Overland Stage-lines depot, watched the dust of the westbound run roll toward them. Both youngsters appeared somewhat drawn.

"Pushing the hell out of it," Sissy offered. "Jest cain't wait to get his boots under Miz Niendorff's table for noon dinner."

"Onlikely," Bubba said. "Not with that varmint bait she serves up. A starving wolf wouldn't tech it. No wonder we're doing so poorly."

"Yes." Sissy heaved a sigh. "I surely wish mama was better."

"She ain't better. She's worse."

Sissy nodded. "A lot," she said.

They watched the stage come on at a high lope. When it hit the bend northwest of town and straightened for the Travelers Rest, they could hear the driver yelling, "Hee-yah, you bastards! Flatten out. Bring her up in style. The hell with the old lady's curtains!"

"Monk Beckham." Sissy nodded. "Nobody but Monk can sound like a catamount full of porky hog quills."

A fierce light appeared in Bubba's intent face. He wheeled on his sister. "Sis, Monk was driving when Lon and Junior tooken stage for Texarkana. And that were a high noon run, too. I got the feeling!" he cried suddenly. "It's in me wild. Yonder comes that letter, Charlotte May!"

Bubba ran to meet the stage, a hundred yards out into the salt piñon. And ran back by its spinning hubs choking on the dust and trying to yell up to Monk Beckham about a letter from brother Lon. The driver cussed him and swerved the teams to keep the coach from knocking the racing boy under its yellow-spoked wheels. But Bubba ran a dead heat with the six-horse hitch, and he was right. The letter from Lon *was* in the Overland mail sack.

Three minutes later and with the dust still settling

nicely upon the widow Niendorff's fresh-clean curtains, he and Sissy McCalister were out in the garden crouched back of Big Red's packing-crate chicken house. Sissy held the letter desperately to her breast, neither child yet daring to unseal the stained and tattered envelope.

"Lord God," Sissy said, "supposing it ain't the one? You know, not saying they're coming home."

Bubba's narrow face grew dark. "It's the one," he said. "Open it, Charlotte May."

The girl did so nervously, and spread the pages of the letter upon the soft summer earth where the June sun fell warm upon them, and bright with hope.

There wasn't a sound, then, scarcely even of breathing.

Dearest Mama,

Louisiana
Red River

Mama, we are coming home.
God attended us at last and your two boys will be with you mebbe ahead of this letter.
A miracle has saved us, mama.
I will tell you of it.
We have been in the thick of it ever sinct I writ you last. Finally, late this March we was sent over into Arkansas, wheres we joined up to the 15th Texas Infantry. Ain't that a hoot, mama? Me and old Jim Junior, we went to ride in the calvary and we ain't see'd the saddle side of a horse the whole cussed war.
Nor ever did we lay eye on General Hood, neither.
We was took by the 15th at Clarkesville and marched to Fort Smith, Fort Smith, mama, imagine. That near to home. Only about a four day ride down to Texarkana. But it were hell there. No food, no clothes, no discipline of the men, mean and poor officers.
And me and Junior wasn't too well there.
Fact, one doctor said to let us go on home as our condition was that despirt. But the other doctor said no, we could go with the levy for Shreveport that General Kirby-Smith was going to send back over into Mississippi to help at Vicksburg. I didn't blame them doctors. They was getting all the men they could out of Arkansas. Elstwise they faced either to starve or get shot in a revolt.

48

Junior caved in about halfways to Shreveport. When they see'd I was his brother and keeping care of him, they throwed me in the wagon with him. There was sixteen of us in there, three of us dead. Three more died on the way to here, where I write this letter.

But we made it, Mama, and there we was in Shreveport just over the river from Texas.

And here comes the miracle.

Our wagon was just unloading dead and living at a mudflat camp outside the city whens a rain-sopped officer and two ragged aides rid up. He stopt his horse and asked our sergeant who we men was, and the sergeant toldt him we was headed east to fight.

Mama, you'd ought to have see'd the flash of eye that officer give the poor sergeant.

He flang back his cape and we could see he was a general, and he said, moving his horse to be near us, "These here men to fight again? In this here war? In this here life? By God, sergeant, fetch me the commanding officer of this section."

Natural, the sergeant went a 'running and come back in a spell with a whipt looking colonel, who didn't seem to know what to do when he seen our general. He was that scairt, I mean to tell you, mama, that colonel was tail-tuckt.

"Sir," the general told him soft, "you will see that all of these men receive their honorable discharges as of this evening. I want them over the river and in the Marshal rest camp tonight. Is that clear?"

"Yes, sir, it is," the colonel said. "But—"

"There are no buts, sir!" the general toldt him. "My aide will draw the authority and you will present it properly where it will be recorded. I will have your name, sir."

"Starr, sir. Colonel John Patrick. 23rd Texas Calvary."

"That's all colonel. Dismissed."

The colonel drawed himself up then, and saluted, and there was our miracle.

"Thank you, General Hood," he said. "By field order, your signature, yes sir!"

And there you are, mama; we never did find General John Bell Hood, but he surely found us and in the very nitch of time.

*Every man of us that could, fell on our knees in that mud and cried like babies.*

*Gen. Hood said to us, "God bless you all, men. You've fought enought for a thousand wars. Go home and find peace."*

*The reason this letter is so long, mama, is that we are already over Red River and sleeping dry and under canvas outside Marshal, Texas. We got a lantern to each tent and things to write with. There's seven of us from the Fort Smith meat-wagon made it here over the river alive. The army will help us with passage far as Ft. Worth or San Antone, whichtever is closest home fer us.*

*We tooken Ft. Worth, you can bet!*

*Mama, we'd ought to be home and all on us back out to the Paint Creek place by the middle of June, or last of it at the latest.*

*This will be the best summer we can make of it, and we will start with you, mama.*

Yr. Lvng. son,

Lonsford McC.

# 10

They showed this letter to mama. They were hoping somehow that its nature would break through into mama's memory. But it did not. For a moment it appeared as if it were going to. Mama seemed actually to try to read what it said, when Sissy held it up for her by the window. But the two children guessed afterward that it was only some accidental expression on mama's face and nothing to do with the letter.

"Gas," said old lady Niendorff, hearing what they said. "It's only gas. Makes her smirky like that."

"The hell!" Bubba cried angrily. "What would you know, you damned old—"

Sissy grabbed him by the nape of his neck with both hands and tried to hold him in the crook of one arm while popping the hand of the other one over her little brother's mouth, but the seed was in the ground.

The widow Niendorff wheeled about and flounced back to them, halting arms akimbo between the children and the silent woman in the rocking chair.

"I heard that, Randolph Barnes," she hissed at the largely surprised Bubba. "It will just be the cork in the jug for you people in my house. Charlotte May"—she stabbed a big-knuckled forefinger at Sissy—"you had best see to other lodgings by the end of the week."

"But ma'am, Miz Niendorff, we ain't no other place to go."

"If we had," Bubba helped out, "we'd a went there long ago."

"Well, you're going there now, young man. I will not take language like that from a child, not in my house, not no more. You've smarted off with me onct too often, and been nothing but grief to me since you come here. Sissy, you're welcome to stay. You can work your way around here. But your mother and this nasty little boy are too much for me."

"Yeah," Bubba said, "and we ain't paid our rent in nigh a year, too. I reckon that's what you mostly cain't stand about mama and me."

"You see, Sissy," the widow snapped. "He is hopeless. Takes after your mother. She was always quick to take insult from none intended. And she was mean-quiet underneath, just like this boy."

Bubba took up the broom that the widow had been toting through the room when she heard Bubba sully her name in anger. With this first handy weapon, the boy swung hard. The broom was a broomcorn heavy-duty type with a handle of Osage-orange wood. Bubba's aim was on, and the handle, out beyond the broom head, caught the widow an inch above the tops of her button-up shoes and fair across both shinbones.

Mrs. Niendorff's screech is still remembered in Red Hawk, Texas. But that isn't what stampeded Bubba. The boy had broken the broom handle and he well knew

51

what brooms cost and particularly what busting that broom was likely to cost him. He had instant visions, the way that town already felt about him, of being put in the jail for the whole of summer vacation from school. You couldn't assault and battery an old woman in her own house and expect to go free for it.

Bubba lit out and took to the brush and did not come in out of it until dark that night, when he showed up scratching at the back door of old Cap Marston's shack out past the edge of town.

"I bin expecting you," the old man said. "Your sister done toldt me what happen't twixt you and the widdy. Good for you, bucko. I only wisht I could have see'd it."

"It were something," Bubba said.

"Well, she took hard words to your maw, and ain't ever I knowed a kinder, nicer lady than her."

"Me neither, Cap. It's just that folks don't seem to understand mama."

"Mama and you, boy. You go together like tree and bark."

Bubba nodded that this was so, then frowned. "What we going to do, Cap?"

"How you see it, Bubba?"

"I been thinking on it all day. And it's come to me."

"How so?"

"We got to take mama home."

"Great Christ, boy, don't talk addlepated."

"Cap, we got to. Didn't Sissy tell you? Lon and Junior are a'coming home. They'll be in Red Hawk any day."

"Charlotte May showed me the letter." Cap nodded.

"Sure, and don't you see how it has to be? Lon and Junior put the trust of mama on me and Sissy. How's it going to look for them to come home and find mama throwed out in the street? Cap, we simply got to get mama back out home and settled in nice, befores the boys get here."

"Hell's fire, Bubba, you're daft. How you going to get your mama out there? You and Charlotte May going to travois her?"

"We got feet."

"Sure, and how far they going to take you with these here damned hippycrit towners follering you out a-horseback? They ain't going to let you and your sister go back out there, nor drag your maw with you. How'd it look if they done that? You know what I mean, letting a little fambly with a Comanch'-broke mama, a sister fifteen year old and showing things what ought to show for her age, them and a thirteen-year-old redhead feist of a boy about half-size what he oughter be, I say, leaving a fambly like that to head back out inter the Comanch' grass, without even no man to go with them?"

"*I'm* the man," Bubba said, not smiling.

"Sure," Cap spat at him. "And I'm General Ben McCulloch come back from the dead at Pea Ridge! Bubba, you got to pull yourself down to a walk, here, and use your head for something besides boiling your brains in."

The conference was interrupted at this point by a soft rapping on the leather-hinged door of Cap's shanty, and it was Sissy come out from the town hoping brother Bubba would be there. "I knowed it!" She grinned, giving the boy a whack between the shoulder blades that made him blink. "Bubba, me and you got the same *puha!*"

"Other folks going to figure out he's here, same as you done," Cap reminded her. "Jest take 'em a mite longer. What have you been thinking, Charlotte May?"

There were sudden tears in the girl's eyes. "Cap," she said, "I'd like to go home. I'd just like to take mama and go home. You know any way at all in the world we can do that, Cap?"

"I can tell you one thing, Sissy. You and your hardhead brother sure enough do buy your *puhas* from the same Comanch' medicine man. He's singing the identical chant you be. It's the homesick song."

The old man's mention of the Comanche fired up the intense look in Bubba's face. He wanted to know at once what condition Cap found the Indians in this spring. Had he heard or seen anything of them? Wasn't it a fact that no Yamparika band had been spotted east of Emigrant or Horsehead crossings of the Pecos, since their defeat at the Paint Creek ranch? Most especially since that defeat had seen their chief killed and his medicine made very bad by a crazy woman? Wasn't it a fact, Bubba ended, that what the townsfolk were saying the past months was true—that the Comanche weren't coming back to this part of Texas in a long, long time, and maybe never again?

Cap had to admit the essential accuracy of this line, and it was plain that he himself, an experienced Indian fighter of yore and longtime mail rider of more recent times, believed the Comanche danger to be past for that area. Indians tended to avoid religiously those sites where their *puha* had failed them in battle. It was very likely a buffalo-grass fact that the Paint Creek home-place of the McCalisters was henceforward and power-fully taboo for the Yamparika.

"All right, boy," he summed up. "I'll give you that. Mebbe you would be fair safe from the Yamps. But they's other roving bands might pass through—mebbe some Lipan or Mimbres Apach', or outlaw Kioway—hell, you never know. No, sir, it ain't no way hair-tight safe out there."

Sissy had caught some of Bubba's eye-shine. "Cap, it won't never be that safe. But Bubba's saying we can do it. That's all. If the Comanch' ain't been there in two years, they ain't coming. You just admitted it. Cap—oh, Cap!—ain't there some way?"

The old man creaked up out of his broad-slat chair, motioned the two of them to come to him. When they had, he put an arm about each of their shoulders and held them to him. "Sis," he said, "and old Bubba, listen here to me. If there was any way in God's staked plains that I could see it your way, I would. But it ain't to be. Even if there was a way to get you two and your poor mama back out there, and the place fixed up decent to live in, the towners still ain't going to leave you do it. They'd be talked about, don't you see? It ain't you they give a hoot about. It's themse'ves. They don't want it

54

said that Red Hawk done let a demented widdy woman and two young childurn, one a busting-out, nubbin-growed girl, go back out to live in the Comanch' grass. And for double certain, not when they ain't a man on the place with them."

Cap sighed, tightened his hug.

"Happen you had a man to go with you, well mebbe it would wash. But you ain't." He paused, releasing Bubba. "And I don't want to hear that horse-dobbie abouten you being a man, Randolph Barnes. You know damn well what I mean. You, too, Charlotte May." He let the girl go now and stood back from them. "You don't know these Red Hawkers. You think the town's small? It's a regular by-Jesus metriopolis compared to the sizes of their minds. Ain't you heard enough of your pore maw being called the Paint Crick Crazy Woman? Ain't you both had your shut of the town meeting simpering 'our own little orphant fambly' at you? Hell, you're the main attraction in town, don't you know that? They ain't going to give you nothing but sweat and sorrow, but they ain't going to let you go, neither. It wouldn't be Christian, you see."

"I don't see cow chips!" Bubba glowered. "They's got to be a way. I'd rather see mama dead than made futher fool of, or to be found out in the gutter by Lonnie and Jim Junior. I was give the guard of her and Charlotte May, you hear? I will see them home again on Paint Crick in time for the boys to find them there, safe and happy, iffen I have to borry a gun and shoot somebody."

Bubba peered quickly about the tangled rat's nest that was Cap Marston's one-room castle.

"Whar's your old Texas Ranger hip gun?" he asked.

"In a good place." Cap nodded warily. "Whar I keep it when I ain't riding the mail line."

"Gimme it." Bubba motioned impatiently.

"I'll give you a swat in your ragged butt!" the old man fumed. "What the hell's ailing you, Bubba? You know I ain't going to loan you no gun. You cain't even handle a broomstick. How you going to hold down a januine 'Big .44' Captain Sam Walker Colt's reevolver?"

"Well, Christ," Bubba said, disheartened. "I reckon that runs us plumb out of friends in this here town, Charlotte May. Come on, let's go."

But Sissy had a strange look to her eyes. She had been watching old Cap Marston as he laid it into Bubba. She had seen the light come up in the wrinkled oldster's face when the talk had turned to the Texas Rangers and Cap's famous old four-pound relic of a rusted ranger fighting Colt. And her young mind went back to those times papa had spoken of Ranger Brevet-Captain Arlo Marston, who led the charge that broke the Mexican left at San Jacinto, and seeing the old man there before her in his hovel outside the mean town of Red Hawk, Texas, and thinking back to papa's proud tales, Sissy's own face lit up.

"Cap," she said softly, ignoring Bubba, "we've found our man to go with us."

"Sure you have, Sis," he said. "And I'm going to marry the widdy Niendorff and git elected to the state guvmint and be the second coming of Sam Houston."

"No, Cap," Sissy said, "I mean it. Me and Bubba and mama have found our man. He's Captain Arlo Marston, of Hays Texas Rangers."

Cap stared at the girl as though he had seen a ghost. A minute before he had been an old forgotten man living out his time at the charity of the community, riding the mail for four dollars a month and horse feed, waiting to die in whatever of dignity memory might call up for him. Now, for another minute, Sissy had summoned back for him the glory days he had thought lay dead with the Alamo and the great victory over Santa Ana, at San Jacinto.

Old Cap was a windy fellow but once he had ridden with history. His only tie with that famous time was the giant rusted old Walker Colt he hid in the tattered carpetbag beneath his bunk, along with the other secret treasures of his vanished past. But the girl with the tawny-gold hair and quick laughter had called up the spirits of Ben McCulloch, Jack Hays, and Sam Walker and, doing so, had brought Arlo Marston again to San Jacinto and the charge on the Mexican left.

The old man looked long and slowly at the Paint Creek ranch girl and her small, scowling brother. From somewhere came a straightness of spine, a thrust of jaw, a burning of rheumy gray eye that had been stranger to old Cap's life nigh these twenty years.

"Lord God, come on," was all he said.

# 11

Old Cap took charge with joy.

When Sissy, hesitating, asked him was he certain he wanted to do it, he only said, "Why, yaller-hair child, you done made old Cap young for one night more in his life. That's pay for what's left of the rest of it, you had best believe. Come on, again. Let's go!"

And Sissy, taking up the spirit, laughed that laugh of hers that was like wind chimes in morning breeze.

"You mean it? We going to do it tonight? Good God a'mighty, you hear that, Bubba? Say hallelujah!"

"The hell." Bubba grinned. "How's she going to go, Cap. Whereaway from here?"

"Foller on," Cap said, and raised the chimney and blew out the wick of his coal oil lamp. "Stay close and go quiet and I'll lay it out for you."

They went out into the windy darkness of the young June night. Cap led the way, keeping to the side of the road. As they went along, he gave his companions their parts. Whatever of local traffic chanced past, he ducked down off the right-of-way into the weeds and lay low with the McCalister children until that traffic was gone by.

"Don't want nobody seeing us together," he said. "We got to move mighty swift and no getting fouled in our own harness, you hear? There's no more than thirty minutes 'fore moonrise. Now what have I toldt you? Quick."

"I got to get mama ready without old lady Niendorff sniffing nothing is up," Sissy answered. "I'm to say it would do mama a world of good to go for a walk whiles the moon rises. As for belongings, take nothing but what she has on. Same for myself. I'm to have mama out behind the store in the alleyway at eight sharp. Bubba—"

Bubba blinked and set his jaw. "Well, me, I'm to sneak into the widow's back yard and shinny up the drainpipe to mama's room and get one of the widow's big laundry bags out'n the linen closet and jam inter it all of mama's and Sissy's and my own stuff that it will holdt and then shag the hell out'n there the same way I come. I'm to be out at the old saw yard come eight on the nostrils."

"Inter the grass!" Cap said, and pushed the two of them down the slope of the culvert they were crossing. They lit in the water and Bubba cussed something wicked and Cap vowed to suds his mouth out with hog lye when the chance came along, while Sissy covered her ears and said, "Goddammit, Bubba, you hadn't ought to use sech words in front of a girl."

"Well, dog it, this stale water smells like mule pee and I don't cotton to being drownded in it just to let that smirky old goat, Wilbur Hubbison, ride over my head on this here culvert. He gone yet, Cap?"

"He's gone, and so had we best be. We'll split three ways. Remember, now, you kids, we ain't larking here. We mean to get your mama out home and all of us with her and to do it tonight by dark afore anybody can halt us. It's going to take luck and guts and gumption. Not to mention a little brains, whicht is where you worries me, Bubba. For Gawd's sake keep your temper corraled and just get what I sent you for, and light out with it."

Bubba and Sissy were sobered now and getting a little edgy. It wasn't that they feared anyone in Red Hawk, except that some one of the towners could spot them and ruin it all for mama. They had to get mama home. That was the main of it. That and get the ranch all spick and dusted up for old brother Lon and Jim Junior. It would be a heartbreak to have any of it go wrong this late in the beautiful June evening.

"We will do our parts, Cap," Sissy told the old man, as they scrambled dripping up out of the stand-water of the culvert drain. "The Lord wouldn't be that mean and small as to foresake us now."

"Amen Jesus," Bubba said, not certain of the usage but absolute on the spirit.

"Here we go, then," Cap said, and trotted away in the darkness. After a moment of lonesome looking around, Bubba and Sissy took their separate ways. Neither of them had the least notion of what Cap was up to for his part of the plan, as he would not tell them of it. "What you don't know you cain't blabber," he had told them. "Jest you two be where you was told, and when. You will find old Cap a'waiting for you."

It proved a night for schemers and daft ones.

Nor did the Lord let them down.

Simms Ellerbrock, owner of the Red Hawk Livery Barn and Livestock Commission Agents, later took his bonden oath that old Cap Marston had never seemed more sober or square onto the pathways of virtue. He had surely convinced Simms that Mexican Jack, who lived in the *monte* out between Paint Creek and the Overland Road west, did indeed have a large stack of buffalo hides which were turning a little too ripe and had to be wagoned to the army buyer down Fort Griffin way on the first cool night, or old Jack he would lose them all. Cap Marston had made a contract for the hauling but needed a wagon and figured the old McCalister rig, which Simms had bought, would do the job just fine. Coming to doing the job right, Cap might also just as well hire out the old McCalister team, since those prairie jugheads were used to the wild stink of buffalo hides and would not spook or make any trouble on the road over it.

The only thing was that Cap had to move fast.

Tonight was the night, or the hides and the haul fee were gone goslings.

There would even be an extra five dollars on the hire

of the team and wagon if Simms kept quiet about it until Cap got the haul made. When a man had got to be as old as Cap Marston, he hated like sin to have folks hearing he had failed again, or been left looking foolish.

His tale had surely sold Simms Ellerbrock, who was as tough as any horse trader to take behind the bushes, but it had all been a load of bushwa, not buffalo hides.

By the time the town wised up to anything at all being off-track, Bubba and his big laundry bag and Sissy and her smiling, nodding mama had both made their meet-ups with ranger Arlo Marston and been piled into the McCalister ranch wagon behind the old ranch team and were, the lot of them, happy as though they all, and not just mama, had mislaid their minds.

There was only one small false note struck during the wagon ride by roundabout to get out of town undiscovered by the Red Hawkers. The widow Niendorff's best large laundry bag had objected to being heaved so heavily and hard into the wagon by the panting Bubba McCalister. It had in fact uttered an unmistakable if thickly muffled Rhode Island Red rooster crow. The same followed by a cackle chorus in chicken-coop Mexican, likewise diminished, which sounded much like three outraged Spanish game hens contending foul play.

"Well, hell!" Bubba had cried indignantly. "I wasn't going to leave them behindt. I ain't yet got one solitary egg out'n them, and I paid thirty-five cents cash money for the trio. *Callate*, Red, you ongrateful sonofabitch!"

"That so," Sissy said loyally. "I loant him the money. That damn Mexican Jack said they was his best birds, too."

"Speak no evil of Mexican Jack!" Cap pleaded, laying whip to Sam Houston and Sugarplum. "He's the one got us out of Red Hawk and homeward bound. Say hallelujah!"

"Say hallelujah! Say hallelujah!" echoed the two children, and even Bubba laughed when Sissy did. But then Sissy faded her laugh and her breath caught and she said to her brother, "Bubba, look at mama. She ain't smiling no more." And Bubba looked at his mother and felt the clutch of his heart, and Sissy finished. "Bubba, mama's crying! She knows we're going home."

# 12

On the twenty-ninth of June, 1863, Lonnie and Jim Junior McCalister were set down at Fort Griffin, Shackleford County, and were there within a long pony ride of home.

The problem was they had no pony to ride.

They had come this far on General Hood's discharge letter. It had got them army ambulance and supply wagon rides all the way from Fort Worth, where army transport of sent-home troops cut off. The letter hadn't been the whole of their passport, though. They themselves had done their part in softening hard army hearts through a whole string of military posts past Fort Worth. It was not possible for southern officers to look at what the war had left of these brave Texas boys and not at least try to see them another day's journey toward home. The fact that all such officers in this beginning third year of the war were local "old soldiers" recruited from onetime ranger outfits, as were their meagre troops, had its effect also. Some of them remembered Sunny Jim McCalister from the ranger days of Plum Creek, the Rio Salado, and even Old San Antone and the border war with Cheno Cortinez. For these old boys to see the sons of their comrade-in-arms shot to pieces and fighting now only to get home before they died on the way was a heartrending thing.

It got brother Lon and Junior one more ride.

The quartermaster at Fort Griffin had heard their story, and when he saw them resting outside the officers' quarters trying to figure their next appeal, he sent a private to bring them over to his supply depot. The army was aiming to establish a new small cavalry post up on the North Overland Road. It would be midway of Paint Creek and Red Hawk and would be built by late summer. A survey party was going up there that same afternoon, and there would be room in the wagon for two Texas boys who had, between them, "give a leg festered to the crotch and a mummified arm shrunk half-size" to the right and noble cause.

Lon thanked God and the Fort Griffin quartermaster and helped load Junior into the survey wagon and sat in there with him under shade of canvas all the way.

It was dark when they reached the Overland Road.

Here, the survey party turned for Red Hawk, rather than camp out on the bare ground with what looked like a hard rain blowing in from the northwest. The McCalisters were given the choice to ride on in with the surveyors or stay out and camp the night "so to be nearer home come sunup." A tent and good blankets were offered, if they voted to stay, as this would be the party's base camp for their survey.

Both Lon and Junior yearned to sleep out where they could smell the rain rolling in over Paint Creek and home. But mama and the kids were in Red Hawk and expecting them. So Lon said they would go with the surveyors. But here, Junior held up a hand from his pallet in the wagon and raised up to his elbows, and called out, "Lonnie, I hear hosses on the lope. Got to be the eastbound run. Hold on."

A moment later, they could all hear the approach of the stage. The driver, seeing their wagon lanterns and coffee fire, pulled in his teams and halloo-ed the camp.

A short out-prairie parlay followed.

The driver proved to be Monk Beckham, and when he told the McCalisters that their mama and kid sister and brother, along with Cap Marston, had moved back out on Paint Creek ten days gone, nothing could have held the boys from going home.

Nothing save for the fact that Junior could not walk and Lon was so sick and weak and wearied himself that he knew God meant them to stay put until morning. The surveyors had an inspiration here. They said they would leave the wagon and all the supplies, including the medicine chest, for the boys to guard. They would go on into Red Hawk on the stage and return next morning early aboard the west run. They would be obliged if the McCalisters would do them the favor, and there would be five dollars each for them in it, as was no more than fair.

Lon ordinarily would have refused this for charity, but again he was too ill. He accepted with a sigh of exhaustion, thanking the men for their kindness. Since the surveyors were carrying Confederate scrip and cared not for cost, they were in turn happy to be away to Red Hawk where their "camp" would be dry as to rain and wet as to bottled refreshments.

Monk Beckham took the surveyors away from the base camp in a rattle of stage-driver profanity and in minutes Lon and Junior were alone with the rising wind and the wondrous smell of the rain blowing in off the buffalo pasture.

The wagon canvas was tight and snug as a Yamparika tipi. The freshening wind gusting against it was sweeter balm than any medicine in the army chest. Even Junior was lulled off through his pain. Lon slept deep and quiet for the first night of the journey home.

Tomorrow they would see mama.

Tomorrow the journey would be over for them both.


# 13


Sometime after midnight Lon was awakened by the snuffling of horses. Then he heard the jingle and squeak of bridle bits and stirrup-fender leathers. There followed the stomping-in-place of halted mounts, held on the rein. There were horsemen out there. They had ridden up on the camp and were standing their horses just beyond the flickering light of the fire that Lon had built up and banked to get through the night. It was that fire, he realized, that had drawn in whatever riders were waiting so eerily quiet for the camp's inhabitants to give themselves away. To make the false move that would give the edge to the strangers.

Lon cussed himself for getting careless. The last thing you did was leave your fire lit at night. And Lon had even rigged a piece of wagon tarp over it so that the coming rain wouldn't drown it out!

"Hello, the wagon," a gravel-growl voice called from the outer night.

Lon didn't have a gun of his own, nor had Junior. What had they to defend? They hadn't a dime between them, nor one good whole human carcass. No horses, no saddles, no personal plunder whatever. On the verge of protesting this innocence to whoever might be outside, the truth of the situation struck him.

Those horsemen out there didn't know how down and destitute he and Junior were. They were looking at the plump team of mules and the fine sturdy wagon and camping gear of the government surveyors.

"Hello," a second, kinder voice said. "We'd appreciate the share of your fire, friends. We're fair used up."

Lon, reassured some little, still hesitated.

"You in the wagon." Gravel voice was back. "This is the law. You got two seconds. Pile out of there, both hands first and showed empty at the puckerhole."

"Coming out," Lon responded hurriedly. "Junior," he asked low-voiced, "you awake? We got company."

"So I hear," muttered Junior. "Gimme a hand, Lon."

"Stay put, little brother," Lon said. "I'll introduce you later."

He crawled to the rear puckerhole of the wagon top and loosened it, showing his hands to the visitors before sliding out to the ground.

He didn't like what he saw—nine of the roughest mean-dog customers a body could recall. Eight followers

64

and a leader. It was the leader that had the growling voice and the pale-eyed, loafer-wolf look to go with it. The leader stared now at Lon McCalister, eyes unblinking.

"Who're you?" he said.

Lon told him, adding, "How about you?"

The leader pulled back his worn sheep-pelt coat, showing a pewter star. "Sheriff over to Pioche," he said.

"Hey," called a weakened but friendly voice from the wagon's interior. "Old Charley Skiles. Sonofabitch, you got a bad cold there, Charley."

"It ain't Charley," the leader said. "Charley just lost the election. I got the job."

"No bull?" Junior exclaimed feebly.

"You got Sheriff Skiles's job?" Lon echoed.

"You doubting it?" the leader asked.

"No," Lon denied. "I jest didn't imagine they'd ever change from old Charley, over there."

"Special job," the man said. "They had a hurry-up call. Bank robbery."

"In Pioche?"

The leader nodded. "Bunch of bad ones wearing Confederate uniforms. Rode in peaceful and the town treating them like returned heroes. Maybe like they been treating you, eh? I can see you been in the war."

Lon gave back the other's nod. "Yes, sir, we was. Me and my brother, yonder in the wagon. He's bad hurt."

The leader looked at the pathetic scarecrow in the butternut rags of a southern infantryman. He shook his head almost as if it grieved him more than it ought for a man in his hard profession.

"If your brother's bad hurt," he said, "what would you call yourself?" Again the commiserate headshake. "Boy, you ain't going to make it to daybreak, you're that used up. Let's have a look at your brother."

In the single blink of the pale eyes that came with this sentiment, the leader's entire attitude changed. The harsh voice did not rise, it just went flat.

"Secure the camp," he said to the men behind him.

They went off their horses as if ordered to take cover on cavalry patrol. Before Lon could move, one of them had grabbed him and slammed him up against the side of the wagon with a "don't move!" snarl, two more had swarmed into the wagon after Junior, and the remaining men had run like wolves to check under the wagon, behind the piled surveyor supplies, out where the mules grazed on picket lines and back to the fire's side.

"All clear," reported a squat, hairy posseman who appeared to be the sheriff's chief deputy. "Will I whistle in the Indian?"

The leader nodded yes, and the posseman put two fingers in his mouth and sent out a bullbat nighthawk's call that even Bubba couldn't have beat. It was answered by its mate out in the prairie blackness, and moments later a bedraggled Indian rode into camp leading an overloaded packhorse.

"Tie the horse to the wheel nearest the fire, wheres those packs can dry," the posseman ordered one of his henchmen.

The fellow took the animal from the Indian, who was a tongue-bound mute. He tied the packhorse and without further command got some wood out of the canvas-slung possumbelly under the wagon and built up the banked fire. As he did so, one of the two men who had gone into the wagon after Junior slid back out and trotted over to where the leader still sat his horse. Lon's man had meanwhile eased off on him, finding no weapon on the youth, and the group of them closed in behind the man from the wagon.

"One in there is puking blood," the fellow told the unblinking horseman. "He don't seem able to say nothing."

"Get him out here," the leader said.

"No, for God's sake!" Lon sprang forward. "You cain't move him quick or rough like that. It'll kill him. He ain't holding on but by a shag."

The leader moved his horse over to where Lon had been quickly seized and held by two of the possemen. He leaned down, concern evident in his frown.

"Son," he said, "get out of the way and let us do our work. Me and my posse are just doing a job. A bank's been heisted, one teller killed, two others that might not make it, and a kid was hit in the getaway on the street." He paused, straightening in the saddle. "Now maybe you two boys got a good story for how the one of you got hurt bad enough to be vomiting blood, and maybe you ain't. It's my business to find out. That's why I'm here. Tranch," he said to the hair-grown deputy, "go ahead and drag the other one out here."

Lon heaved to break free of his captors and they pinioned him easily, debilitated as he was. Even so, the leader instantly lashed out with a cowhide boot toe hard as shank iron, taking the youngster full in the jaw and throat. The men let Lon go and he sagged to the ground and fell over on his face in the dirt, not moving.

"Go on," the wolfish leader said. "Haul him out."

They brought Junior from the wagon and laid him on the trampled grass beside the fire spot. He was a fish-belly color and breathing open-mouthed. The leader growled for a third posseman to kneel down and examine the sick man.

There was an odd skill in the manner with which this night rider lifted the closed lids and studied the fixed pupils beneath. An unexpected expertness in the way he pressed ear to the raggedly breathing chest, felt with his hands for any boarding of belly muscles, failing of the carotid pulses or lower-limb pressures.

As he worked, another posseman noted the return of body movement to Lon McCalister, and went over to the youth and peered down at him, and called back to the man who wore the sheriff's star, "This one's coming around."

The kneeling man looked up from his examining of Junior McCalister and announced quietly, "This one isn't."

Lon was struggling to a sitting position, staring around confused and frowning. The intense pain exploded from the throbbing jaw and he threw up violently. The examiner left Junior, came over to Lon. When the vomiting stopped, he took a rag wet with the cold water from the wagon's barrel and soaked it on the back of Lon's neck. Lon came out of it in a moment, though still dazed.

Attempting to speak, he found the lower jaw wouldn't respond. He slurred a sound like the Indian mute's, and the kind-voiced examiner said, "Don't try to talk, son," and then felt the jaw and its angles and jointings, nodded to himself, and added, "Not broken. You're lucky." He waved to his watching fellows. "Spread him," he said.

A posseman took each of Lon's four limbs and stretched the youth suddenly tight. The examiner kneed over astride his chest, seized the base of his lower jaw from both sides and with sudden, wrenching force, pulled the jaw forward, down, back in, and upward. Lon screamed a profanity of agony but heard the audible *pop* with which the jaw went back into its socket and was instantly relieved of the bursting pain.

"Dislocated," the examiner said, getting up from his chest. "There is nothing that could have been done for a fracture. You can thank the Lord for small favors."

Lon sat up, feeling the repositioned jaw. It still hurt, but nothing he couldn't bear. "I think," he managed with some initial difficulty, "I'd ruther thank you, mister. And that wasn't no small favor. I'm beholden—"

Lon broke off, for the first time noting Junior lying on the ground nearby. There was something wrong in the way Junior looked. His arms were rigid, knees drawn up, chest moving spasmodically to the ragged breathing. Of a sudden, Lon McCalister felt the presence of death.

Lon didn't know what he did next, but it began with the wolf-eyed leader of the pack growling at him to get to his feet. When he did so and started instinctively toward Junior, the leader grabbed his coat collar and spun him around. "Hold on," he said. "We'll take care of him." But Lon didn't seem to hear him. Once more, unthinkingly, he twisted to free himself of restraint.

"My brother!" he cried out. "God a'mighty, what've you did to him? Leave go of me, goddammit. Junior, wait!"

The leader nodded as though in altered compassion. "Tranch," he called. "Help out here, please."

The hairy deputy at once moved in and the leader willingly let Lon go. The ranch youth took one weaving step toward Junior. Instead, he encountered Tranch. He never saw the deputy's knee come up to smash him in the groin, he only remembered the blinding pain of it. When he went down everything was a whirl and blur. Enough of consciousness remained to register the thudding of his body into the dirt and then the dull sodden crunching of the booted foot into his ribs, again and again and yet again. After that, the blackness came.

When senses returned, Lon saw the leader bending above him. He remembered thinking how strangely the light eyes reflected the firelight. Dimly, Lon thought again of the wolf in this gaunt man; he had never seen human eyes shine back the light like that, only animal eyes. It was unsettling. Junior would have said it gave a body the fantods. The thought of Junior revived Lon's memory.

"You hear me now," the leader said. "We ain't done a thing to your brother. Just don't you push us again." Straightening, he nodded. "Go ahead on and see him."

Lon staggered up, tottered toward Junior, collapsed back into the dirt. He pulled himself on his elbows the remainder of the way, and took his brother's hands, now knotted over his belly as if to hold back the cold that crept upward within him. "Hold on, Junior; it's Lon—"

Junior may have heard him. One large fist closed over Lon's hand and squeezed weakly, but that was all.

Lon turned his face upward, where the quiet-voiced examiner had come to stand above him.

"He's in ventricular fibrillation," the examiner said. "Irreversible."

Lon was paper-white. He himself appeared as though he had fought his last mile homeward. "What does that mean?" he asked.

"Your brother's dying."

"No, no! He ain't!"

"He's got to," the examiner said. "Once that particular flutter of the heart sets in, it's over."

Lon tottered to his feet once more. "Could he make it to daybreak?"

"He might. He should have died twice already."

Lon turned back to the posse leader. "Sheriff, we're almost home, him and me. Our place is just over yonder rise, maybe ten mile. I can take the wagon where there ain't no ruts to foller. Let me put my brother in it and bear him home to mama. We can make it by first light."

The leader and his posse exchanged looks.

"Just over the rise, eh?" noted hairy deputy Tranch. "Now ain't that interesting. No road inter the place, you say, but you can get us and the wagon to it without no trouble. Sheriff, we got us a case-ace here."

The leader pursed his lips. The movement showed a wide mouth of maloccluded teeth, the canines prominent and yellowed. "Who's home with your mama, boy?" he said.

"Kid brother, kid sister, plus a old man helping out."

The leader looked off west. "Big storm coming," he said. "Going to be a gully-cutter, sure."

"Wash out everything." Tranch nodded.

The others of the posse nodded too but said nothing, watching the sheriff.

The latter turned from his look at the piling westerly cloud bank. A riven of lightning ran the prairie, off southwest, the growl of the thunder thumping in seconds later. "Son," the posse leader said, "you brought that kick on yourself. It looked to me that you would break free and I couldn't be certain you didn't have a hideout blade, or even pistol." He shrugged, spreading his hands. "You know this ain't any regular posse, nor me the regular sheriff. We've been brought in for this manhunt, kid. These are picked hunters. You're lucky one of them didn't drill you. It's the main reason I had to kick you, to get you down alive before somebody else put you there dead. You understand that?"

Lon gazed dull-eyed at the waiting possemen, who now were half circled behind the leader. Once more, he had thoughts of a wolf pack. But he knew that was likely his mind going bad on him, because of the terrible fear for Junior dying. This temporary sheriff was for certain an experienced man and hard used. It only made sense he would have with him the wolfiest pack he could pick up. That was plain. Something about that pack still bothered Lon, yes. But he also knew that any more delays, false fears or real, could only end forever Junior's chance of living to see mama.

"Boy," the leader insisted, "you understand what I say?"

"Yes," Lon McCalister answered. "Will you and your men help me get my brother home?"

"Watch us," was all the wolf-eyed leader said.

It was but a matter of minutes before the possemen, moving with a familiarity that told of striking a thousand camps in the night, and hastily, had the surveyors' base site picked clean as a dead cow's skeleton. Junior was placed on a canvas tarp in the wagon, Lon driving, the Pioche posse flanking the vehicle and following where Lon *gee-ed* and *haw-ed* the fat mules from Fort Griffin. At the last came the mute Indian leading the packhorse.

It seemed fitting somehow.

The Indian couldn't talk but he could whistle.

He was doing that now, maybe knowing something the white men did not. Or could not. It was a hauntingly beautiful melody—sad, poignant, lovely, filled with the distances, freedoms, and homecoming wonders of the buffalo grass. And it was the last song and the last sweet sound that Junior McCalister heard.

# 14

In the last of the thinning night, just before sunrise, Lon McCalister was awakened by one of the possemen. The fellow had come aboard the driver's box of the wagon to spell Lon, who was letting the mules wander.

"You was nodding off," the posseman explained, taking the lines from the thin youth. "Captain didn't want you falling off and harming yourse'f. You're hurt enough."

"The captain?" Lon mumbled sleepily.

"Well, boss, you know, the sheriff."

It was the first time the fellow had spoken in Lon's earshot, and the first Lon had noted that he was a black man. "Hey," he said. "You're a nigra."

"Always was." The black posseman grunted.

"Yeah, well, thank you. I'm all right now. Gimme back the lines."

He reached for the mule team's reins but the Negro posseman held them off to the side and shook his head.

"Doctor wants you to crawl back yonder in the wagon and see to your brother, boss. Boy's been mighty quiet in there."

"Thank God. It's the first good sleep he's had since Red River. I'll stay up here."

The black was a big man, with a mean, deep bass voice. "White boy," that voice now said, "get your ass-bones back there and see to your brother like I say. Doctor's orders."

Lon didn't argue. But, crawling back through the front puckerhole, he asked, "How you going to keep the track without me? You might drive off the edge of some gully."

The big Negro laughed. "Boss," he rumbled, "every time that lightning stabs I see the country five miles around. Ain't no gullies where we're heading. Just this big rise. And 'yond that, 'cording to you, we'd ought to see your plantation."

"Ranch," Lon corrected. He got himself settled next to Junior's head and shoulders, where he could still see out and talk out the puckerhole to the big black man. "No cotton out here, 'boss,'" he mimicked the driver.

Lon didn't like this mean-voiced Negro. He was a man, Lon was, who had no trouble with black people as such. In his West Texas, buffalo-grass upbringing, Negroes had been scarce, and slaves nonexistent. But this fellow gave off a bad feeling. Lon had heard more than plenty of times from the southern whites in the Confederate ranks the warning term "bad nigger," and now he was wondering if this posseman wasn't one of those bad ones. Likely, he was. Likely, also, he was a slave in times back. *Most* likely, he was one of those slaves first set free by Mr. Lincoln away back in September of '62, so they could raise hell behind the Confederate lines.

Well, that idea hadn't worked and Lon McCalister was not going to let this black scoundrel run anything on him. That was why he'd thrown that "boss" business right back at the hulking Negro. Yes, and it seemed to have worked, too. The black posseman was tending to the mules like he hadn't heard Lon ape him. Pretty quick, and fair polite, he turned to Lon and asked, "How's the boy in there?"

Lon hadn't moved to see to Junior, not wanting to disturb him. Now, however, he reached a hand to touch him, first on a shoulder, which seemed oddly rigid, then on to the forehead to feel for fever. There was no fever, nor ever would be. Junior's face was cold as quarry stone.

Lon knew terror then. His mouth opened and his lips framed the words, *Oh, dear Jesus God, not now, not this near to home*, but no sound issued. Instead, Lon fought silently to still the hammering of his heart.

"White boy." The Negro driver's reminder had an edge to it. "I asked you, how's your brother."

Lon needed time to think and must stall to get it. "He could use a good warm blanket," he answered the driver. "You got a spare in them packs on the horse yonder?"

"Naw," the black posseman answered. "Them's mostly our uniforms. Them and the nose bags for the hosses. We ain't enough grub left to stuff a flea's butt. Blankets, hell. We ain't see'd a blanket since Fort Worth."

The response was careless but it took Lon McCalister by the throat. *Mostly our uniforms?* What uniforms? Sure not rangers, they didn't wear uniforms. Not Yankees, they were a thousand miles off. Confederate uniforms?

Lon sat scarcely breathing, praying God the black man

would not pick up the blunder. "Me and my brother ain't slept under blankets since futher than Fort Worth," he finally said. "Nobody cares about southern boys anymore."

"Nor southern niggers," the black driver agreed. He had not caught his mistake, Lon was certain, but the implication of that mistake still had the young Texan by the throat. If those *were* Confederate uniforms hidden lumpily in those packs yonder on the Indian's horse, was this the very gang of renegades that had robbed the bank in Pioche yesterday? The possibility raised the neck hairs, misfired the heart, shut off the breath.

But Lon's mind was suddenly cleared. He knew one thing for certain sure. Providing it was the gang, he must escape if any of the Paint Creek McCalisters were to survive what rolled their way in the survey wagon and among the troop of horsemen with it.

"Friend posseman," he said, leaning forward, "you see that outcrop of rock and brush ahead and to your right?"

"I see it," the black driver said, waiting for a lightning streak.

"Steer close to it as you can," Lon told him. "There's deep sand just to the left, and we could bog the wagon."

"What's 'yond it?"

"Just the rise. You're nigh the top-out. There's a spring in them rocks. You'll see the seep from it running off to our right."

"I seen it before. The water good?"

"There's better," Lon said quickly. "It's salt."

The water was sweet as hickory nuts but Lon did not want the wagon to stop at the spring.

"Mules need to drink," the black man muttered.

"They can stand in Paint Creek to their bellies, and it ain't half a hour further on."

"That's your ranch, Paint Creek?"

"Yes. Ours and the Comanch'."

"You got Comanche Injuns out here? The real ones?"

"Sure. Watch it, bear in on the rocks more. Crowd them mules over. You'll sink to your hubs in that sand."

The black posseman swung the mules, which did not

care to leave the perfectly firm track they were on, but went anyway. When he had taken them and the wagon past the spring and had the mules digging in for the last upsweep of east rise, he turned and peered at the silent puckerhole, and called quickly, "White boy, how old's your mama?" Receiving no reply, he asked, "How about your baby sister? She big enough?"

There was still no response from the wagon and the big Negro hauled up the mules with a curse.

"Captain!" he called sharply to the posse leader. "You'd best check the wagon. Something's turnt iffy here."

The leader pulled his mount off to one side and ordered two men into the wagon. They were back out even faster than they had crawled in. "The live one's gone," they said.

"What the hell do you mean 'the live one'?" the leader rasped.

"The other one's still in there," one of the men answered. "He's deader than a hung carcass."

There were oaths and counteroaths but in the end it was the same. Lon McCalister was nowhere in eye-reach of the wagon, nor lightning view of the plain as far as the next three shimmering flashes revealed.

"He cain't go far," one of the men said. "It's going to be day soon. We can jump him, sure."

"Not so sure," the leader denied. "We'll push on to the ranch. I don't like the feel of things." He frowned at the storm cloud still stalled off to the west. "Not a drop yet of that rain that was going to wash out our backtrail. The damn posse from Pioche will have hit Red Hawk easy by now. That old fool of a sheriff won't have quit. He will be after us."

"We got to have some rest," said Tranch, the second-in-command. "The horses, too. But that damn skinny Texian kid dealt us off the bottom. We've rolled to here over clear prairie leaving grass tracks and dirt prints a blind Chinee could foller in moon dark. That kid knowed it weren't going to rain. He's traitored us, sure."

"Christ, you ain't saying he deliberate a-purpose led

us to foller him off over the prairie, so that we'd leave tracks for the sheriff?" one of the men said. "Why, hell, Tranch, it were you who suggested it, not the pale kid. Maybe you'll get promoted to general."

"Yeah, sarge," another put in. "It *were* your idee."

Tranch turned a baleful stare on his challengers. "Captain," he said aside to the leader, "we got us some insubordinating going on here. We still running by military regulation, Articles of War, Confederate States Army?"

"We are," the leader said. "Girty, you and Fowlis back off. Sergeant Tranch was correct. We are in no trouble here compared to what we might be had we not run into these Texan boys." Thunder rolled to block out his words, and he nodded westward. "The storm's yet going to hit in time. And even with that old sheriff hanging onto us like I say, he can't have trailed us through the night. Yes, we *can* rest at the ranch, sergeant."

"Well, all right," Tranch grudged, then brightened. "Leastways, we'll find horse-feed grain and a hot breakfast. Yeah, plus some real live warmed-up female women to go with it! Har, har." Sergeant Tranch was the first to appreciate his own delicate humor and usually, as now, laughed alone. "Iffen so, remember your rank. What the captain leaves, Tranch cleans up. What Tranch don't finish, you pigs can root in."

"Well"—another posseman grinned—"so long as I don't hafter foller no black pigs. They muddies the pond!"

The Negro driver stared at his fellow. "Once upon a time, Massah Pike," he said, in his deliberate mockery of Negro field-hand servility, "you going to knock on my door and find me home."

Here, the patient man who had ministered to Lon McCalister moved forward. "Captain Fragg," he said to the leader, "a suggestion. I believe we should make the rest halt quite brief, then split up."

Fragg eyed the speaker.

"Why so, Major Canfield?" he asked.

"As a physician, I can tell you, sir, that the men are nearer their limits than we may suspect. We have been

76

decimated by the desperate condition of this Texas country, by the wounding of our troops in combat raids, and by the ceaseless driving of the law behind us since necessity forced us to deeds no decent men would perform. We have been forty-eight hours without sleep or even surcease of riding since the Pioche robbery, alone."

Captain Fragg broke in upon him scowlingly. "Get to it, major," he demanded.

"Well, sir, it is my opinion that we do not have the time you feel we do between us and that sheriff's posse from Pioche. A child died there. And a woman employee in the bank proper. That will be a hanging posse, sir."

"Jesus God, I know that. What's your point?"

"The men are at one another. The horses are ridden down. The ranch ahead may well be—I say it *will* be—the last chance we have to recoup mentally and bodily and to take evasive action." He looked steadily at the desperate pack now gathered behind its pale-eyed leader. "I hear talk here of women at the ranch. If this prove true, the problem will be crucial. Discipline, captain, entire and severe, will be mandatory. If there is to be any question of taking these women, of having them or even of considering it, it will be the end for us."

Fragg looked at him, nodding. The wolfish stare remained watchful, but the growling voice seemed patient. "I know, and the men know just as good as me, that you been to military college and are more than just a doctor. You know some soldiering, and that's a fact. But whatever they done taught you of battlefield tactics in that fancy school don't mean nothing out here, and ain't since we set out from Brazosport and the Gulf." He paused, still nodding. "Out here, you *are* just a doctor, Major Canfield." Now the growl deepened, the pale eyes narrowed. "It is getting light," he said. "In a bit we will be at the top of the rise. From there, we can see any move of the Texan war hero to get to the ranch ahead of us. If we don't see him and all seems clear, we will change into the uniforms and ride down like the good Confederate soldiers we are."

"Har, har," applauded the coarse and hairy Tranch.

Major Canfield straightened. "And the women?" he demanded of Fragg.

Fragg went for his horse and remounted to lead the way. The others quickly did likewise. Canfield was left standing by the wagon. He heard Fragg say something inaudible to the men, and heard again the vulgar "har, har" of Sergeant Tranch paying duty to the wit and wisdom of his captain.

The black driver leaned from the wagon seat. "Mister Henry, suh," he urged the doctor, "tie your hoss to the tailboard with mine and climb up here with me. We had best get set to go our separate ways from these scum. There is mean, dirty trouble lies over this ridge."

The major heaved a sigh of exhaustion, tied the horse, came back, and got up with the black man. "Scipio," he said wearily, "we must stay with the troops. Fragg is a madman. He has betrayed the cause, but we must not. California remains the last chance for freedom."

The big Negro started the mules. The wagon creaked up the last of the grade to the Paint Creek divide. Neither man spoke for some moments. Then the black driver looked over at his companion, uneasiness and something darker in the strain of his deep voice.

"Mister Henry," he said, "I cain't promise you about the women. Lord God, It's been so long. I ache in both loins that fierce it bends me over. I just don't think I can stay shut of them, Mister Henry, Jesus help me."

Henry Devereaux Canfield did not look over at the big black man but spoke to the graying dawn about them.

"Scipio," he said, "the Texas boy said he had his mama and a young sister, yonder. You remember your mama, Scipio Africanus? And your sister? How old was Florene when the Yanks came through? I forget. Twelve? Thirteen?"

"Lord, Lord, don't do that, Mister Henry."

"I'm not doing anything, Scipio."

"Yes you are, yes you are. Oh, Jesus."

"We buried your mama, Scipio, after you ran off. She told me something to tell you, if ever I saw you again."

"I don't want you to say it to me."

"I'm not; it's your mama saying it."

"She never. You're the one."

Canfield let the wagon rumble upward another rod or two, then said softly, "She said you were the proudest thing of her life that night the Yanks came, the way you kept them from Florene, the hell you had to pay for it."

Canfield let the words trail off, waiting.

"I know what I paid," the big Negro said.

"And I," Canfield murmured. "I sewed you up."

"They slit me," the black driver said. "Four cuts. I still pass fire when I pee."

"That's not what I want you to remember, or what your mama wanted you to, Scipio."

"Hadn't it been for you home on leave to tend me, Mister Henry—"

"Scipio, you're not listening to me."

"What you want?"

"I want you to remember what your mama wanted you to remember—her pride in you."

The huge black renegade rolled his eyes meanly. "That ain't no good to a man six months without a woman. Don't talk no more of mama, hear?"

"I hear," said Henry Canfield. Then, looking away from Scipio Africanus, "I wonder if mama does."

# 15

As they neared the divide of east rise, the day was scattering the night, painting the storm cloud rose and golden.

Fragg ordered the halt well below the crest. He and Sergeant Tranch went forward afoot to reconnoitre the terrain. Being careful to keep down, they saw below them the ranch described by the escaped Texan youth. Of the youth himself, although they lay ten full minutes watching, they saw nothing. From the lay of the prairie, open for miles in all directions, they understood he could not have come to the ranch before they reached the crest above it. Presently, they slid back from the rise, returned to the halted wagon and waiting troopers.

"It's all clear, yonder; nobody stirring," Fragg reported. "No sight of the soldier boy, neither. But I think we'd ought to ponder the situation, me and Major Canfield. Tranch, take Girty and Fowlis and go back up to the rise. One of you go south a quarter mile, the other, north. Tranch, you keep the middle. If any of you sights the Texian kid, finish him quiet. If your prowl don't turn him up, get back down here on the double. We're moving out."

"You got a plan, captain?" It was Corporal Tulliver G. "Walleye" Pike, leering, wandering-eyed third-in-command of the renegade pack. "Course we knows you always has. Har, har!"

"Shut up, Pike," Tranch ordered. "Captain ain't talking about *that*." He quelled the others with a glance, nodded to Fragg. "Go ahead on, captain."

"Take your men and get up on the ridge like I told you," Fragg growled. "The council's twixt Major Canfield and me. It's tactics and battle order. You'll know more when I say you will. Now scatter out, and get back fast."

Tranch, Fowlis, and Girty departed on the trot. Fragg swung back to the remaining group.

"Corporal Pike," he said, "take Hoad and Creech and the nigger and scout back through that spring-branch gully down yonder. Make certain the Texan kid ain't died in that brush, and see if there's any tracks you can pick up to show he skirted out from there. And, corporal. Watch the nigger. I've an idea he's winding himself up to make a run for it."

Pike passed the order to Scipio, who clambered obediently down from the wagon box with a brow-knuckling, "Yassuh, Massah Pike, suh."

The corporal cursed him and snapped, "It's *Corporal* Pike, you black bastard. Let's hear it!"

"Yassuh, Massah *Corporal* Pike."

"Oh, Christ!" Pike gritted. "Let's go."

The four men took off down the slope and Captain Fragg turned to his regimental surgeon.

"Dr. Canfield," he said, quietly enough, "we got us a campaign to go over here. I been thinking about what you said. You know, about making a decision here at this ranch of the Texian's. Go ahead and talk of it."

Canfield studied the captain. "Do you mean it?" he asked softly.

"It's why I sent the men away." Fragg nodded. "They can't be let in on anything like this. You know I've leaned on your military education and your college learning ever since you come to me with your idea, way yonder to the war, in Mississippi. But I can't let the men see me asking things of you. I got to be the field leader."

"Yes, that was the agreement, Fragg."

"I know it was, Major Canfield. You wasn't never any more intent nor dreaming on the new place and the new way than I was. When you tended me in that field hospital, in Tupelo, you saved more than my life. You saved my soul. I had been yearning to hear what you was saying to me, but never could put the words to it. Your dream to raise up a company of hurt and dispaired southern soldiers after the war and go out to California and make a new country neither Confederate nor Union that wouldn't have no wars, well, that lamp you lit inside me, it just shone me through the dark night of that there hospital, and on into our company here, which, God knows, has fallen on ribby times and needs a council to set it right again, full desperate."

He stopped to draw breath, shaking his unkempt head, narrowing and then opening the pale eyes.

"I know you've had your fears of me, and of the men," he continued. "And that ain't to be wondered over. We have had to do much that wasn't in your war books at the college. We have lost three fourths of our company, most of the best men in it, but I want you to know that I am still with you, major. I can command what we have

81

left here, if only you will trust me to do it, and will stay with us. Now, sir, what do you say of consent to that?"

Henry Canfield thought frowningly about it.

He wanted to believe Fragg. God knew he did. Just as he had wanted to believe him from the inspired moment when the pale-eyed CSA cavalryman had suggested that Canfield's California dream need not wait until after the war—indeed, that it must not. That its hour was then, no matter the risks.

Dear Lord, the memory! Canfield had been in a field dressing station plunged in a fit of melancholy such as only a combat surgeon of forward troops might explore in the life-amid-death work of sewing together mute pulps of grapeshot-minced humanity, when fate intervened and he experienced his view of the higher destiny. The station was near the town of Tupelo, Mississippi, the immediate patient a captain of Alabama irregular horse soldiers who, unknown to Canfield or to any of the medical staff, was wanted by the Confederate high command for murder, desertion, and crimes of high treason.

But the patient had known his situation and had played Dr. Canfield for what he saw him as—the fifth ace in a rigged game that would gain Captain Braxton Bonaparte Fragg the chance at freedom that he so richly did not deserve. Seeing plainly the gentle Carolinian's idealism through things Canfield said, as well as in attitudes revealed in his treatment of the wounded and dying all about Fragg, the captain began to arrange his cards.

Gamblers must take risks, particularly in the opening of the game. Fragg's initial ante was to divine that the medical officer—Canfield was regimental surgeon of the Fifth Carolina Horse—was ready to break. He next bet his life that Canfield would not turn him over to the dreaded military police of the Mississippi Command.

To Fragg's advantage was his already gained knowledge that the sensitive doctor was a serious man of peace.

Such men, the war had taught Fragg, were the dupes of all who would use them, and for whatever purposes of evil, particularly of evil taken in the name of peace and freedom for all humankind. Hence, Fragg began to play at once upon the major's high idealism and then, and only then, to ask of the soft-spoken physician if he, Fragg, might entrust to him a dream of hope for humanity far beyond the terrible fields of war. Should the major agree to the trust, he would learn that such visions as he himself clearly held—that war was an obscenity of hell—were shared in secret by many others caught in this cauldron of hades that the South called the last cause of the right and noble. Would the major say yes to the captain's plea for mankind?

Sensing nothing here other than what the wounded cavalry officer set forth upon the surface, Canfield had agreed to the confidence. He listened as Fragg proposed, unvarnished, that the medically and militarily educated major and the near-illiterate, battle-taught captain of guerrilla horse cavalry join their splendid hopes and secretly enlist a company of fellow dreamers and rebellers against the maiming, disease, slaughter, and insanity of war. With this hidden force of heroes, Fragg and Canfield could win their way to the West, and so to California, where the last, best chance of establishing a nation-state of true freedom and just peace without slavery yet existed.

At this point Henry Devereaux Canfield had made the error of his life; he had accepted, whole cloth, enough of Fragg's incredible premise to ask the captain how he imagined to bring off the practical exigencies of such an unlikely trek.

Here, Fragg was at home. Before the war he had been a guerrilla horse raider up in the border country of Kentucky and Missouri. He had ridden then, and into the first year of the war, with the likes of Quantrell, Morgan Walker, David Poole, and the wild man, George Todd. He had learned his deadly trade well and was prepared now to give Major Canfield not only the convincing ways and methods of both organizing a troop and of moving it through enemy country—in this case, through their own country, whose loyal minions would now become their lifeblood pursuers—but to provide the surgeon an already executed route-march map of the escape road that would get them free of Mississippi and landed on the Gulf coast of Texas. Fragg even had ready for Canfield's astonished study a further map of the then-known area of Texas, including the accurate portrayal of Marcy's north-route Emigrant Road to California, via the trans-Pecos, into New Mexico and Arizona territories, and so to the golden land of California and the New Republic of Peace.

At the time, Canfield had questioned the plan by quoting to Fragg the failures, in California, of other pro-Southern causists with the same dream of a newborn nation, independent of either the Confederacy or the Union. He named the Committee of Thirty, the Knights of the Golden Circle, and the Knights of the Columbian Star, all bona fide and powerful conspiracies to launch an outer nation. But Fragg had swept them all aside with the argument that these groups had not been secret at all, but as public as the War Between the States itself. Their crusade, his and Canfield's, would be *different*; their New Republic of Peace *would* be secret and thus could be made to thrive "out there, where hope has not yet died, and bold men can yet win the victory for God and the new country born in His name."

Weakened, sick with exhaustion and revulsion against the carnage of torn and broken bodies that was his daily battlefield, Henry Canfield had "seen the star!"—as Fragg had described their mission. He had even, in the uplift of relief at his decision to strike west with the gaunt captain of guerrilla horse, committed his mind to Fragg's ultimate deception: He allowed the renegade to persuade him that this dream was Canfield's idea, to which Fragg had agreed, rather than the other way around.

No one save a dedicated idealist such as Canfield could have been so used. But the regimental surgeon and high-born southern cavalier believed in the possibility of the projected nation-state because he hungered so desperately for it. He did not know that peace was possible, he only knew that further killing was impossible. When Fragg

84

spoke, Canfield asked only after their respective roles in the conspiracy, and the death sentence of desertion that it required, and the cavalryman sketched in for him the basic nature of the scheme, appointing him the company doctor and spiritual arm—Canfield was an ordained Baptist lay preacher—while Captain Fragg organized and led the little company of heroes upon its desperate journey.

There were no delays after that.

The company was recruited out of scoundrels known to Fragg, all either deserters or contrabandists, and some forty strong set forth one dark and blustery March night hidden by bribery amongst bales of Confederate cotton down-river bound for New Orleans.

At the Louisiana port, they transshipped by dark again, and successfully, to a leaky tub of one stepped mast and a blockade-running pirate crew of five, to be sailed over the Gulf of Mexico to Texas.

Upon being landed at the Galveston Island outbank cove of Santa Louisa, just below the smuggler haven of Brazosport, Fragg promptly ordered the crew shot and the ship fired and set adrift. Henry Canfield's horror and bewilderment at this monstrous action were traumatic. He was restrained from immediate announcement of separation from the raider band only by the warning of his loyal CSA orderly and forager, Scipio Africanus, the Negro who had been born and raised with Canfield on the latter's Sea Pines Plantation in the Carolinas. Scipio had understood the desperate nature of Fragg and his human wolf pack well enough to know that his former master and owner would be shot as instantly as had been the pirate crew once he made mention of going another way than their own murderous one. From that moment, the regimental surgeon, if he did not yet comprehend Fragg's full wickedness, understood at least that he, Canfield, was virtual hostage to him.

It was against this nigh incredible history of their coming to the crest of east rise that late June morning, the lovely summer of 1863, that Henry Canfield now ended the uncomfortably lengthening pause through which he had reviewed his trusting of Braxton Bonaparte Fragg, and answered Fragg, at last.

"It's true that I have been shaken by the cruel needs of living upon the land, as we journey west. I've not understood your methods in each case, and in some I can never forgive the company's conduct. However, we have come this far and, as you say, are much reduced in number. I judge, too, that you imply this attrition presents a problem in morale but state positively that you can control our remaining force despite its low spirit."

"You have got it accurate, major," Fragg said carefully.

"May I then suggest, captain," Canfield replied, "that the problem is not one of morale but of morals."

"Morals, you say?"

"Yes. And that consent you have said you wish from me comes simply to this: If we are to reach California at all, much less with a useful force at our command, this present company must be disbanded."

"Disbanded, major?"

"Yes, and now, before we ride into the ranch, yonder. These men are planning a rape of the women there, and we cannot tolerate such a breakdown in discipline. You know the Confederate Military Code on looting and rape, Captain Fragg."

Fragg nodded silently. He knew the code surpassing well; its application to himself would mean the firing squad. The surgeon was becoming a problem. Still, the company had need of his medical arts and, above these, of the respectability his fine southern figure and soft Carolinian accent gave to their charade as uniformed troops of the CSA, under Canfield's command. Yet, in the end, Fragg wearied of the game. Somewhere in the growing dawn behind them, the Pioche posse was riding.

"Well, major"—he tried a final time for patience with the highbred fool before him—"what percisely you mean when you say we got to disband? You for a fact suggesting that me and you desert the others here, in defense of whatever women might be at the ranch?"

"You and I and my forager, yes."

"The nigger?! Good Christ, he'd be the first to force the women!"

"I think not, Captain Fragg," Canfield said stiffly.

"Well, Canfield, you think what you want." Fragg was short with it now, no military pretense. "This council has told me that I was dead-center right about you and your nigger. You were scheming a break." Fragg eyed him coldly. "We will see to that after we see to them women." He swung about to face Tranch, just returned.

"Break out the uniforms!" he barked. "We're soldiers still. Battle call! Issue flag and bugle."

Hearing the pack's growling laughter, watching its members scatter to do the leader's bidding, Major Henry Canfield shook to the chill. The cold fear left behind by the guerrilla captain's parting stare at him spread outward from the pit of his gut. He understood finally how Fragg altered his character to suit the need of any moment he might encounter. And he saw that Fragg's need as of this moment was no different from that of Sergeant Tranch, or Corporal Pike, or even that of poor bedeviled Scipio.

Captain Braxton Fragg was not going to order off that attack on the ranch women. He was going to *lead* it.

# 16

"Bubba, get your butt in here and help with mama! Now you know we got to get her ready."

Sissy stood in the open kitchen doorway, hands on hips and challenging. At fifteen, flushed with work, hair piled atop defiant head, blue eyes sending sparks, she appeared to Cap Marston the most beautiful thing he had ever seen.

Old Cap was just coming out of his horse-shed bachelor quarters, where he had made camp since bringing the McCalister children and their mother back out to the Paint Creek homeplace. Breaking his eyes from Sissy for a moment to look back at his new home, he gave a grateful, small nod.

It wasn't a bad place for an old man to live in. Especially since that damned rascal Simms Ellerbrock had snuck out from Red Hawk with a theft warrant and the pullet-livered town marshal to serve it for him on the poor defenseless widow woman. The warrant claimed back Simms's rightful property of the old McCalister ranch wagon and its wolf-bait team, plus a due bill for total-time rental of the rig according to livery law, cash money or go to debtor's prison.

Now for a fact a man had to admit that the air and natural aroma in and about the horse shed had been a hundred-and-eleven percent improved with the collar-galled old horses seized by Simms and taken off to town again, and that not to mention the buffalo gnats and heel-flies that had gone with them. Yet Cap had to growl and spit all the same at the idea of putting the widow of Sunny Jim McCalister behind bars as a common horse thief.

Then the old man's eyes found Sissy again, still sunshine-framed in the kitchen doorway looking fiercely about for her missing little brother, and inner lights of love relit the seamed and craggy face and old Cap Marston nodded one more small nod and was content.

He was particularly happy that the two kids were so worked up over what he had told them earlier—the lie that he had dreamed, real as life, that this was the day Lon and Junior were coming home. Indeed, that they would be there first thing this very bluebird morning. But he had a twinge of remorse. The fact was, the "dream" had come from Mexican Jack, who had the news "hard" from Monk Beckham the night before and thought it prime enough to detour his saddle mule all the night-long way to tell his friend Cap about it.

"Bubba!" Sissy came one stride out of the kitchen door. "Where the hell are you at?"

Cap rubbed his eyes, the better to appreciate the early light in the girl's disarrayed hair. He ought not to have lied to the children about that visitation, but had he told them Mexican Jack was the source of the information that the boys had been brought up to Overland Mail Road by some surveyors from Fort Griffin, they wouldn't have believed it. A stranger, maybe. A Mexican, never. Especially *that* Mexican. Still, it would all be mighty nicely ended if it worked out that both Cap and Mexican Jack were right, and old Lon and Junior would show up with the sun.

For the moment, it made an old man happy enough just to look at the lovely young girl that Sissy McCalister had bloomed into. And, looking, to know that he was at least partways responsible for Sissy's being there that morning to clean up the place, dress mama in her very best, and find Bubba, if she could, in time to greet Lon and Junior when they came riding over east rise. It was that fact—Cap's prime part in getting the family back out on the homeplace in time to have it spruced up for the returning soldier boys—that eased the rheumatics in his spine bones and even softened the screech that Sissy McCalister now put up in search of the errant Bubba.

"Randolph Barnes, goddammit, answer me this minute! I cain't clean house and wash mama and get her fresh dress on her without you give me a hand. Sing out now or by God I will—"

Whatever it was that Sissy might have done of mayhem on brother Bubba, it was delayed by the latter's respond-shout of righteous ire.

"Hell's fire, Charlotte May, will you shet up? I got to keep watch on this here Juarez Sally chicken. Damn if she ain't about to lay a egg!"

"You put that above welcoming Lon and Jim Junior?"

Sissy's question was one more of astonishment than continuing exasperation. But redheaded Bubba was still steaming. After all, Lon and Junior weren't even in sight yet. And the Juarez Sally chicken was no farther than one more cackle and a squawk from dropping the first hen egg ever laid west of Red Hawk, Texas. Or at least west of Mexican Jack's *rancho grande*, out in the salt sage.

"She's squatting! She's squatting!" he yelled back at

his irate sister. "Jesus H. Christ, I got a chicken here going to be a mother!"

In the dooryard, Sissy McCalister gave up. Arms that had been akimbo dropped to sides. The oval face that had been fevered with flush-blood now calmed to the rose-blush and sun-gold tan of the ranch girl's striking complexion.

Bubba was right. One of his precious Mexican chickens about to give birth drew priority over two older brothers who hadn't showed up yet and, indeed, might not show up at all, old Cap's gift of prophecy not being one that you could exactly set your watch by. Accordingly, she cocked an ear to the sudden silence out by the hen coop and called anxiously to know if Juarez Sally had delivered yet.

Her first answer was a startling crow by Big Red, which naturally led her to believe Sally had come through. But the old rooster's *doodle-doo* was followed by an equally startled curse from Randolph Barnes, who appeared directly, tramping head down toward Sissy and the kitchen door.

Nearing her, the boy tried to evade his sister and go in the door past her. His expression was one of mixed outrage and indignation, even of philosophical confoundment.

"Hey," Sissy said, concerned. "What happened?"

Bubba stopped, and now she could see that the bewilderment had overcome the anger in little brother's face.

"I had my hand right under her when she done it," he said. He kept one hand behind him, leading Sissy to believe that this hand held the miracle of Juarez Sally Day.

"And she laid the egg right in your hand?" she asked.

Bubba looked up at her, sunburned brow dark with betrayal. The freckled nose contorted. The missing front tooth gapped in grimace. He brought forth the offending hand and opened it wide.

"Hell no," he said, defeated. "She shat in it."

# 17

There was a further tactical delay on east rise.

As Fragg broke off with Canfield to order the men into uniform, Gabby, the mute Indian packer, was just wandering in off the rearward prairie. Fragg cursed him for falling behind, and the Indian, who had appeared about to convey some intelligence, only shrugged expressionlessly in receipt of the abuse and kept his peace.

His action did not elude the wary eye of Scipio Africanus, now returned with his fellows from searching the spring draw for sign of the missing Lonnie McCalister.

"Very well," Fragg said, "let's move out. Nigger," he added to Scipio, "you and Major Canfield get to your wagon again. I want you two where I can see you. I am aware what you been planning. You had both better come to understand that Braxton Fragg is in field command here."

"We understand, captain," Canfield said. "But we are in no way preparing a flight. As I have just told you in council, having come this far, I am committed. As for my forager, I believe only death could separate him from my service."

Fragg nodded thoughtfully, as though this might be arranged. Then he turned suddenly apologetic. "Begging your pardon, major," he said to Canfield, "but we are going on to California. You seem to have forgot our quest, but I ain't. I need your help, that's why I warn you. It's only so you won't do nothing foolish and so bring harm to the cause."

"The 'cause,' captain?" Canfield echoed. "Can we yet be serving the same crusade?"

Braxton Fragg's gaunt face seemed literally to glow from some inner fire. "The Republic of Peace, major," he said, low voiced. "The true freedom from war, ever."

Canfield shivered involuntarily.

In that moment his and Scipio's lives hung on whether Fragg was deliberately performing a role to lead on Canfield and the powerful Negro or whether—and this was far the more frightening thought to any doctor of medicine—the pale-eyed captain of guerrilla horse literally believed what he was saying of his steadfast devotion to the once-beckoning Republic of Peace.

Very carefully, the gentle Carolinian returned Fragg's nod, and the guerrilla leader's dark lips lifted over the yellowed teeth.

"If it appears to go beyond you now and again, major," he said, "it's only that there's places wheres my experience outranks yourn. That ain't never to question your seniority but only to forward the cause."

Confusion invaded Henry Canfield once more. He could not seem to separate the several sides of Braxton Bonaparte Fragg.

Why was that?

It was evident in the baleful eyes, the growl of the heavy voice, the erratic behavior that swung from the purely vicious to the fawning benign. Yet he, Canfield, kept questioning his own observations. Wanting not to accept what he saw.

"That's gracious of you, captain." He nodded, at last. "As a matter of fact, we have held joint command by agreement from the outset. In the same manner, we have from the beginning shared our vision of the new republic. Indeed, Captain Fragg, it was you who reminded me that the dream need not await war's end." Canfield paused, sensitive features alight. "I believe that the history books will show, sir, that it was Captain Braxton Fragg and not Major Henry Canfield who carried forward the last banner for peace."

The look that Fragg shot him at this flight of victory re-winged was that of the wolf outside the shearing pen. It was as if to study the fatness of the flock inside against the height and closeness of the fence pales. Ought he to jump now or await a better time, an easier place? Fragg's answer was a field compromise; the holy fire of inspiration for California and eternal peace was dimmed, but not altogether quenched, by the cold water of reality.

"You tech me, major," he said, "genuinely you do. But we've a cause to serve and it cain't be left to linger."

He held a final beat of pulses, eying Henry Canfield.

Watching the two men, Scipio Africanus made silent nod to himself. If he, Scipio, were of right and sound mind, then Captain Fragg was no more daft than Major Canfield; he was only far, far more dangerous. Or was he? Which seer was the greater menace to other men: the one who *said* he believed in the vision, or the one who *did* believe in it? Scipio knew about visions. His people called them voodoo. And they raised more general hell for more folks than any number a man could multiply of outrightly bad things done deliberately and by their own names. Be those names bribery, the burning of barns or houses, looting, the bearing of false witness, horse stealing, lusting after a neighbor's wife, blackmail, murder, or even the raping of a white woman, those things could be dealt with. They could because they were known. But the hell that went on inside a man's soul? The dark that lived inside his skullbones? Even in good and kind men like Mister Henry? Ah! not even God knew about that; only the Devil did.

"I understand," Scipio heard Henry Canfield answering now. "What are your orders, Captain Fragg?"

"They ain't been changed," Fragg growled. "You and the nigger back in the wagon. We'll tend you later."

Scipio tensed to the stated threat. If his old Carolina master made the wrong move here, that hell Scipio had just been thinking about could spill out like the guts from a slaughter-winched hog. But Canfield steadied.

"Thank you, Captain Fragg," was all he said to the guerrilla officer. "Scipio, take the lines. Do precisely as Captain Fragg has directed. None of your tricks, now, you black rascal. Up you go."

Scipio Africanus frowned his understanding.

He reached the driver's box in one lion's stride from front-wheel hub to the reinsman's seat. Putting down an aiding hand for Canfield, he virtually lifted the company surgeon to the seat beside him. Canfield thought he heard him growling but was not certain. And Scipio said not a solitary word in clue. Indeed, there was no more talk among any of the company after that.

To horse and showing the thirteen-starred battle flag of the Confederacy, the cavalrymen jingled at a sharp trot up the remaining grade of east rise. They came to the crest as the sun gloriously broke free of the prairie's rim behind them. It was a West Texas sky for sure: the bluebird weather to the east, where they had come from, the still ominous purple-and-black cloak of the storm shrouded to the west, where they were going. The air was electric with distant lightning. The wind came fresh to the horses, belling weary nostrils. Man and mount could smell the rain away off. The pace increased without command of any rider.

But Fragg had one more halt to call.

Just below skyline, he stopped the command to summon up his bugler, Corporal Pike, and to arrange his troops in final proper line of march for the emergence into view of the ranch. In the opportunity so granted, Canfield turned to Scipio.

"I want to know what happened back there in your search for the McCalister boy," he said. "That Indian appeared to know something. Do you think he saw the lad?"

Scipio cocked an eye toward Fragg and the troop before answering. "Injun never seen the Texian kid but was certain to tell Fragg he did. Tame Injuns like him will boast on scalping a pack rat. But Fragg jumped old Gabby before he could grunt his lie out. So old Gabby, he friz up on him. He'll not thaw, neither."

"You sure?"

"He won't say nothing; I guarantee it."

"You scoundrel, he's a mute!"

"Yessuh, that's why I trust him."

Canfield accepted the standoff. He never knew when Scipio Africanus was behind or far ahead of him.

"How do you know the Indian didn't find the boy's body?" he parried.

"I'm just right certain he didn't." The black forager shrugged.

"Right certain?"

"Yessuh. Now you knows when old Skip he hides something, ain't no dumb-tongue Injun going to find it."

"You found the body?"

"Yessuh."

"And hid it without the others seeing you?"

"Best I could, yessuh."

Canfield bowed his head. "Thank our dear Savior for that kindness," he said. "Both lads are beyond harm now."

Scipio shook his head. "One is and one ain't," he said.

"Scipio!" Canfield guarded his excitement. "The boy's alive?"

"Was last I saw him. I took and shoved him up under a rock outcrop, safe from rain and wind."

"Praise God," Canfield said. "We must go back for him."

"Don't even think on it," Scipio warned, startled.

"But we can't let that boy lie out there and die!"

"No, suh, nor we cain't make him lie out there and live, neither. We done already give him his best chanct."

Canfield considered it. He could see the black forager was in better diagnosis than himself. Moreover, he could also see Captain Braxton Fragg looking their way and scowling hard. To ward off a visit from the captain, he waved to him and offered an acknowledging salute, as though to say, yes, I see you; we're ready here.

Fragg seemed satisfied. "Pull up your wagon, close ranks," he called to Canfield.

Big Scipio, not waiting for a relay of the order, clucked to the mules. The team dug in, the government wagon creaked forward. Dr. Henry Canfield reached to pat the former slave's knee. There was frank emotion in the tribute.

"Scipio," he murmured, "it was a very brave thing you did. What if you had been caught at it? Suppose Fragg yet finds out? You've risked everything hiding that boy."

The big black shook his head. "No," he said. "I just remember me being young as him once and somebody else hiding me whens there was people looking to take my life."

Canfield nodded slowly. "I remember," he said.

"Surely you do," Scipio answered. "You was the one saved me from them nigger killers."

"You were innocent, Scipio."

"Was that Lonnie child guilty?"

"No, no, you did a wonderful thing for the lad."

Again, Scipio shook his head. "Never done it for him," he said. "I done it for you." They drove on, slowing as Scipio maneuvered the wagon in behind Fragg's disreputable column. "I owed you it," the big Negro finished. "Life for a life, just like mama used to read me from the Book."

"That's the Old Testament, Scipio," Canfield contended. "The tribal vengeance preachment. We don't believe that."

"Onliest testament I know," Scipio said. "Eye for a eye. Tooth for a tooth. Old Moses, he been there."

Canfield was made uneasy by the look in the muscular slave's dark face. "Do you also believe that if thine own eye offend thee, pluck it out?"

Scipio put back his head and laughed, once, softly. "No suh," he said. "I'll do the plucking on somebody else."

"You use what you want from the Bible, then?"

Scipio rolled him a sideways look. "Mister Henry," he said, "the Bible ain't nothing but the book of life; you takes some and you leaves some, and you prays to hell that you done grabbed the best you could."

Henry Canfield once more surrendered the field to Scipio Africanus. "I'm glad we named you after a great soldier," he said. "You'd have made a catastrophic preacher."

"Glory, glory!" rumbled Scipio, and whipped the mules to follow Braxton Fragg and the guerrilla cavalry.

# 18

In column twos, the ragged horsemen topped the crest of east rise above and across Paint Creek from the McCalister ranch.

"Bugler," Fragg said, straightening, "sound the approach."

"The what?" blinked Pike.

"Blow something!" Fragg snapped.

Corporal Pike raised the company bugle, an instrument that, like Fragg's command, had known nobler times. He puffed into the right end of it, however, and a recognizable blaring of martial tones issued from the bell.

"Color sergeant," Fragg said to Tranch, "raise the guidon."

Tranch shook out the molding draggle of his commander's old regiment, the Fifth Alabama Horse. Hoisting it, he shoved its staff under his off knee, clamping it awkwardly there to fly in some semblance of a proper military rake. "Guidon on, sir," he said, saluting left-handedly.

Fragg went in the lead, alone. Behind him came Tranch and Pike, his noncommissioned officers. They were followed by the troops in column twos: Private Oliver "Hound Dog" Fowlis with Israel Girty, Private Ralph Waldo Creech with Archimedes Hoad, known as Crawdad. After the four ordinary soldiers-of-the-line rumbled the supply wagon and company ambulance, with driver-forager Scipio Africanus and regimental surgeon Major Henry Devereaux Canfield. The pack string, under lagging order of the self-enlisted Indian mute, Gabby, brought up the rear.

A sorrier command would have been difficult to gather, or indeed to conceive in the mind. But, far down the slope of east rise and over across Paint Creek, Bubba McCalister, racing around the corner of the ranch house in response to hearing the unbelievable sound of a brass bugle blowing in the sunrise stillness of the buffalo grass, skidded to open-mouthed halt.

"Jesus Christ, Cap!" he yowled at lung top. "Soldier boys!"

The old man, so summoned, came limping at full sprint. He was armed with his old ranger spyglass from the Battle of San Jacinto. Bringing the glass to bear on the still-distant company, he exclaimed in startled turn, "Sonofabitch, them's Confedrit troops, boy! Run and fetch your sister and bring your mama 'round to see. That there has got to be Lon and Junior's outfit!"

The youngster hesitated, overmatched by the moment's choke of pure joy. Then, recovering, he issued a thin and wretched screech designed but never destined to be a he-coon rebel yell, and ran for the ranch house rear door. He went *ki-yiying* the entire distance for Sissy to rustle her butt and to "bring mama round the south side"; Lonnie and Jim Junior were coming down east rise with a full Confederate escort.

In the enchanted lull of the wait for the distant soldiers to draw near, the heart of Randolph Barnes McCalister was close to overflowing its cup in tears. Yonder came his hero brothers. The war was over and Bubba's world was back together again.

When, next instant, Big Red the Rhode Island rooster flapped up to the ridgepole and stretched to crow his personal welcome home, Bubba just plain-out broke down.

Sure he cried.

"Crapsakes," he later defended. "Who wouldn't?"

How wonderful could one day come to pass?

The others of the little group beside the paintless ranch house seemed caught in the same web of wonderment. Perhaps it was the flash of the early sun in their eyes. Or again it may have been the sound of the brass bugle, the flap of the company guidon in the freshening prairie breeze, or simply the unstringing of emotions of hope too long and tautly held. Whatever it was, it trapped not only the family's hearts but their heads as well.

Ordinary precautions of life in such a lonely, unpopulous land went ignored that morning. The wish was both father and mother to the glad assumption that they who came yonder down east rise this thirtieth and most joyous morn of June, 1863, were friends. And why would they not be, this day when Lon and Junior were expected home? What other southern soldiers than friends of the boys could these troops be?

The McCalisters saw the renegade column ford the creek from east rise and start up the grade of west ridge toward the house. The faint frown and shadowed eyes of Mary McCalister masked her feelings from all but God. Sissy's face was radiant, masking nothing. She didn't see Lon or Junior but she just knew that Cap was right and that these were her returning brothers' comrades-in-arms. Perhaps the boys were resting in the canvas-topped wagon driven by the huge black man. They might be weary from their long march home. Or maybe they were following along behind somewhere. But Sissy knew that somehow Lon and Junior were bound up with these tattered and weary-seeming heroes of the war coming now up lower west ridge to the ranch house.

But of a sudden Bubba McCalister was not so sure.

Bubba was thirteen now. Still young enough to be betrayed by a chicken befouling his hand, but not that young anymore as to wag his tail to every man-grown stranger riding in off the prairie.

Matter of fact, Bubba didn't like the way these men were looking at mama and Sissy, as they drew nearer the house and he could make out their faces. It developed that old Cap Marston, standing with the redheaded ranch boy, didn't care for these appraisals either.

"Bubba," he said, stiffening, "slip back around the house, easylike. Go and get my ranger Colt. It is hid in the trunk back of the stove. Fetch it to me, *fast*."

"Old Redeemer!" whispered the boy. "Jesus Christ."

He was gone within the moment of his big-eyed whisper back around the corner of the ranch house. He was quick and shifty about it as any shy coyote. But the men who were riding into his world that day were not coyotes. They were wolves. And they were after Bubba McCalister on the instant that he moved to escape them.

# 19

Fragg saw the boy slip around the house. *"Get him,"* he side-mouthed angrily to Tranch, and Tranch spurred around the house the opposite way to cut Bubba off. But here Fragg's sharp glance noted the alarm the maneuver had put into the face of the young sister. On the instant, his voice and bearing altered. "Do not harm the lad, sergeant," he called after Tranch. "These are our own people here."

Tranch, Texas born and ranch reared, laughed and shook out his coiled lariat. Out of sight of the others he saw Bubba running for the horse shed. Tranch could have heeled the boy with a ground loop, dropping him unshaken. Instead, he threw an overhead loop, cinching the racing youth under his arms, dallied two hard wraps around the saddle horn, sat his horse back on its hocks.

Bubba cried out, went high into the air, came down on the flat of his back, breath-bursting hard.

Tranch paled beneath the hair mat of his beard. Fragg had warned against harm to the boy. And the kid wasn't moving.

"Hey, you ain't kilt," he accused the flattened youngster. The declaration was rewarded by a stir from Bubba, together with an earthy profaning of Tranch's mother. The affront relieved the renegade's fear of his captain's possible displeasure. With an oath of his own, he spun his horse about and dragged the boy, still on the flat of his back, through the ranch yard dirt to where Sissy, old Cap, and mama were now cornered against the south side of the house by the leering rebel band.

Bubba, spitting sand and rock and recognizable bits of ranch animal excreta, came wobbling to his feet. Tranch, greeted by his fellows with hoarse laughs for his roping of the "redhead bull calf," made the reflex cowboy motion of slacking his loop. He had brought the calf back to the fire and busted him good doing it. By all rights the little sonofabitch had ought to stand still and shake where he was. But Bubba McCalister wasn't your run-of-the-roundup shorthorn calf. He was West Texas breeding, longhorn ladino strain clean through. He came up shaking all right, but not from being busted and dragged. Bubba was mad.

He felt the slack that old cowboy Tranch unwittingly gave him and saw at the same time that the others of the bad crew had swung their attentions back away from Bubba to mama and Charlotte May. With his coyote's instincts for the sliding maneuver, and silent, the boy slipped the noose and stepped out of it. He was free at this point but the thought of fleeing had not occurred to him. Bubba had other solutions in mind.

Leaving the empty loop behind, he glided down the length of the lariat as it lay on the ground trailing behind Tranch's horse. Picking up the rope no more than ten feet from its owner's saddle, the boy swiftly coiled its length until he had the loop up to his hand again. Beyond Tranch, the others were commencing to crowd in on Fragg, who was speaking to mama. Bubba heard two or three things said about both mama and Charlotte May by the men behind Fragg's back that brought the furies into his blood. But he was not distracted. The weapon of deliverance was at hand.

Leaning on the house within his reach was a catclaw switch he used to herd his chickens with. It was nothing but a ratty branch, but it had thorns on it from being untrimmed, and Bubba treasured that chicken stick right then above even old Redeemer.

Stretching, he managed to dislodge the stick from the house. It wobbled, appeared about to fall the wrong way, then wobbled back and fell toward Bubba. He caught it, juggled it, held on. Hefting it, he eyed the target. Distance seemed about right. And trajectory.

He shook out a smallish loop of the lariat, whirled it, and threw it to fly over the head and settle mid-body of Sergeant Tranch. In the identical moment and with every accuracy he could give it, Bubba shoved the thorny-headed chicken stick up under the tail of Tranch's quietly standing horse.

The horse squalled as if rifle-shot.

It went up not only straight into the air but horizontally sideways out from under its hairy rider. When the poor thing lit once more upon the earth, it did so in full gallop and still squalling. As Tranch had not bothered to unwrap the hard dallies about his saddle horn, he was nearly cut in two when the horse reached the lariat's full length away from him. The wrench jerked him out of midair and slammed him down onto the prairie hardpan with fearsome force. All that saved him was the application of the ancient law of irresistible momentum against movable body. Tranch followed the runaway at the end of his own dallied lariat, bouncing and slamming about crazily. He struck dirt, rock, sand, gravel, adobe mud, natural gas, everything but oil, and surely would have been worn down to a human nubbin had not the horse turned in its own hysteria to run back toward the startled guerrilla group. Here, Girty and Fowlis, versed in the arts of subduing panicked horseflesh, spurred out to wedge Tranch's horse between their own mounts, so slowing the animal before the sergeant had been ground lifeless.

Even so, hell was immediately owing.

When the rock chips had ceased flying and the gritty dust again settled to earth, it was not alone the worn-raw parts of Sergeant Levi Tranch's hide that were missing.

Bubba McCalister was gone entire.

## 20

Bleeding, Tranch staggered to his feet. He shook from him the nearly fatal noose of the lariat and went for his lathered, still trembling horse. He was talking thick-tongued to himself. "Smart-ass little frigger, I'll peel him alive!"

Fragg's graveled voice countermanded him. "Sergeant Tranch, hold where you are!"

Tranch, still furious, held. He knew that grating tone in his captain's order. The man who went step one beyond its threat played with disaster.

"Yes, sir," he said, saluting. The mere gesture hurt. Tranch was a man pretty well used up in that moment. He would then and there have challenged any less sinister commander than Braxton Fragg. But Levi Tranch was only a bad man, not a mad one. He waited uncertainly.

For his part, the captain was quite in control.

Only clock ticks before, when he himself had noted the redheaded boy's absence, the bugging of fury in his pale eyes had made Tranch's present rage seem benign. Now he answered the sergeant's salute offhandedly and kindly as some unwashed, ragpicker Robert E. Lee of the West Texas llano.

"Your language, sergeant," he said. "Please."

"Please what, cap'n?" Tranch scowled.

Fragg tipped his hat to Mary McCalister. The ranch-woman stood with Sissy and Cap Marston. They were still huddled instinctively at bay against the house, although no move had been made, actually, to cause their alarm.

"Apologize, Tranch," Fragg continued. The guerrilla leader nodded toward the anxious women, waiting.

Tranch studied the problem and brightened. "Oh!" he said, relieved. Chucking his head toward Mary McCalister and her tawny-haired daughter, he knuckled dirt-caked brow and grinned. "'Scuse it, ma'am. I wouldn't say nothing deliberate undecent front of you nor Little Sister. It's the times makes us rough and mean."

"Thank you, sergeant," Fragg said. "Now as for the lad, let him be. He will see quick enough, wherever he's hid, that we are friends. He'll understand our first treatment of him was normal soldier caution. All little boys like soldiers. He will be back, ma'am," he ended, with a flourish of foul hat to Mary McCalister.

Tranch stared at him, unbelieving. "Damn," he said, "am I hearing you straight?"

"Perhaps you had best be, if you are not," Fragg suggested. "Let the poor boy alone."

"But he like to kilt me, goddammit!"

"I won't warn you again, Tranch!"

"About what, for Christ's sake?"

"Your unnecessary language, sir. The ladies—"

This time Fragg made a full bow from the waist to the now relaxing Sissy McCalister and her suddenly smiling, nodding mother. Even old Cap Marston was warmed.

Maybe these men were not the skulking dogs they had seemed. Maybe they really were the comrades of Lonnie and Junior. The least that could be offered them was the benefit of an undoubtful welcome. The old ranger almost bowed back to the gravel-voiced leader. Praise the Lord. Could be these were good Confederate boys just down on their luck. God knew that happened in wartime. War not only made men do ugly things, it made them look ugly, too.

"Thank you for the ladies, sir." The old man waved to Braxton Fragg. "Miz McCalister's been poorly. Don't speak much. But we thanks you kindly."

Tranch shook his head. Hearing the exchange, he could not accept it. Captain Fragg, the butcher of Bogalusa? "Bloody Brax," the trail hound of the Fifth Alabama Horse? The night rider of Natchez? The seditioner? The deserter? The bank robber? The shooter of small children? *Him* turning good and' righteous? Sitting there on the same horse off which he had killed the old sheriff's hair-ribboned daughter, telling Levi Tranch he had best mind his tongue in front of these dog-shanty cow-ranch women? And doing it at a time when a tough, crafty kid, wise to the country and meaner than a teased snake, was off and running full-yelp for help?

It was a few too many for old Tranch.

Accustomed as the sergeant was to Fragg's wide swings of character, this instant piety and light put on for the ladies McCalister was a brown frowner for Levi Tranch. He couldn't make it out. No sir.

But Captain Fragg, if quite mad (as the Confederate army police called him), was no fool. As a survivor, a gut fighter, a runner-down and cutter-off of human prey, he was a genius. In this case, even while the alarm of the ranch boy's escape was still spread on the worried faces of his men, Fragg had noted something not yet remarked by any of the others. And it changed everything.

Off over west ridge the prairie sky had gone black as gangrene. The immense storm cloud that had threatened all the past night through was coming now. It was building into a rolling, ugly mass, moving to pass over the McCalister place and break on east rise. Both the ranch people and the restless marauders surrounding them were too intent on the game of hopes and fears and human hungers being played between them to scan the weather.

What the hell. It was a bluebird day where they were. Let the game get on. Cut the cards for the women. Who went first on the daughter. Who settled for the looney mother. How were they going to handle the big nigger? You couldn't let him on until everybody else had finished. Well, hell. High card would get the girl. Low card would shoot the nigger. *If* he unbuttoned. Rest of it would just have to sort out, wild card.

But Fragg, seeing the ominous storm, knowing it meant total washout of their trail coming into the McCalister place, even of where they had left the Overland Road, knew he had time to play his own game.

The redheaded kid that had run off? Where would he go that it could make any difference that day to Captain

Braxton Fragg? After the boy finally did hit the stage road and hailed down a coach, he would still have to roll on into town for help. Meanwhile, Fragg and his California column would be riding again. And riding rested of appetite, restored of horseflesh, freshened in all those things that the capture of a good commissary and some of the local women guaranteed to guerrilla cavalry the wars of the world around.

Graciously, humbly almost, Fragg dismounted and came to stand diffidently before Sissy, mama, and old Cap. Requesting the men to move back, he called Canfield to join him from the wagon. When the latter had done so, Fragg sweepingly introduced him to Mary McCalister.

"Major Henry Devereaux Canfield, ma'am," he said. "Duke University School of Medicine, regimental surgeon of the Fifth Alabama Horse, Confederate States Army."

He went on to fulsomely anoint Canfield as "surely the best suited of our rough number to reassure and comfort your little family, ma'am, in the unfortunate and unhappy matter which now must be disclosed." He then doffed his filthy hat with a flourish for the again blank-faced ranchwoman, introducing himself.

"Captain Braxton B. Fragg, ma'am, your honored servant. With my poor men of the Fifth Alabama. All that remains of us alive." Replacing his hat, he straightened and made way for Canfield, who, confused, failed to step forward in time. The pale eyes flared and Fragg shoved the major with force sufficient that he stumbled and had to catch himself. The guerrilla leader's face was again and immediately apologetic. That is to say, if a starving dog wolf can appear contrite. "Major Canfield, ma'am," he finished. "He will tell you of your two brave boys, which was our hero comrades and which we done our loyal best to bring home to you."

Canfield, put thus under the fieldpiece of necessity, rallied like the Carolina blueblood he was. His innate grace under fire kept the ranch group attentive to his words. The fact that he was a doctor guaranteed respect after the grim fact of those words—precisely Fragg's intent.

Henry Canfield not only gave the medical details of Junior McCalister's death, but in the accounting absolved Fragg's scabrous pack of any blame for the tragic irony of "the noble lad expiring so near to his beloved home and family." Yes, and despite every effort of Captain Fragg to honor the fervent prayer of the departed youth's older brother, Lonnie, that the troop would force on through the night with the wagon carrying the dying soldier boy. "There was no chance of saving your son, madam," Canfield said softly. "He was a victim of the war, as surely as had he died on the shell-torn, terrible field at Shiloh Church. It was his heart at the last that surrendered; his spirit never gave up." Canfield lowered his head. "We have him in the wagon, ma'am. He is at peace and did not suffer."

Mary McCalister smiled and nodded.

Sissy sobbed aloud.

Old Cap Marston looked drawn, frightened of what he now must ask. "And what of the other boy?" he said. "What happened to Lon? Is he in the wagon too?"

Braxton Fragg moved forward. He put Canfield aside with an unconscious sweep of the arm.

"No, old-timer," the heavy voice said. "We think the other lad is all right. He slipped away from us."

"Slipped away?" said Cap, cautiously.

"Well, you know, just up and left. Disappeared."

"Disappeared?"

"Look, old man, don't take me out on my every word. It won't profit you."

"Yes sir." Cap squinted, nodding that he gathered the guerrilla's meaning plain enough. "Didn't mean no implyments, captain."

Fragg eyed him a moment, returned the nod, satisfied.

He then related Lon's vanishing at the spring on the east rise grade, or near there. As the older youth had been ordered by the doctor to rest in the wagon with the younger lad, his own condition being one of severe depletion, Captain Fragg believed that Lonnie had awakened to find his brother dead. Shocked and bewildered, he had simply run away. Slipped into the night. Disappeared. Exactly as the captain had just said. It remained a virtual certainty, however, that the youth would recover his composure in good time, and little doubt find his way home, forthwith. Why, Fragg proclaimed soberly, the lad was likely at that very moment making his way to the ranch. Dr. Canfield had assured him, Fragg, there was naught in the missing lad's medical condition to worry over. In no case was he in so sorry a state as had been his poor brother.

In the progress of this balm spreading, the guerrilla leader had neatly turned from dour old Cap Marston back to empty-eyed Mary McCalister. He touched the tall woman's arm now, concluding earnestly. "There is one thing, though, ma'am," he said. "It would be the kindest thing we might do to put the brave lad in the wagon to rest before his beloved brother Lon gets here. The doctor thinks we had ought to spare your Lonnie this sorrow. It would just unfairly torture the lad all over again, you understand."

Sissy McCalister, so long held in the silence of dismay at these strange rough men and their sinister captain, now flared in defense of the one thing in the prairie world that was hers in trust of Lon and Junior.

"Dammit, quit talking to 'her!" she burst out, confronting Fragg. "She don't know what the hell you're talking about. Cain't you for Christ's sake see that?"

Cap Marston edged up to join the defiant girl. They fronted Mary McCalister as though physically to protect the vacantly frowning ranchwoman. "Talk to us, captain," he said. "Me and the girl takes care of missus."

"Har, har!" burst a growl from the rear ranks. "We will relieve you of that duty. We'll take care of the missus for you, old man. And missy too, by God! Har!"

It was Corporal Walleye Pike, and Fragg turned upon him like a mad dog. It seemed the officer would shoot his corporal then and there. Walleye himself was convinced enough to begin backing away, gray-gilled, holding up both hands as though to ward off Fragg's fury.

Again, the captain held. He ordered Pike to report to him when they had bivouac set up, and in the interim the others of his troops had best bear witness to their military conduct. Fragg would tolerate no offense to these women, nor violations to their property. This was still the Fifth Alabama Horse, and its men would act like Confederate cavalrymen or face flogging.

"Major Canfield," he said, turning from the mutter of the troopers, "please to prepare the body for burial. I will have the grave dug. Old man"—he wheeled on Cap Marston—"where would you think the missus would like the boy to lay? You and the girl figure it; we ain't much time for the digging."

They all saw the great cloud now. It had crawled off northering of the ranch house, crossed the Paint Creek drainage, and was spilling angrily over the crest of east rise. Thunder and the riven of heat lightning began to run the prairie four sides of the people at the house. In the order of ten or fifteen seconds the boiling cloud front cut off the sunlight. In the fan of its passage, great fat drops of rain commenced to spackle and patter the bare ranch-yard dirt.

"Detail!" barked Sergeant Tranch, unbidden. "Shovels from the wagon. On the double. Hup! Hup!"

"Major," Fragg called to Canfield, now making his way to Scipio Africanus and the parked survey wagon. "Have the nigger bring the wagon up here. Quickly, please. There's more cloud coming behind this that passed over."

He turned to find Cap Marston at his elbow. Beyond the old man, the leggy young girl was leading her mother back into the house. The wind blew the girl's dress between her long, coltish limbs, from behind. The bobble of the young buttocks thus limned made Fragg tremble.

"Yes?" he snarled, showing his teeth to Cap.

"Yonder," the old man said, pointing. "Put the boy there on the knoll with his father. You see the stone up there, just 'neath the poplar tree?"

Fragg signified that he did, ordered Cap to get the women to graveside quickly. "Dr. Canfield is an ordained minister," he told the old man. "He will read the service. Tell the ladies. It will comfort them."

"Thanky, captain." Cap tugged at his hat brim, limped off around the house to hasten Sissy and mama. Fragg watched him go. But he wasn't thinking of those rheumy old tailbones in their baggy sag of torn overall seat.

He was seeing Sissy going away again.

And the pale eyes went ugly.

# 21

The stage, outbound west from Red Hawk, Texas, slowed and drew to the stand in mid-road. The six horses blew light mists of bit froth and tossed their heads, still full of run. The government surveyors got down from the halted coach, minds not yet cleared of the previous night's bout with two quarts of Old Crow. They stood with backs to the prairie, blearily waving up their farewells to the driver. It would be more than time enough to turn and face the dreary fact of their base camp, and two war-sick Texas boys left to guard it, when the stage had gone on toward the Pecos.

The driver, with that "friendliness" generic to old Texas stagers, did not speak to his debarking fares of what he saw beyond them. It was not in his contract with Overland to advise passengers on altered conditions of the road. Thus the three Fort Griffin men watched the Concord rock into motion and dwindle small down the dim tracery of wagon tracks, unaware of the totality of their abandonment. They were in pain, plus some remorse, unwilling yet to bid the morn good day. It was only when a final swell of prairie hid the westbound run from view entire, that they came about to paw at sandy eyes and blink in disbelief at where their camp had been.

"Damnation," one of them said. "Our returning war heroes must have run off with our Confederate government property."

"They did a good job of it," the second averred. "Nothing left but the ashes of their camp fire."

"It's a mirage," the last of them concluded. "We will see it reappear in a minute. Just blink real hard."

But the camp, except for its burned-out fire spot, was empty. Blinking and wishing their wagon and its dump of supplies would materialize out of the crystal prairie air did nothing but further irritate already pinkened eyes. The surveyors were still standing about in various colloquy and curse as to their next move when, up from the southeast, swept Sheriff Charley Skiles of Pioche with his unshaven eight-man posse. The conversation now came down to cases.

Getting the surveyors' story, the sheriff and his chief deputy quartered the camp, quickly found the wheel marks of the reloaded wagon bearing away westward. Observing these tracks to be overlain by the hoof signs of no less than ten escort horsemen, the sheriff called his posse into trail meeting.

"All right," he led off, "here's what we know."

Three government men, supposedly good and reliable citizens, had reported their field-camp supplies, wagon, and team of big Missouri mules missing and presumed stolen. Easily followed sign of same theft ran off west by north over empty prairie.

The camp had been left in the guard of two young soldier boys. These lads, in Confederate uniforms and claiming to be honorably discharged for grievous wounds in heroic service to the South, had identified themselves as brothers, which they did not look like at all, and had said they were bound for the McCalister ranch on Paint Creek, some miles over the prairie from the Overland Road.

It would now appear, from the evident rendezvous of the Pioche bank gang with the two youngsters, that the latter were scarcely war heroes. Little doubt they were deserters, or worse, and certainly scouts or spies for the bank robbers. How they had obtained the names of the McCalister boys, Lonnie and Jim Junior, both of whom were known in Pioche, was a dark question. Most likely they had fallen in with the boys along the road home, gained their confidence, then murdered them and assumed their identities to provide a cover for their advance work in spotting banks for the renegade murder gang.

It thus became, the sheriff exhorted his weary listeners, a double duty of the Pioche posse to follow on at this point. To the original enlistment of hounding down the killers of a woman and a child in cold blood on the streets of Pioche was now added the even more pressing responsibility for coming up to the killers before they, in turn, reached the McCalister ranch.

"This is a hanging posse," the veteran lawman reminded them. "The husband of the woman killed is in this posse, as is the daddy of the little girl. We won't be taking any prisoners back."

He paused, judging the temper of his men, and saw that it was wasting.

"Sheriff," one of the worn-down riders said, "you're asking more of us than we've got to give. I cain't make it no futher. And what you've cut yonder is a blind track. There don't none of us know just where is this McCalister ranch, nor even for certain sure where is this here Paint Crick. Hell, there's a drainage every ten mile out here. Every draw full of sand and rock is called a crick or a branch. We could foller that wagon track and them pony prints from here to hell and back around the barn three times, and never see hide nor hackamore of the bastards. Now I'm right sorry, Charley. I know how you got to be feeling. But this here is as far as I go."

Hard-eyed, aging Charley Skiles, the painfully flesh-wounded sheriff of Pioche, hit in the gun battle with the gang outside the bank, stared the speaker down.

"Anybody else?" he said.

A second man nodded, not looking the old lawman square on. "I'm with Jake," he muttered. "We don't none of us know the country. We're out of our own country. We got no food. No more grain for the horses. We're wet from last night's rain, and all you got to do to see how wet we're going to get again is look off northwest."

"Sure as hell, Sam's right," another posse member

noted. "It's blacker than print ink, yonder. And yonder is right where them wagon tracks lead."

"Well, Orlie," the sheriff said, "we got bright sun and clean sky behind us. That's fifty-fifty. You can't get better odds chasing kid and woman killers." He turned to an older, blue-jowled man, giving him a narrowed-eye look. "What do you say, Mr. Hardeman? It was your bank got robbed."

A. J. Hardeman gave him back the tough look.

"Ask Harrel Simms," he said. "It was his wife got killed."

Skiles didn't blink. "Simms?" he said.

Harrel Simms, a slender, youngish fellow, pale and drawn with his tragedy and the grinding hours in saddle to avenge it, found the strength to hold steady.

"I give over to you, sheriff," he said. "Annie was all you had."

The grizzled lawman took it like a knife, deep in, but didn't give. "Simms," was all he said. "Thank you."

He eyed the others of the posse.

"Meeting's over," he said. "Let's count heads." He looked off where the thunder growled. "Quit, or go on."

The men stood hesitant, exchanging glances.

During the spreading ring of the uncertainty, one of the surveyors announced that he and his friends had opted to wait by the road and take the eastbound stage back to Red Hawk. They would rather go with the posse but had to find transport to Fort Griffin to make their proper reports.

"Sure," the sheriff said. "You bet you do." He turned again to his reluctant posse. "Well, men?" he said.

Waiting for their answer, Skiles knew doubt, desperation, heartache, and emptiness for Annie Skiles, the seven-year-old only child of his old age. He was weakening himself. His wound stiffening fearfully. If the posse voted now to quit the chase, it would be over. He was too old and had been hurt too much and recent, and was just plain too far out into unincorporated Texas territory, for further pushing on past a posse vote to quit.

"Skiles," banker Hardeman said out of the silence, "we got a tie here. You're the breaker."

Inwardly, the old lawman flinched; all that the men saw was a twitch of muscle along the stubbled jaw. Then a nod and a resetting of battered Stetson. Swinging his horse, he pointed him along the wagon tracks. One by one, all the members of the Pioche posse fell in behind him. The surveyors waved them farewell and good luck, looking somewhat sheepish. None of the riders heeded them. Yellow was a good color for kitchen curtains. Not much else.

In the lead, young deputy Will Hatch rode up alongside Charley Skiles. "Sheriff," he said, "you're looking puny."

The old man glanced over at him. "Don't let it steer you wide," he said.

"Meant it friendly." The deputy frowned. "You know I did."

"I know a few things." The sheriff nodded.

"You don't know half you think you do." The younger man scowled. "Not about me, you don't. I ain't after your job, Charley."

"But you'll get it, eh, Will?"

"Sure, mebbe some day. You know, sometime."

"Yeah, like the first time I stumble."

Will Hatch shot him a look. It wasn't a mean look nor sneaking. Just tough and young and tired of waiting.

"Only if you go all the way down," he said.

Charley Skiles touched up his horse, didn't say anymore to Deputy Hatch or to the posse. The dark cloud bank was coming in on them faster than they were closing ground on the bank gang. It was push all the way, now, or lose the trail. Back in the pack of the posse, low-voiced muttering jumped up into out-loud doubts. When the rain began in fat splatters, ponchos were redonned, hats screwed down tight. Reins were shortened on nervous horses.

Skiles was going faster all the while.

The rain came on, steady, cold, dismal. The range-wise among the posse members understood the lull. The gut of the dark cloud bank hadn't split yet.

Three of them, Jake Jacobs, Sam Peckingham, Orlie Dobbs, trail leaders, rode up beside the sheriff.

"Charley," Jacobs said, "how long you figure those tracks will hold in this rain? What rain we got right now, I mean. Not what's coming. Three, four mile, you say?"

"Five, mebbe. Longer for the wagon. Why?" Skiles dropped his horse to a walk. "Your boys melting, Jake?"

"Some of us. I'll say this: If it comes on to pour full-spout, those tracks will wash out in five minutes, never mind five mile. If this thing hits like it's a'threatening, it's *adios muchachos*. We're gone home."

Orlie Dobbs came in quickly, drawing the cinch on it. "Just wanted you to know, Charley."

And Peckingham added as fast, "Yep, she's soured."

The old man looked at them, spitting water from the draggle of his mustache. "Will you give me to trail's end, miles or washout, whichever?" he asked them.

Jacobs checked his companions, who nodded unhappily. "You got it, Charley," he grudged. "Slop on." But when he turned to relay the call to the possemen now crowding up behind them, division appeared. Two of the original eight men had had enough. A. J. Hardeman and Harrel Simms were turning back while they could still follow their own trail out to the Overland Road again. They gave Charley Skiles his grief, and Will Hatch his hard mouth on the bit, but they were both husbands and fathers. They had ridden out the string of their duty to community. They would have to leave it to the army or the rangers to catch up to the renegade Confederate band. Yes, and to do what hanging was to be done. For the two of them, it was just what they'd heard Jake telling Skiles: "*Adios muchachos.*"

The dissidents, so spoken, turned about and were gone into the drive of the rain. The sheriff studied the remaining men.

"Hmmm," he said. "That's passing odd; I don't see banker Hardeman 'mongst your number. Ain't that strange?"

"No," growled Ortmann, "it ain't. Let's move out."

They went on. The wind increased. It lay flat to the prairie, throwing the water into their faces like waves in a field of twenty-foot wheat. It was suffocating. The horses were having trouble blowing their nostrils free to breathe. Their riders began losing sight of one another for fleeting seconds. It wasn't going to do it.

"Rally in here on me!" Skiles bawled. "Rope up. Pass your lariats. Tie to Will, he's dallied on me. Come on, I can still read trail between gusts."

Roped in a line, the men went forward another half mile and were done. Hand was not visible arm's length from nose. Every draw and dry gulch was roaring with runoff water, some a foot deep, some two inches, some over a tall horse and booming. At the last of it, their mounts simply hunched loins, put rumps to wind, and quit.

# 22

The men sat there, letting the horses bunch.

With water running boot-heel deep on the prairie flat, there was no prayer in hell for continuing. God or Old Nick, one, had washed free the sins of the killer gang. What was left of the Pioche posse might as well throw in and go home. When that black rain passed over and the sun came again, it would shine on a thousand miles of buffalo grass as clean of wheel rim or horseshoe iron as the far back side of the moon. Charley Skiles, thinking of this inevitability, accepted it.

"Leave 'em roped," he said, "and guide on me. I will give old Kickapoo his head and see where he winds us up. He's the best horse ever I see to get back to the barn. All set? *Yaahh*, Kicker! Oats in the nose bag, boy."

Kickapoo, sired by a mesquite-bean wild stud out of a Percheron plow mare, was long in tooth for a fact. But his wise old head still worked, and the brimstone blood of the mustang stallion that had seduced his dam lent fire yet to the great splayed hooves. In minutes he had drifted quartering to the storm and counter to where any rider would have sent him, and found the shelter of east rise spring. But a problem arose there.

Indeed it arose out of the very rocks of the spring-branch outcrop that spelled safe haven from the cloud-burst to the exhausted remnant of the Pioche posse.

One moment old Kickapoo was leading them into the wind shelter of the ancient limestone upthrust, nickering compliments to himself. Next second, the old horse was emptying his nostrils of water with an expelled snort of alarm and a sideways buck jump that dumped the sheriff on his arthritic hip among the small broken stones of the bony ground. The second following that, the other horses piled into the backing Kickapoo, who then stepped on Charley Skiles trying to get away from them. Posse obscenities mixed with high-pitched neighing and violent breaking of gas by the spooked horses ensued for the next five wild seconds. Then, through a thinning moment's hole in the wind blow of the rain, the cause of the jam-up was seen—a blurred human figure tottering up from under a ledge of the limestone, above the spring. A figure that croaked inhuman sounds and staggered on toward the tangled posse. And a figure that then pitched forward and fell face down in the bank mud, even as Charley Skiles was still cursing old Kickapoo and raging for somebody to help him up onto his feet again.

Two of the now dismounted possemen, Dobbs and Peckingham, went to Skiles's aid. The third, Jacobs, ran on to the fallen man. Ortmann and Dean Oates followed Jacobs. Only Will Hatch stayed on his horse, unhelping.

Jacobs turned the stranger over to prevent drowning in the liquid mud. Sheriff Skiles, up and limping badly, got his night-hunting bull's-eye lantern from its right-knee saddlebag. Crouching under the now-quieted Kickapoo's ample belly, the old man lit the lantern with a match from his waterproof wrap. Coming over to the down man, he slid back the bull's-eye shield, played the beam on the face of the storm ghost. It was the face of a dead man, or a dying one.

"Anybody know him?" Skiles said.

Nobody did.

The old sheriff nodded. "I do," he said. "It's the oldest McCalister kid, Lonnie."

The others looked at the motionless body, then up at the almost equally gray face of Charley Skiles. It was plain they did not think the old man was tracking true.

"Whoever he is, he's gone," Will Hatch said from his horseback view. "He's soakeder with blood than rain."

Carlos Ortmann, a sometime Texas Ranger, leaned over, ear to chest of the apparition. "I heard a heart bump," he said, glancing up. "There's another."

Skiles shouldered in. "Skin his eyelids back," he told Ortmann. The latter obeyed, and the sheriff shined the bull's-eye directly into the opened eyes. He and Ortmann exchanged looks. The pupils seemed to have shrunk. "Keep them lids back," Skiles said, and reached to touch the outer corner of the naked eyeball with his finger.

"Jesus," breathed Jacobs. "He's alive."

"If he ain't," Skiles growled, "you'd best not believe the lid-blink on the next 'dead' grizzly you poke in the eye to see if he'll squint. Get the boy up on my horse."

"You mean put him up behind you, sheriff?" Jacobs asked.

"No, Jake, put him in the saddle. Then rope and strap his feet under the horse's belly. Pad the horn with my poncho. I'll walk by old Kick's wither and keep the kid from flopping off. Come on, we're getting out of here."

"The hell," Will Hatch said abruptly. "You got your brains wet, Charley. It ain't safe out there."

Charley Skiles stepped around the unconscious man to shine the lantern up onto Hatch. "Funny, Will," he said. "Damn if I see any Pioche star pinned on you."

"Aw, for Christ's sake, Charley," one of the possemen began, but the old man shut him off.

"Rope the kid on old Kick like I say," he gritted. "This hip is seizing up on me every minute we stand here augering. Happen I don't walk out of here, I mebbe won't walk out of nowhere. I'm ordering it, hear. Will—"

The deputy moved his horse forward. "Yeah."

"I'll say it once more." Skiles nodded. "Bad trail or no bad trail, this kid has got to be took back to town. He won't last out here. We get him to the doctor in Red Hawk, he's a chance."

"No chance, Charley," denied young Hatch flatly. "And no doctor. We'll wait the rain out here in the rocks."

"We?" Skiles said softly.

"Me and the men. You too, if you're half bright."

Skiles studied the possemen.

"Well, well, well," he said. "I'm impressed, Will."

He turned to the patiently standing old Kickapoo and gave him a pat on the overfed rump. "Come on along, old Kick," he said. "Pioche done got herself a new sheriff."

Kickapoo whickered agreeingly. He rubbed his vast jughead on Skiles's shoulder, nibbled the old man's ear with leathered and hairy lips, started forward. As he went over the treacherous bog of the open prairie, he continually rolled and walled his good eye to the rear, checking to see that his "passenger" was riding all right and, more important, that the stubborn, not half-bright, and wounded old man was keeping pace and spirit beside him.

Dimming into the now slacking rain, the sight was too much for the Pioche posse. As one, except for one, they mounted up and followed old Charley Skiles. Deputy Hatch played it hardass for about ten seconds and threw in.

"What are you standing here for, knothead?!" he snapped at his half-drowned pony. "YaahhHH, damn you."

Four hours later, worn white and shaken by the long walk out, Charley Skiles led his forward possemen out of the ground fog left behind the rain, not fifty yards from the Overland Road and the campsite of the government surveying crew. There, he found Banker Hardeman, Harrel Simms, and the three surveyors crowded about a halted eastbound coach. The surveyors, spying the sheriff of Pioche, made haste trying to jam into the stage, yelling for the driver to whip up his teams. But Charley fired a shot from his hip gun over the head of the driver and promised to do better for the surveyors did they not cease and back off of boarding the stage, as just then he had some questions to ask.

Moreover, and firstly, he had another passenger for the Red Hawk run.

"Any of you know him?" he asked the government men, indicating the slumped body on the big shaggy horse.

One of the surveyors blurted out, "Sure, that's one of the two damn deserters we gave a lift from Fort Griffin. Said they were the McCalister brothers."

"They was," Charley Skiles said wearily. "This one's Lon. You see the other boy anyplace?" The men shook their heads. "Dammit," he said. "Lonnie, here, come up through the downpour staggering and trying to talk slur-like drunk. Trying to tell us something desperate hard. Like to warn us of something. Or somebody. He never got it out. Went into the mud and stayed there."

The sheriff looked up at the stage driver.

"I want him took to the doctor, in Red Hawk."

"Red Hawk!" The driver was incensed. "I'm already running two hour and ten minutes late. I ain't a'going to do it. You cain't hold me up here on the prairie. I ain't paid to pick up drunks. Get the hell clear of the road; I'm rolling this rig."

He reached for his whip in its socket.

Skiles slung another shot out of the long Colt forty-four. The whip stock shattered in the driver's hand. He screeched like a runover coyote, thinking he had been hit. He had not, and Charley Skiles dismissed him.

"All aboard," he instructed the surveyors. "I will hand the kid in to you, gentle." The government men scrambled to get into the coach. Skiles started to lift the dead weight of the unconscious youth, but his knees jellied up and the prairie commenced to blacken about him. He fought off the faintness, gesturing for his men to complete the job, which they did. By now, however, the driver had recovered, seeing no blood.

"Hold it the hell down there!" he bellowed. "Who's going to stand good for the kid's fare? Company bills me for any deadheads I load on. This ain't rightful."

"Sure enough, it ain't," Skiles agreed. "You bill it to Pioche County, the sheriff's office. Boy's a material witness. We'll need him agin that bank gang."

"Who's we?" the driver insisted to know.

"Me, mister."

"Oh, sure. And who be you? Super of the Overland?"

"Sheriff of Pioche. Move out, damn you."

"Bullwater!" the driver blustered.

Skiles took ahold of the coach. The prairie was spinning again. But again he fought off the blackness.

He pulled the Colt once more, shifting it upward.

"You don't get this boy into Red Hawk 'fore he dies," he said, "I will bill you, calibre forty-four, due and payable whenever I find you."

"All right, all right, for Christ's sake. Latch the door and get back."

Skiles stepped away unsteadily. At the last moment, he leaned into the coach rear window. "Hold him gentle like I said," he advised the surveyors. "I wouldn't want to hear you'd let harm come to him. But I know you won't. Genuine heroes always do their part." He eyed them icily. "You bastards," he said, and pulled his head out of the window and yelled "*Heeyahh!*" up at the driver and stumbled back as the rear wheels slewed and threw gravel and mud all over him.

With the driver whipping hard, the six-horse hitch moved the heavy Concord quickly up to road speed. As safe distance was gained, one of the surveyors, the young mouthy one, leaned out the rear left-hand window with a dirty-sign wave for Charley Skiles, and a derisive string of cowardly obscenities, ending with, "Bill the U. S. of A. Government, you crazy old bastard!"

"Yeah," sighed the old man, "sure."

And with that he went down into the slop of the road. He wasn't unconscious, he was just done in. Deputy Hatch, who was holding old Kickapoo, said quickly to Ortmann, who rode the fastest horse, "Run down the stage and hold it agin. We'll put the old man on it with his precious McCalister kid." Skiles heard him, but he was too far gone into exhaustion and near shock to call him out for it. When they helped him up to the rehalted coach and put him into it with Lonnie McCalister and the nervous surveyors, he made no objection except to admonish Jacobs to take good care of old Kick. Just as the driver was about to lay the leather to his teams again, he leaned down and demanded to know of the posse who to bill for the old sheriff of Pioche's fare. It was Will Hatch who answered him.

"The new sheriff of Pioche," he said. And then to his men, as the big Concord rocked into final motion and disappeared into the swirl of the misting fog, "Here, somebody take this damned old horse of Charley's. He's sawing his mouth raw to run after that stage."

Jacobs reached to take the reins from Hatch but, in the exchange, dropped them. The big, rough-coated animal at once reared and kicked and galloped off into the fog, neighing for old Charley and the Overland stage to wait for him.

"I will go and round him up," Jacobs volunteered.

"Let him go," ruled acting sheriff Will Hatch. "Ain't Charley always told us what a barn finder he is?"

"Naw, he might never get home, Will," Orlie Dobbs said. "Leave me and Jake go after him. We'll catch up to you in Red Hawk."

"Ain't going to Red Hawk, Orlie. This posse's run out. I'm taking it home."

Ortmann, the tough ex-ranger, frowned over that.

"What about Charley, Will?"

"He needs the rest. He's old and he's wore clean out and they'll treat him nice." Hatch reached into his vest and they saw him bring out the old sheriff's star, which

he had unhooked from Charley Skiles unseen by any of
them. There wasn't a word from any man of the Pioche
posse as he pinned the star on himself outside the vest.

"Any questions?" Will Hatch said.

There were none.

And only one general observation.

"Looks good on you, Will," nodded cool-eyed Carlos
Ortmann. "Little big, mebbe."

# 23

With Sissy and mama gone into the house to dress for
Junior's funeral service and Bubba disappeared, only Cap
Marston remained to watch the ragtag Confederates. Cap
made himself as small as possible while awaiting their
next maneuver. Captain Fragg did not keep the old man
overlong in suspense. The moment the women were out
of sight, the reasoned tone with which he had been
calming Sissy and Cap vanished. "Now, by God, we will
see!" Cap heard him curse low voiced. The throaty grating
of the oath broke the old man out in goose bumps. All
his original fears of the drifter band returned.

With the threat, Fragg remounted his horse and
spurred him the short distance to where Scipio and Henry
Canfield were obediently bringing up the survey wagon
with Junior's body. In his approach, the guerrilla leader
drew up on Canfield's side, a seeming awkwardness as
he then had to speak across Canfield to address the Negro
driver, his obvious target.

"Scipio," he announced, the kindness of the words just
loud enough to carry to old Cap at the house, "please to
take the Indian and go fetch the redheaded tad back
here. He is understandably stressed but we don't want his
mother and sister fretted over it. Not so long as we can
help it, we don't. Ain't that so, Major Canfield, sir?"

Canfield, plainly surprised, bobbed his head. This was

an unexpected relief, surely enough. Evidently his earlier pleadings to maintain discipline at the ranch had worn in on the brutal Fragg. About here, and for the sake of the handsome ranchwoman and her flax-haired daughter, a decent man could thank his God.

"Yes, yes, of course," he murmured in belated assent to Fragg's query. "Carry on, captain."

In response, the guerrilla leaned across Canfield to continue with Scipio in words that did *not* carry to the house. The posture, leaning in so far from the saddle, would have dismounted a less skilled horseman. Fragg made it seem graceful, natural.

"Nigger, didn't you hear me?" he said icily. "Go and get that goddam kid. Now, by God, now!"

For a fearful moment Henry Canfield thought the big Negro would not take the order. The whites of his eyes showed mean. The look in the black face would have slowed a saner man than Braxton Fragg. But Fragg, leaning even farther in across Canfield and, quick as a cottonmouth, shifted his right hand a fraction and in it appeared a Colt Navy Model revolver. Both hand and weapon were perfectly screened from the view at the house, by Henry Canfield's body and by the drape of the guerrilla's long CSA cavalry coat. But the freed slave and the master who had freed him could see the weapon well enough. Its muzzle was less than a foot from the temple of the regimental surgeon. And it was evident then that Braxton Fragg did not make awkward approaches or commit tactical blunders in his cruel profession. He had taken Dr. Canfield hostage in full sight of those at the house, and not a one of them, even of his own men, understood the fact. But Scipio Africanus understood it.

And still he didn't move.

"Nigger," Fragg repeated, the yellowed teeth showing, "if you don't do as I say this instant, your fine-haired master's brains will fly. They will fly out on your side of his skull. And splatter you. Now do you hear me, nigger?"

"Yes, suh," Scipio said.

He gave the reins to Canfield, stepped down from the

seat box, and went to the rear of the wagon. There, he untied and mounted his saddle horse. As he turned the animal with a hand signal to Gabby to follow him, Fragg added a qualifier. "And, nigger, if you don't come back with the boy—" He deliberately suspended the threat and Scipio knuckled his brow, humble as any field hand.

"Yes, suh, cap'n, I understands."

He started away, then checked his mount, frowning.

"There's onliest the one thing, cap'n." He saluted and sat there, blinking stupidly. Fragg showed the stained canines once again.

"Yes, yes?"

"Anything happens to Mister Henry whiles I'm gone—"

Scipio suspended the words exactly as Fragg had done with him the moment before. The guerrilla went dark with fury at the aping. But the big Negro and the Indian packer Gabby went away on the trot before Fragg could loose his outrage. In the intervening clutch of seconds, Henry Canfield spoke quickly, diverting him further.

"Captain," he called, "had we not best get on with the business of the burial? It is a hard thing we must do. Especially for the poor tortured mother. It will not soften for her by delay. The demented suffer more than we know, captain. They weep inside."

Fragg stared at him a long moment, then said only, "You fool," and started his horse for the lone poplar above the ranch house.

Canfield drove the wagon on up the slope, parking it just beyond the grave that was already there on the lookout knoll beneath the tree. Wrapping the reins, he made sure Fragg did not see him get down on the far side of the wagon and go back to check his own horse at its tie on the tailgate. This matter was narrowing down and the regimental surgeon, for all his genteel upbringing and despair of war, did not want to be caught on foot away from his mount. Even a swamp-wolf guerrilla cavalryman did not outride a proper Dixie old-blood landholder. Canfield got the horse loose, hand-led him around the wagon and to the offside of the poplar tree. He tied him there with a loose knot. It was only then that he realized Fragg had followed him all the way.

"Didn't mean to startle you, major," the guerrilla said. He was on foot leading his own mount. "But I did want a word with you before the men get up here."

"Yes, of course, sir. And you did startle me."

"Well, sir, I mean for you to believe that the matter of the pistol was a field-command decision." He said it as though there had been no menacing Colt and no contemptuous "fool" aimed at Canfield. "The black was on the point of refusing a direct order, you see. Surely, that was plain to you; the problem with the nigger, I mean."

"No, I'm not certain it was, captain."

"Now, major, sir, you know I would never try any such of a show-off trick on you. But in a quicksander like this, you know, sir, with the men all humpy as so many jack mules to be atop them women, sir—well sir, a combat officer has got to do some peculiar things now and again. Ain't that a field-manual fact, major?"

"At least, captain," Canfield said, "I am pleased and thankful that you are worrying about those poor women in yonder. I appreciate that. Now, sir, may I not go to the house and bring them out? I'm sure they could use a stout arm just now."

"Go ahead." Fragg grunted. "Just don't stretch the courtesy."

Canfield caught something in the other's tone, and halted as he started off. "What is it you mean, captain?" he asked. "Stretch what courtesy?"

"Fooling with the women, sir. I just told you the men are pawing the dirt and peeing in their pants to be at them. I can't hold them off all morning, sir."

"Damn you, sir!" Canfield exploded. "I had your word about the women. Come, man, in God's name. We must control these troops. If not you, then I, sir!"

"You!" Fragg burst out.

Canfield drew himself up. "I will personally shoot the first man that moves to harm those women. Now you must understand that I mean this, captain. And I must understand that you are with me in my determination. Now then, sir, are we agreed? Yes or no."

Fragg seemed aggrieved by the question's evident calling into doubt of his fitness to command.

"Now, major," he said earnestly, "you well know that I wouldn't want to see that poor crazy lady hurt no more than you would. Her nor the girl, neither one. No, sir."

He stood taller having said it, a man who had been reached, brought to his best. The bony fingers ran the vanished creases of the butternut leggings. They smoothed the rumpled lapels of the long Confederate coat. Reset the angle of the ragged Jeb Stuart hat.

"Of course we will bury the boy in the wagon first," he said emotionally. "That's only fitting to any mother."

He paused, the pale eyes of a sudden unblinking in their regard of the gentle Carolinian.

"*Then* we will come to the women," he said.


In the brush-choked gully just beyond the poplar tree overlook of the McCalister ranch, Cap Marston lay on his belly and shook like a wet dog in cold wind.

The old man had bravely risked the danger of being discovered in order that he might sneak up the draw and hear what went forward at the gravesite between the two leaders of the invading Johnny Rebs. Having just heard the dark ending of their conversation, it was slight wonder that he shivered so. Nor could he believe what he then saw follow of frightening behavior on the part of the doctor, a man old Cap had thought of some quality and indeed high character.

No sooner did Fragg issue his chilling words about the ranchwomen than he wheeled about in dismissal of the company surgeon, striding over to deploy his arriving troops in proper order about the gravesite, already being readied by Sergeant Tranch's diggers. The doctor, for all his noble declaimings, stood stock-still with an empty blink playing his face for all the world as if he had not, in the finish of it, understood a word of what he had just heard of terrible menace.

After a moment, he too strode off, in his case down the slope to the ranch house where the two women were now seen exiting in dark shawls and with slow steps.

Cap held at the gully lip a last moment.

Watching the grave being dug and the genteel doctor walking down the hill to escort the women to the poplar knoll, the old man raised himself on his elbows. He watched Sissy coming up the hill, her young grace and golden beauty strangely alight in the storm's electric rivens. The words formed on his withered lips, framing the cry that he would like to have flung her—*Honey, honey, God help us, they're mad as hatters, both of 'em!*— and he thought he saw the slender girl glance up and catch sight of him in the fringe sage of the gully, and he imagined to hear her clear voice crying back to him, *Oh, Cap, what must we do?*

Then a thumping crash of thunder shook the earth of the poplar tree overlook, and rod lightning chained the skies over Paint Creek in blinding flares. Covered by this cannonade, old Cap slid back into the bottom growth of the draw and tottered at best speed downward toward the ranch yard, where he might join the two dear women and come with them to the grave.

# 24

Purple, gray, and black, the storm clouds piled and scudded wildly above the Paint Creek drainage. On the poplar knoll where papa lay and Junior soon would rest, the stillness of the mourners was heightened by the sudden dropping away of all wind. In the eerie quiet, the garish light of the electric bolts lit the stark faces, made the still air smell of burned ozone. All knew the wind fall was momentary, a pocket of vacuum in the rainburst all about them. But Cap said softly to Sissy that it was God's will and that it was done in respect to Jim Junior.

And the willowy girl smiled a drawn smile and whispered that it was too bad mama couldn't know it, as she surely would have liked that kindness from the Lord.

"She knows it," Cap whispered back. "Looky at her."

Sissy looked and mama was standing with face upraised to the dark clouds, a sort of great calm on her features. It was sure enough as though Mary McCalister were thanking her Maker for the pause in his rushing power while her son was lowered to last reward. "She knows, she knows," Cap said again.

Sissy answered that she almost believed mama did understand, even if but for that moment, that it was her second son being buried there beneath the poplar tree. Then she and old Cap hushed, as Dr. Canfield raised his hands and came to the edge of the hole where the troopers had just finished letting in the body of Junior McCalister.

But Dr. Canfield could not find his Bible for the reading. In vain he sought through the pockets of his Confederate officer's coat for the book that was never hand's reach away from his need of it. Still, he could not find it. Ordained minister that he was said to be, experienced lay preacher that the men knew him to be, he yet appeared lost without his book. Indeed, for that anguished moment at graveside, it seemed there would be no prayer for the dead. Then, in off the prairie, rode Scipio Africanus.

The black man took in the tableau, dismounted, and went to Canfield's side. There, he cast down his glance and said, deep voice rumbling like some soft thunder of its own, "Leave us pray."

Fragg first shot him a look that said more of hate than hallelujah. Then, instantly, he reversed. Nodding at Scipio, he removed his hat, turned gaze to heaven. Sergeant Levi Tranch lifted upper lip in an audible growl of contempt. Corporal Walleye Pike rolled widespaced eyes and mouthed some out-loud foulness. Tranch promptly cursed him, causing Fragg to snap at his profaning sergeant, in turn, to stand to in proper silence.

Rebellion smoldered, threatened to ignite.

In the stilly damp of the open grave, the men grew restive. They were randy to be at warmer game than this sanctimonious nonsense of Fragg's ordering respect for a damned nigger. But before their humbling might escalate to a more open ugliness, Scipio raised dark face to darker skies. Throwing wide his great arms, he called forth against the returning outcry of the storm:

"The heavens declare the glory of God and the firmament showeth his handiwork. The law of the Lord is perfect. The testimony of the Lord is sure. O, Lamb of God, who lieth down here, the Lord hears thy bleating. He is with thee in this day of thy trouble. He harks thee from his holy pastures. He will reach down and draw thee to him with the saving strength of his right hand. He will call thy name and ye shall be risen to stand upright by his side. Do not cry out. 'My God, my God, why hast thou forsaken me?' For the Lord thy God sayeth unto thee, 'Behold, I am here, come ye with me. And ye shall live in the kingdom of Heaven forever, selah.'"

Scipio lowered his outspread arms. He bowed his head. Not a man of the troopers moved, except to trade glances and compress lips, and then to look downward as the black man looked downward. In the strange subdual amongst the men of the Fifth Alabama Horse, Henry Canfield found his dignity and his voice.

"The Lord gave and the Lord hath taken away," he said. "Blessed be the name of the Lord. Amen."

Hurriedly, the men finished filling in the grave.

The storm began to roar again. The rain returned with the wind. The women and old Cap stumbled down the hill. Canfield turned to follow them. One of the troopers, muddy shovel a-shoulder, caught up to him.

"That was some prayer that the nigger give," he said. "Where was it from?"

Henry Canfield looked at him.

"The heart," he said, and hastened on to help the women where the hill steepened, just above the house.

# 25

Bubba could run. He could run in bursts and fits and streaks like a young bird dog or a weanling colt. In good times he would kick out and leap sideways and capriole into the air like a kid goat. But if it was bad or dangerous times, Bubba just plain-out ran.

This was a bad and dangerous time.

Bubba smoked past the horse shed on his way to north gully before Tranch had even hit the ground for his first bounce at the end of his own lariat. But then Bubba remembered that north gully was not where Cap had told him to run for in the first place. He remembered where he had been bound when Tranch had roped him and dragged him back to the others. It was to the horse shed. The horse shed and The Redeemer, old Cap's four-pound Walker Colt revolver. Unbroken of stride, the ranch boy wheeled to his left, circling to put the shed between himself and the drifter scum. Then he raced straight in behind the shed.

Skidding to a halt at the rear wall, he cussed at the solid planking, which held no window opening. He knew both side walls were also without windows. All three walls bore rifle slits only. And not even a runt butt like Bubba McCalister could squeeze through a West Texas "Comanche slot." Such "windows" would only pass a .50-calibre rifle barrel with bare sighting space left over. Damn! He had to get around to the front.

Bubba could hear the commotion going forward where Tranch's horse was being controlled beyond the main house. Next minute they would realize he was gone and would be after him. He must get around the shed, into its saggy leather-hinged door, dig out that old gun of Cap's and get it back to Cap—somehow—before those bastards came for him, Bubba.

And they were bastards. Evil and wicked and lusting, like the Bible said. Elsewise, old Cap would not have sent Bubba to fetch The Redeemer for him. The old man was so crickety with his years that he couldn't run himself. That's why he had sent Bubba to go and get the gun for him. It wasn't for any doubt that Cap meant to use it. He was a Texas Ranger proud times ago. Hell, he would do it. He would blast those sons of Dixie bitches right out of their boots, dast they to touch Sissy or mama. He would, that was, if Bubba didn't fail him in fetching the gun.

Still, he hesitated, fearful of risking all.

What would Lon and Junior have done? Got down the gully and gone for outside help? Somehow got word to town of the bad lot that had ridden into the Paint Creek homeplace? Bubba shook his head.

Anybody knew what Jim Junior would have done; he'd have bellowed like a longhorn bull with his bangers caught on a cat-claw thornbush, and charged the bastards head-on. Brother Lon wouldn't have yelled, and likely would have circled. But by Christmas he *would* have gone to them. Neither of them would hide like Bubba was hiding, safe back of the horse shed, gnawing on his knucklebones and whimpering that he wished his two big brothers were there in his place.

Bubba spit dry. He set his jaw. He got ready to run again, knowing his true course now.

"Redeemer," he whispered hoarsely, "here I come."


The storm rebroke in full squall as the men ran their horses into the shed, from the burying. Following them, Scipio guided the stolen government survey wagon in under the roof of the adjacent lean-to hay shelter and made the vehicle secure. Tying the team without unharnessing, he slipped the animals' bits, fed them what scraps of last summer's hay still lay about the dirt floor. He talked low to the mules, rubbed their draggled ears, smoothed the silk of their muzzle skin. They talked back to him with grunting mule sounds, and he said, "Yeah, ain't much difference in a mule and a nigger, less'n you'd say the mule was smarter." There was a stir, a footfall, behind him. His hands slowed

"Nigger."

The one word broke flat in the stillness and he knew the voice and turned to face Braxton Fragg.

"What'd you find of tracks yonder?" the guerrilla leader said. "Of the boy's, I mean."

"There's kid tracks everywheres 'bout here, cap'n, but no fresh ones that reach the gully. I sent the Injun on crost the draw. Told him to quarter 'round futher out. That's case somebody might be coming in on us." Scipio shrugged dismissingly. "Redhead boy ain't left the place, cap'n. He's holed up sommers to hand. We'll dig him out for you soon's the rain lets up."

"You had better," Fragg said. "I don't want that kid left loose, you understand me?"

"What you gonna do with him, cap'n?"

"Shut him up," Fragg grated.

He wheeled and went back to the horse shed. There, he called his troopers together in the reasonably dry retreat of Cap's bunk room. The men came grumbling that the damned old codger and Major Canfield were in the main house with the women, all warm and toasty as squab in a dovecote. Meanwhile, they were out here in the goddam slop and raindrip of the horse shed. Captain Fragg, they plainly hinted, had better have some hotter-bottomed answer for their condition than that old bush-way about CSA field orders and regulations.

Fragg said earnestly that he had such an answer and would start his proof by detailing Girty and Fowlis to the house, where they would be charged with guard of the women. They would also make certain that Major Canfield was up to no damn-fool gallantries, such as trying to aid the women to escape. If the Carolinian were to make any such unmilitary move, Girty and Fowlis were to shoot him. At the same time, if either of them so much as laid a dirty finger on the captive females, they would be shot—by Fragg.

Girty and Fowlis departed at the trot.

Fragg then instructed the others that "Canfield's nigger" had told him the Bubba boy had not escaped. It was possible, however, that he had. It was also possible that the older brother had survived his escape from the wagon and might even now be up to some mischief in their rear. He, Fragg, had decided there could be no sensible gain served in blind pursuit of either McCalister youth. Already they knew they had little time to spare. Either or both of the escaped brothers could reach help. The older one, for example, might encounter the Pioche posse in the field. Even though the storm made this unlikely, they could not count it out. As for the red-headed kid, which of them knew where neighbor help might be reached? It could be two miles off or twenty-two. Again, no good commander of irregular horse would risk the guess. The troop must move on.

"What about the women?" Private Creech demanded in immediate surly challenge.

"Yeah," his comrade, Private Hoad, rasped. "You ain't thinking to 'regulate' us out'n our little pleasures, be you, captain? Or lecture us to your noble ways?"

"Har!" Walleye Pike exploded. "Not him, not hardly. Remember them women we caught on the road outside Palo Pinto?"

"Heaven save our souls!" Hoad cried in mock alarm. "I had hoped never again to think of that turrible naughty thing he done there. Har! har!"

"Damn you," Fragg growled. "Hold off."

He was thinking of the women, admitted. But he was a true guerrilla doing it. Not brainless scum like he commanded here. Canfield had been right. Any serious breakdown of discipline now would make for fatal delay. On the opposite military hand, why not take the women along? Let them be camp baggage. That should appeal to the men. Give them something to think about on the hard march Fragg knew they faced.

Braxton Fragg might not himself deny his own lust, but he understood, as the men did not want to remember, that every one of them was wanted for the rope. And that went from the south coast of Georgia to the sunset edge of Texas. Their best chance was California. More likely it was their *only* chance.

Arizona? New Mexico? Apaches and worse. The

Yankee general Canby had them under his thumb. It was Union country clean out to Yuma and the crossing of the Colorado River into California.

But, ah! once they got to the golden state!

Canfield had been right about that, too. Admit it. California was the last throw at new lives for Braxton Fragg and his Fifth Alabama Horse. It was so because their old lives were not worth five cents Confederate anywhere along the twisted bloody trail of desertion, sedition, murder, and rape that they had left behind them in the flight to the west. Damn, and damn again. What to do?

"*Captain.*" One of the men spoke to him sharply. "You all right?"

Fragg passed a hand over his face, nodding. "Just scanning the way ahead," he said. "We've far to go and can't stay here. We will need to take the women with us. Camp women, they'll be. Fair turns for all. No favoring. What do you say, men? Have I ever shorted you in booty or spoils?"

He had not, and the men knew it. Yet they stirred like hornets angry in the nest. Scipio Africanus, who had only then come quietly to the bunk-room door, heard the sound and stayed outside. Unnoticed, he scanned the room's interior, marked the sullen faces, watched the wipings at wetted mouths, grimaced to the fierce aching of his own loins for a woman. Lord God, the tempting was fierce.

As it will where man's tensions exceed his strengths, an errant detail intruded itself to distract Scipio's passions. Something in the room caught at his forager's eye. It was a thing not right, not where it ought to be by normal rules. The forager, of all men at war, is trained to see any such item not in its correct place, or rightful relationship, with those other things around it. Especially in a house. It would be a thing hidden to keep it safe from just such buzzards and jackals and hyenas of warfare as Scipio Africanus had been. In this case, it was the room's stove. More exactly, it was something *inside* that stove.

Scipio had missed it at first sweep.

Then, noting it, he had dismissed it. But it wouldn't stay dismissed.

While the men hesitated in their mutinous anger against Fragg's threat to resume the forced march out of Texas, the black forager stole another glance at the stove. This time he knew he saw it—a tiny sifting of ash trailing down from the firebox to the floor. A pack rat in there disturbing the ash? Field mice maybe? Well, it was a hell of a big rat or mouse, if so, for its beady eyes were blinking back at Scipio Africanus out of the top vent grill of the sheet-iron door.

Scipio wanted to laugh. That was the feisty redhead ranch kid hiding in that old stove. It purely had to be. Damn! The nerve of the little sonofabitch. And the pure backhouse luck. Sweet Jesus!

The stove just happened to be cold. It just happened to be a heating stove, not a cookstove. And it just happened to be a big-bellied sodbuster model built to burn a bushel of cow chips or cornhusks, or any other blessed combustible but wood, in this westering land where trees were scarcer than harpsichords in a whorehouse. Say hallelujah!

Scipio looked at the beleaguered Fragg. Then at the men—Hoad, Tranch, Pike, and Creech—smoldering in revolt.

Lord, Lord, could a man betray that boy to such a pack of mongrel swamp dogs? Just hear them snarling at Fragg now. Why, they'd kill the boy, should Scipio give his hiding place away. They even sounded as if they were about to kill Fragg himself. And Scipio might be next!

But even as the angered men began to close in on the cornered guerrilla leader, threatening him aloud with death if he did not give them the women, they were stopped by a high thin scream echoing from the main house.

It was a woman's scream, crazed with fear, and at its wild sounding the pack went on the rush out of the horse-shed bunkhouse room.

## 26

Leading the race from the horse shed was Scipio
Africanus. The ex-slave knew that no woman would be
in peril with Master Henry Canfield yet in charge of
guard troops. Something very bad had happened in the
main house, and one thing more outside it. Captain
Fragg's harsh discipline had been sapped and mined: the
woman's scream had lit the Devil's fuse and all hell must
blow up now.

Scipio reached and hurled himself at the kitchen door.
It was barred from the inside. Again, Scipio lunged at it.
The heavy inner bar cracked like a roof timber giving
way The door flew inward, rebounded, and was smashed
aside by Scipio. From behind, Fragg and the men piled
against him. For an instant, the clot of their collision
jammed them all in the doorframe—and they saw the
carnage inside.

Mary McCalister and Sissy were under brute criminal
attack. Dr. Canfield lay unconscious on the floor. Beyond
him Cap Marston sprawled, badly hurt and moaning in-
coherently. Of the attackers, Fowlis had Mary McCalister,
Girty was at the girl.

The ranchwoman was strong, giving skinny Ollie
Fowlis trouble. He had her blouse ripped half away. One
breast was fully bared and Fowlis, crazed at the sight,
was savagely attempting to take the woman on down with
arm strength to the floor.

Israel Girty had the girl's skirt and petticoat torn down,
uncovering the young body. Froth literally laced his thick
lips, and he was growling like an animal.

But the girl, wiry and quick, fought him back with
clawed fingers and found his glaring eyes. Girty screamed
and grabbed at his face, blood cascading between his
fingers.

At the sound of his comrade's cry, Fowlis turned an
instant from Mary McCalister. The ranchwoman, man-

wiser than her valiant daughter, drove a knee upward into the genitals of the trooper. Fowlis uttered a strangling cry of blind pain, vomited, staggered back. It was in this foul moment that Scipio broke free of the pack at the door-jamb and charged.

Seizing Fowlis away from Mary McCalister and tearing Girty free of Sissy, the powerful Negro went berserk.

He thudded and smashed the two renegades together as if they were puppets of cloth and meat. In seconds, they were helpless. Scipio dropped them from him to turn and meet Fragg and the others, who, trying to save the lives of Fowlis and Girty, were attacking him. By their num-bers and with any weapon to hand in the ranch house—fireplace poker, cast-iron skillet, jack-oak chair, table leg, anything—they hammered the black giant into dazed submission. When at last he slumped to the floor, Fragg called the men off, faced about to sweep the room with pale eye.

Mary McCalister had forced herself back into the farthest corner. She had made no attempt to close the front of her ripped-away blouse, appearing unaware of the exposure or of her huddled posture. Still, somehow, her expression had changed. The emptiness that had inhabited her face for so long was broken. For glinting moments now, in her staring about the room, there were seeming glimmers and small flashes—of what? Sanity?

Fragg could not know, nor did he care. He shifted the cold, light eyes from the mother to the child.

The girl was against the nearer wall, behind the heir-loom bed. She had taken up the patchwork quilt to wrap about her lower nakedness. A spreading of the quilt, un-noted by her, revealed the upper thigh. Fragg could see the beginning curve of satin buttock above it and he remembered the way the wind had blown the girl's dress between her legs, walking away from him. He could still see the bounce and jiggling of what the skirt had hidden from him and the wind. Now, there it was, all of it, over against that near wall. Just under the worn old quilt, warm and waiting for Braxton Fragg.

His voice came thick and ugly, thrown over-shoulder to the men behind him.

"I want the girl," he said. "Take the other."

He heard, in answer to his order and as he started for Sissy McCalister, the growling of the pack in its closing in upon the mother. The sound but drove the last of his own controls into the primal darkness of human depravity.

Sissy saw her fate in the change of face and voice in the guerrilla captain. Heard the same knell for mama in the wordless mouthings of the men behind the leader. Oh, God, it was going to be now. There was nothing, no one, left between mama and her and the raider pack. "Mama, mama!" she cried, but it was not mama who answered her.

As she called out, Fragg and the men heard another voice. It carried to them, shrill and high, the single outraged word, "No—!" And they hesitated.

Into their midst a shadow fell. It was a small shadow, and forlorn. It cast itself from the frame of the shattered kitchen door, close by Fragg and the wall where he had Sissy cornered, and passing him to fall toward the yonder members of his pack who crouched over mama. Each of the intruders saw the shadow. All of them swept their glances upward to seek its source, and found it jarringly.

Bubba McCalister stood dark against the outer light, daubed in upon the worn threshold like some small avenging angel of death.

In the boy's hands was a gun.

A very large old gun.

It was The Redeemer, Cap Marston's rusted Texas Ranger Colt revolver, the famed Sam Walker .44.

The great curved hammer was hooked back and Bubba was releasing it. The gape of the bore was leveled at the pit of the gut of Captain Braxton Bonaparte Fragg, who had wheeled about to face the boy. Not half a dozen feet separated the guerrilla leader's hairy belly from the pitted muzzle of the gun. Fragg paled. His eyes showed panic. And then the great hooked hammer fell.

In the heartskip of time between trigger's release and

hammer's striking of primer cap, Fragg dove twistingly to the floor. The redheaded boy had no chance to shift his double-fisted hold of the four-pound gun. Fragg thus escaped beneath the whistling ball. He did not elude the volcano of the ancient charge's thunderous fireball. Its explosion charcoaled his face and hands, cooking them black. Fragg was, agonizingly, a gruesome minstrel-show buffoon, black-faced by gunpowder burns. But the wolf, burned, was unchained now, and the pale eyes blazed, unseared. Fragg was far too quick for the ranch youth to trigger a second, surely fatal, chamber of the Walker Colt.

"I'll kill you, boy," the guerrilla leader snarled, and leaped for Bubba McCalister.

# 27

Bubba exploded from the kitchen door like a kicked-up quail. He flew across the rear yard. Behind him one raging jump came Braxton Fragg. The boy saw no haven, no possible hole to hide in, save the old dug well.

Into it, on the fly, he went.

The heavy oak bucket was where it usually was, hanging from the winch, midcenter of the shaft. Bubba hit the bucket and grabbed the rope. Down they went—rope, bucket, Bubba, Redeemer, and all—fifteen feet to the water below. Fragg instinctively seized at the spinning winch handle. There was an instant's banging of the ratchet, a yell from Fragg as the handle flayed him unmercifully, then an answering yell from below, as Bubba struck the water.

Fragg, cursing at his wounded hands, made a double-fisted clumsy draw of the right-hand gun of his belted pair of Colt Navies, blasted the entire cylinder down the well shaft. The powder bursts and bullet ricochets within the limestone casing of the old well sounded like a full barrage of Confederate Napoleons. When it subsided, there was nothing but watch-tick quiet from the well. The boy below was either shot dead, drowned, or playing possum down there in the inky dark of the old shaft. Fragg had no intention of guessing which walnut hull the pea was under.

"Tranch!" he yelled. "Winch up the bucket!"

"What the hell for?" the sergeant wanted to know.

"We'll let you back down in it," Fragg said, kneading his bruised hands. "We got to make certain of the kid. If he ain't drownded, drown him."

The sergeant wavered but saw a way out.

"Yes sir." Tranch saluted. "Pike!" he shouted to his corporal. "Get your butt in the bucket. You heard the captain!"

"I didn't hear him say nothing to me," Pike countered.

"In the bucket," Tranch commanded, drawing his Colt.

"All right, all right," Pike defended. "For Christ's sake you don't have to get your pistol out about it." He wheeled on Private Archimedes Hoad, standing at his elbow. "Crawdad," he ordered, "winch up the bucket."

"Who fer?" Crawdad wanted to know, but the order had reached the last rank and, grumbling or not, Hoad drew up the bucket, anchored his feet against its bail, and seized the rope preparatory to being winched back down.

The deep voice of Scipio Africanus interrupted. "Hey, looky yonder, cap'n," he said to Fragg. "It's old Gabby, a'coming on the fly."

They all looked off and saw the Indian horseman riding his poor bone pile at top gallop down into and out of north gully, coming from across Paint Creek and the direction of east rise.

"What in the hell is he doing?" Fragg snapped.

"He's waving the blanket," Scipio explained. "He done toldt me that's the Injun signal for big trouble. It means run in the ponies and get ready to clear out."

"Oh, bull chips," Corporal Pike said. "Get on into the bucket, Crawdad."

But Crawdad Hoad, if unlearned, was not ignorant.

He scrambled hurriedly out of the bucket and away

141

from the wellhead. "Bull chips yourself," he said to Pike. "I know a scairt-white Injun when I see one. I'm getting my mount."

There was a moment's seminar at the wellhead, while Gabby cleared the gully and came on for the ranch house. It was during this lull that, inside the house, Sissy McCalister recovered from her overriding fright enough to see that she and Mary McCalister were free to run for it. Out the open kitchen doorframe she could see Fragg and the group at the wellhead. Just outside the door she could see where Fowlis and Girty had collapsed in their wounded crawl outside for fresh air. Both old Cap Marston and the genteel southern major, Dr. Canfield, were still unmoving on the house floor.

"Mama!" Sissy cried, low-voiced. "Come on! God's give us a chance."

She seized her mother's slack hand, but Mary McCalister held back. Sissy knew panic but fought it back.

"Mama," she said, "I will race you for the gully. If you win, I'll wash your hair and make it pretty."

The gaunt woman smiled and nodded, and Sissy took her hand again and ran with her out the front door and down the slope to north gully. She took an angle toward the creek to put the house between the line of their flight and the men around the wellhead. She prayed for Bubba as she ran with mama, but she had the feeling that her wild little brother was already with the Lord. Now it was only herself left, and poor dear mama. So she prayed hard for the two of them to reach the gully and get into its cover before any of the men might see them.

She did not pray hard enough.

None of the men behind the house did see the fleeing women. But, up-gully of them a pistol shot away, Sissy saw the gargoyle-faced Indian pack hand of the invaders cross over and ride for the house—and he saw them.

"Run faster, mama!" she panted. "God surely ain't going to let them get us all."

At the wellhead, Corporal Pike let go the bucket as

Private Hoad scrambled free of it. It winched down in free fall, banging off the limestone casing, making a smacking splash below. None of the men seemed to hear or heed it. The Indian was sliding his lathered pony to a halt now and making his strangling throat sounds with the stub of his tongue and throwing his Indian hand-language at Scipio Africanus with every mute show of urgency and alarm.

"Out with it, nigger!" Fragg rasped. "What's the red bastard saying?"

"Bad, bad, cap'n." The ex-slave's black face mirrored the Indian's extreme excitation. "Gabby says there's a mort of men a-coming up the rise yonder. Thinks it's the same posse been chasing us from Pioche. Says they've somehow got back on our track line and are closing fast." Scipio paused, palmed his hands. "That's about as swift as you can go in Injun talk," he told Fragg. "We'd best foller old Crawdad, yonder, cap'n. Get the hosses and light our shucks. I'll fetch the mules and the wagon."

"The hell with the mules and the wagon," said Private Ralph Waldo Creech. "The hosses will do me just fine; I'm gone!" He did start, too, on the run to follow Hoad toward the horse shed and their picket line. But Corporal Walleye Pike bellowed after him.

"What! And leave the women?" And Creech slewed around in his retreat and came back and said to Fragg, "Christ, I'd forgot. What *about* the women, captain?"

"We're taking them," Fragg said. The old command returned to voice and style. The pale eyes had their wolf light back in them. "They're our best insurance against the posse running up on our rear."

"Hostages, by God," proclaimed an admiring Tranch.

"Yeah," chortled the relieved Pike. "And camp ladies aplenty to go 'round, to boot. Cripes, you cain't beat them accommodations."

"We still must move out quick." Fragg scowled. "Get your horses, all of you. Nigger, fetch the mules and the wagon up to the ranch door. I'll get the women ready to load."

He turned for the house but Scipio called after him, "Cap'n, permission to water my team, sir. They ain't had a drop. Hosses got a dip at the crick, remember."

"One bucket!" Fragg shouted back at him. "Split it between them."

Scipio wheeled and raced for the hay shelter. The mules had not been unhooked, and he got them and the wagon lined out for the wellhead. As he did, the cursing men, leading the horses of Fowlis and Girty, galloped past to form up at the rear door of the ranch house. In the same moment, Fragg came storming out of the house.

His oaths made those of the weary, unrested men seem as child prayers. The women were gone. The bastards Girty and Fowlis had let them get out the front door. They could have gotten into one or both of the main gullies, across the creek, or God knew where else, including any one of the two dozen minor washes visible from the house. It was a trap. A military box. They could not risk the time to root through every cover the escaped women could be in. Now it was life itself they had to save. No hostages. No camp women. Nothing.

"Mount up!" Fragg screamed. "Mount up!"

He dragged and kicked Fowlis and Girty to their feet, near weeping with blind rage. The men clawed themselves into saddles. Tranch ran up with Fragg's horse. The guerrilla leader reached for the reins, then spun about and re-entered the house. Two revolver shots, spaced by the time of three strides between them, thudded out from within the house walls. Fragg came back out the empty kitchen doorframe. His left-hand Colt Navy was still out, still smoking. He jammed it into its holster, took his horse's reins from Sergeant Tranch.

"No hostages," he said. "No witnesses."

At the wellhead, Scipio had halted the mule team to draw the single bucket of water allotted them by Fragg.

He heard the two shots come from the house. His vision, however, was blocked by the horsemen outside the door. He did see tall Fragg's head and Confederate hat moving out of the house, toward the horses.

Then it was Tranch yelling across the yard to Scipio to rustle his black hide over to the house. Yes, and bring the damned Indian with him. Captain wanted bad to talk to them both.

Gabby was sitting his pot-bellied paint off to one side, waiting for the white warriors to get their party in order for the next raid. It always interested him to watch the white man. Especially when he, Gabby, rode in with a dangerous message. An Indian camp would already have been running by this time. But the white men were still arguing about it. Well, that was their way. That was why they got caught so much. He, Gabby, would grow *tekivitchi*—skinny and wrinkled—but these mean ones never would. They would all die in their best years. Still arguing about it.

He saw the black one signaling him and guided his pony after that of the *hombre negro*, toward the white men at the ranch house.

On the way, Scipio gave him the hand signs to be careful. He nodded that he would. But careful of what? The black man had been living too long with these white ones. He was getting crazy too. But Gabby liked the big Negro. He would be careful.

Fragg wanted to know swiftly of the Indian scout, through the interpreting of Scipio: Had he seen anything of the two white women? The mother and daughter of this ranch house? Scipio, as a matter of course, started to tell Gabby some lie about the nature of the guerrilla's question, but it was too late. In their association with their native guide, all of the men had picked up some of the hand signs used by Gabby. In particular, the wily Fragg had made note of certain obvious signs. Such as the one, for instance, denoting woman. Fragg now made the sign unconsciously in talking to Scipio. Gabby picked it up and, before Scipio could lead him falsely astray, he broke a wide, gap-toothed grin over his ugly face. "Unh! unh, unh!" he gargled excitedly. Repeating Fragg's sign, he leaped from his pony, seized the low eave of the house, hauled himself to the roof. Running up the slope to the ridgepole, he struck dramatic pose and pointed, clearly

145

enough for any white fool to read, that the women had gone "that way," into north gully.

He was sliding back down off the pitch of the roof and into his disreputable Mexican saddle in the next instant and wheeling the paint pony and gesturing rapidly to Scipio to "follow me." With that, he was gone, and so were the mounted men of the Fifth Alabama. It was all that Scipio could do not to back-shoot the tomfool Indian, but the fat was in the breakfast fire and an ex-slave had to do what remained that he still might do, to right the evil which he had helped bring to this good white family.

Returning to the well, Scipio, fussing with the bucket, made as though he were having difficulty winching it back up. Under the pretext, he called guardedly down the shaft.

"Redhead chile, listen to old Skip. You hearn all this augering up here just now? 'Bout taking your poor mama and sister away from here? You know what that means, don't you, boy? And you going to answer me now, ain't you? Gimme a sign. Splash. Spit water. Do anything to let me know you're alive down there—"

No answer came up from below. Scipio glanced toward north gully. He was in time to see the guerrillas flush the woman and her daughter out of the gulch, twist them up on their feet, and start back toward the house dragging them alongside the horses.

Behind him, Scipio heard a watery splash, far down. He at once called down the well but received no answer save the echoing of his own tense inquiry.

Scipio laughed. They heard him clear out by the gully. But they already knew he was a crazy nigger. None of them heeded him further. Yet the time shrank.

"Boy," Scipio said, "I like your style. With a little better luck, you could of been a black chile. Now listen to me, last time. I cain't he'p you but to tell you what I'm telling you. There ain't no posse coming to save your mama and sister. I made that up for the Indian and told him to ride in and say it. That was to spook old Fragg. Maybe to get him to leave your mama and sister here, even if they was used bad.

146

"That ain't going to be. In the house yonder I don't hear nothing. Your friend the old man is in there, and my old master from back home. They was shot by Fragg. You hear me? Your brother Lon ain't coming home, either. There's nobody coming, redhair' boy. You're the last one left alive that can he'p your mama and sister.

"I'm dropping the bucket back down now. Grab for it. That's so you can clamber out on the rope. Look sharp!"

He let go the heavy bucket, permitting it to winch down. He heard it strike the water, but no other sound.

"Good-bye, redhead chile," Scipio Africanus said. "I seen you in that hay stove yonder to the old man's bunkroom. You got quality, boy. You and your sister and your mama." The deep voice broke off. "Watch out now!"

Next moment Fragg and his men swept up to the well-head with the two women. There was a delay as Sissy fought her captors again. Fragg, cursing, had both women roped and tied like tree-caught catamounts and dumped brutally into the wagon over the high tailgate. Sissy was weeping but no sound came with the bitter tears. Mary McCalister made no sound either, not of weeping, not of anything. The voice of Captain Fragg rasped the orders. Scipio climbed to the driver's seat, lashed at the mules with the lines.

"Ho-ohhh!" Fragg cried, and the Fifth Alabama Horse swept out of the ranch yard of the Paint Creek homeplace. Where Gabby led them they found firm going despite the deluge of the past hour. They increased their speed, pushing on out into the buffalo pasture.

When, tense minutes later, the well rope stirred and tightened and Bubba McCalister climbed up out of the old well, there was no living human soul visible in all the silent ocean of grass about him.

Bubba was alone with what the black man had told him he would be—the saving of mama and Sissy.

He was the last one left.

If he did not help mama and Sissy, no one would.

But wait.

Maybe old Cap and the black man's master were not really dead there in the house. Maybe they were just hurt.

Bubba ran to the house. He still had with him the Walker Colt that Cap had carried on the left, at San Jacinto. He went only two steps inside, through the doorless kitchen frame. Cap lay to his right, the other man to his left. The backs of both their heads were blown away. Blood and flies and the smell of gunpowder filled the room. The stillness was terrible.

The boy came back out of the house. He became aware for the first time that he still grasped the great old .44 Colt. Deliberately, he triggered it, full around the cylinder. Each fall of the hammer made a wet and punky sound. No charge fired. The gun was useless.

Now truly he was alone. In despair, he raised the old gun as though to go and throw it down the well, then halted suddenly.

In the breaking sunlight of the passed storm, a ray shone upon something he had never before noted about The Redeemer. It was some words engraved on the long barrel. Bubba squinted, lipreading the inscription:

> Be not afraid of any man,
> No matter what his size—
> When danger threatens, call on me—
> I will Equalize.

The boy's narrow face grew less dark. The intent eyes raised up. He looked off to the west where mama and Sissy had been carried away. He hefted the ancient revolver in his hands, and he nodded. He was not alone.

And he need not be afraid.

"Redeemer," he said, and his voice echoed with a flat loudness in the deserted ranch yard, "come along on. There's nobody left but us to do it."

He went swiftly to the bunkhouse and retrieved old Cap's ranger holster with its powder-flask belt from where he had hidden them—and hidden with them—in the hay stove of the single room. He put the gun in the holster, then found no way to secure the belt about his small body. It seemed natural when he slipped it over one shoulder and under the opposite arm. In this Mexican *rurale* style, he could carry the great weapon successfully and even with some bit of dignity. The next part was the hardest.

He went back across the yard to the house. Inside, he didn't look at the flyblown bodies. He got his old hat and ragged coat from their peg by the door, took a grubsack and put into it some stale bread, a rind of bacon, an old tin can to boil water, and a little packet of pinto beans. Only then did he take the crazy quilt off mama's bed and put it over Cap Marston so that the flies would not get at him so bad. Kneeling beside the old man, he spoke to him.

"Cap, I ain't time to do more. Cain't let them get out of sight-tracking range. Got to keep a line on them for when the posse catches up to me. You'd order me to do that. Iffen they gets over the Pecos and me not having kept them in sight, well, you know, Cap. I got to go now, or they will lose me sure." He stopped. He hadn't said it all. Something, some last farewell, was wanting.

He lifted a corner of the quilt. It was to see the old ranger's face and to let him see Bubba.

"Cap," he said, "me and you was true friends."

He got up quickly and went to the door. There he took worried pause to stare at the final, flyblown peace of Henry Devereaux Canfield. "We only got the one quilt, sir," he apologized, and went out of the house and away up the first slope of west ridge. He quartered the grade to cut distance, knowing where the vanished guerrilla riders must go with the wagon. He did not trudge or walk his way but went at a trot, like a Comanche boy. In a very little time only, he too was disappeared from any view of the ranch house.

# 28

The Pioche posse followed Will Hatch five miles south and east from the stage road, and then Carlos Ortmann put up a hand and said, "That'll be far enough."

There was an angry curse from young Hatch and a company-growled question of what the hell was going on, but the men stopped their horses. And they looked to Ortmann, not Hatch.

"Boys," Ortmann said, "*hasta luego*. I'm going back."

Young Deputy Hatch swung his horse belligerently. "Back where?" he demanded.

"To Red Hawk."

"You're crazy!"

"Likely I was, riding out on Charley," Ortmann said. "Get out of my way."

With that, he shouldered his mount past Hatch's and galloped off, leaving his fellow possemen to look at one another and listen to Deputy Will Hatch.

"Let the loco-ass Mexican bastard go," the young officer snapped. "He's just blowing frijole wind."

Dean Oates nodded, reined his mount around. "I reckon I'll just go along and blow a little with him," he said.

"Hold on, Dean," Orlie Dobbs called out. "I just got a whiff of them frijoles, too."

"Me likewise," shouted big Sam Peckingham. And then young widower Harrel Simms. And weathered old Jabez "Jake" Jacobs. And, at the very last, even quarrelsome Pioche banker A. J. Hardeman. They all strung out in turn to spur their horses after the lead of Juan Carlos Ortmann. For the second time that day Will Hatch was left alone on the prairie with his battered pride and, in this latter case, with the suddenly tarnished star of Sheriff Charley Skiles pinned lopsided to his vest. But this time he was going to hold fast.

"Go to hell!" he yelled after his vanishing possemen. "You're all crazy—!"

In Red Hawk, surprises awaited the re-gathered men of the Pioche posse. Old Sheriff Charley Skiles had rallied from his exhaustion, was well enough recovered to be down at Ellerbrock's livery barn haggling over the high prices of rental livestock. Specifically, the posse, sweeping into town, found Skiles at the livery trying to hire a saddle mount to replace old Kickapoo.

From the sheriff they learned that not only was he fit to ride, and fit to be tied if they didn't let him ride, but young Lon McCalister had come to on the stage into Red Hawk and told everything on the Confederate-disguised bank and murder gang.

Right now the boy was doing some 98 percent better up at the widow Niendorff's boardinghouse, where he'd been put down into a bed to rest. In fact, it would not in the least astound Charley Skiles if the hollow-eyed, gut-tough eldest of Mary McCalister's three sons insisted on being sworn into the posse, which was fine with Charley. If he later fell out of the saddle they would just have to let him lay and hammer on. The main thing was to jump the bank gang at the ranch, before they either harmed the womenfolk or had time to rest their horses and get back on the run for the New Mexico Territory.

That last was center-bore vital. Not even Charley Skiles could stretch his jurisdiction far outside West Texas.

"We got to get them short of the line," he told his returned followers. "The shorter of it, the better. They can cut off at White Sand Hills and have only twelve miles to go."

Along about here, Ellerbrock feisted up at the out-of-town horsemen and wanted to know if the palavering posse was going to buy some feed, or wanted stall space, or intended one decent way or another to leave a little money with the Red Hawk Livery Barn and Livestock Commission Co. Agents.

If not, he, Ellerbrock, would be fair obliged if the Pioche crowd would just get their damned horses out of the way where they were barring his barn doors to whatever of less cheapskate trade might be wanting the services of his establishment.

To this show of West Texas neighborliness, swarthy, gray-eyed Carlos Ortmann reacted by jamming the muzzle of his Colt Army Model of 1860 into the open mouth of the liveryman and suggesting he pay attention. What was wanted here was not just a good horse for the honorable sheriff of Pioche County but likewise a using horse for his young friend, Mr. Lonnie McCalister. It might not fatten the coffers of Ellerbrock's firm to furnish these saddle mounts without further debate but it would most surely lengthen his life span.

"Now," Ortmann said, "you are already sucking on my front sight, and if you want the rest of it, here goes. That is the sound of a single-action Colt revolver being cocked that you hear. The next sound that you don't hear will be the back of your head flying off. You got two good horses, amigo?"

It developed that Mr. Simms Ellerbrock's mother had not wasted her cooking on any feebleminded children. The liveryman got the point of Carlos Ortmann's discourse. The two mounts were saddled and led out. With Old Charley Skiles helped up on one of them, and insisting on leading the other one, off went the posse up Main to the widow Niendorff's.

There, the sheriff hollered up to Lon McCalister. The youth, still pale as blue-john milk, put his head out of one of the upstairs bedroom windows. When he saw the posse down below, with the old lawman holding a spare horse, it was the medicine he needed. Even his war-wounded bad arm made movement and showed strength it had not since North Tennessee and the rending battle for Fort Henry. Using it, even if with gritted teeth, he got out of the window and slid down the front-porch roof. Skiles led the horse up onto the boardwalk under the overhang and Lon dropped shakily into its saddle. For a moment, from his bed-rest weakness and the pain from the newly used arm, it seemed he must faint and slide on under his horse's belly into the dirt of Main

Street. But there was fire in his dark eyes, steel in his lean belly. "Sheriff," he said, "iffen me and this old crippled wing can make it, we will point you the shortest way to Paint Crick ranch."

"Son," the sheriff said, "I don't see no crippled wing. Point away. Carlos, stay with him. Let's go."

Ortmann nodded and, with Lon, took the lead. The posse drove back out Main the same way it had come into Red Hawk. There was one stop between the town and Paint Creek. It was just outside the settlement. There, a voice hailed the riders from the sagebrush and Will Hatch loped up sheepishly. He didn't say anything but unhooked the star from his vest and handed it back to Charley Skiles. The old sheriff took it and put it in his coat pocket, also saying nothing. Then he relented.

"We got to push on, Will. Was there anything else?"

The deputy still had his head down. "I'd like to go along," he said. "I'm owing it to you."

"You don't owe me nothing, Will."

"Well, the boys, then."

"Them neither. Let's go, Carlos."

"Sheriff!" The old man checked his borrowed horse, and Will Hatch said, "Maybe I'm owing it to myself."

"That"—Charley Skiles nodded—"is possible. Fall in." Then, to the waiting Ortmann, "Ride out, Carlos."

# 29

Old Kickapoo ran on after the Red Hawk stage for at least seven or eight slowing furlongs. He neighed and snorted for the old man who had abandoned him to halt the coach and get off of it. Enough was more than too much at Kickapoo's age. Besides, this was a game he and the old man had not played before. Kickapoo didn't know what the end of it would be. Pretty quick, however, the rough-coated mustang plow horse stepped in a prairie owl burrow. He went down hard enough to jar him but not hard enough to break anything important.

But now he knew how the game ended.

He got back up slowly, sent a last, somewhat wobbly whinny after the stagecoach. Then he took a look around to see where he was, or rather to see where his friends, the other posse horses, were. If the old man meant truly to run away from him, Kickapoo would simply go along with the others. Horses being the gregarious creatures they are, any company was better than none whatever. Old Kick had a sense that something less than honorable had been done his rickety rider, but the out-prairie was a terrible lonesome place to be and a horse had best not be too choosey, lest he find himself all alone in the wide-open middle of it.

Kickapoo shook his vast and ugly head, shot eyes and ears to another, and then yet another, quarter of the grassland compass. His friends were gone. The Pioche posse had disappeared while Kick was running second to the Red Hawk stage. The old horse knew they could not have gotten too far, but the land was gully cut and up-thrust in this area sufficient to let a horseman, or a whole band of horsemen, get out of sight back of a rise or down into a dip in the shake of an old Percheron mustang's ratty tail.

Kick stomped his great splayed forefeet and shrilled a couple of high-pitched trouble whinnies, but got no answer. Well, the wind was stiff against him. It was coming back of that goose-drowner of a rainstorm that had now passed over, pushing the storm out of the country and letting the sunshine of the June morning flood back into it. No wonder a horse couldn't whinny against such a snapper of a breeze. It was just Kick's luck.

But in drawing in a few lungfuls of that same rainy-fresh prairie wind, the old horse suddenly realized his luck might not be bad. Luck came in two sizes, the other one of which was good. Kickapoo took in another long suck of the wind. It came into his whiskered nostrils freighted with all the wondrous smells of the far Pecos buffalo pastures. And one of those smells aroused in Kickapoo feelings of horse heredity which he had never known before. It was a smell that made the old horse tremble. Fling up his roman-nosed beer keg of a head. Wheel about and bow his neck and lash at the ground and paw the grass.

And then he saw what made the smell.

Up out of a nearby draw, where the passage of the homebound Pioche posse had spooked them into seeking cover, broke a many-spotted, flowing-maned, free-running band of mustangs—wild horses, running wildly!

The blood of Kickapoo's feral sire thundered through his aging Percheron arteries. He reared up for the first time since colthood and cut loose with a sound he had never before heard himself make. It was the piercing whistle of the wild-born mustang. And, bombarding out of their gully covert, his wild cousins took wheeling pause to whistle back to old Kick, in exciting kind. *Come on, come on, if you're coming!* those wild whistles seemed to say. *We've far to go this day, and mean to go it fast!*

Kickapoo rushed down from the knoll atop which he had stood to survey the prairie. Kicking to the side and running with the full-out abandon of a yearling, the old horse took out after the wild band. Its members, in re-spooked turn, took alarm at the jingle and chain rattle and banging of saddle-borne equipment carried by Sheriff Charley Skiles in his manhunting work. Nor were the wild ones reassured by the flaps of the saddle itself, and its stirrup leathers, lifting like wings to flop old Kickapoo on his startling way toward them.

With a mustang bawl of alarm, the old herd mare set off in the lead of the band, while the fiercely whistling stallion galloped in rearguard of the retreat.

Kickapoo did not feel the rejection but only imagined these were wild-horse games. Redoubling his great gamboling strides, he followed happily after the wild half-brothers and sisters. If they were pointed toward the Pecos, away from Pioche and Red Hawk and the settlements, what of that? A horse went where the blood of his

wild sire led him. Even if his mother had been a plow
mare. And his master a sheriff of the law. That was
yesterday. Last year. A whole horse life ago.

*Wait!* the old horse whistled, *wait for me—!*

# 30

The country westering into the far drainage of the Brazos
River was rough. It was rumpled as a messed bed. It was
cut by a thousand nameless draws, crosscut by another
unmapped thousand gulches and arroyos. And it was dry.
It was as scant of water as whiskey at a Shouting Baptist
prayer meeting. It was badlands, getting worse.

Commencing to stumble and go unsteadily now, after a
blur of hours along the track of Fragg's guerrillas, Bubba
kept telling himself that he knew all this about the
country and could whip it anyway. But Lord God it was
hell to get through afoot.

The Roughs of the Brazos was horseback country, laid
out and made that way by the Man up Yonder. He hadn't
meant for grown men, much less thirteen-year-old boys, to
*walk* it. Not and catch up to mounted and mule-drawn
men.

But the redheaded boy gritted his teeth and went on.
The way was mean, and would be meaner, but Bubba
McCalister would not quit. Yet by late day, when he had
to get in under a salt juniper and take water and rest, he
already knew enough to have down-mouthed the stoutest
spirit.

The worst thing of all was that the damned Indian
guide had proved to know about the old Comanche trail
that ran past Kiowa Peak. This was the route the
Yamparika used to hunt buffalo and raid the Texas
settlements. The years and the tens of thousands of unshod hooves had worn a trail as smooth in most places as
a government graded army-wagon road. Also, with the

uncanny instincts they had, the red men had laid out their "Comanch' Road" to beat any army engineers. It made the best of a very bad country, and the fact the mute Indian knew what it was and where it ran—from the Texas settlements' edge to the settled fringes of New Mexico, crossing the emptiest space on the maps of the United States of America on its way—was bad enough news to dispirit any tracker.

But Bubba would not quit.

This didn't mean he wouldn't have to rethink everything. He would. It was one thing when it had seemed the murderous gang would go by the Overland Road, where water was spaced, and some shelter, too, at the relay stations of the stage line. That took a lot of the risk and the raw fear out of it. But now all Bubba's knowledge of the stage road was useless. The fact he had stowed away last summer on one of Monk Beckham's west runs, hiding in the baggage boot just long enough to avoid suffocation and likewise to be far enough out from Red Hawk that Monk couldn't turn around and take him back, was going to be wasted now.

Damn it to hell. Bubba could read that route off in his mind, remember every rock and rut by eye.

Paint Creek to Double Mountain station at Double Mountain Fork of the Salt Fork of the main Brazos. Along the fork out onto the Staked Plains, to Headwaters Crossing of the Rio Colorado of Texas. On to Salt Fork station, where the road went over the river at Solitair Mountain. Next, to Big Spring station and on to Mustang Spring station and so into the White Sand Hills where, by the No. 1, No. 2, and No. 3 water-hole stations, you would go on to Emigrant Crossing of the Pecos, still in Texas.

Or where, Monk Beckham vowed, you could take the Outlaw Cutoff a scant fifteen miles due north by west and be over the New Mexico line, with but another fifty-five miles on to the Pecos River, at Malaga Bend, deep safe inside New Mexico.

Which, if you were an outlaw on the run, Monk said,

was the prettiest fifty-five miles ever you would see, and the ugliest if you weren't.

It didn't matter to Bubba now, either way. He wasn't going on to Emigrant Crossing *or* along the outlaw trail into New Mexico. He was going a third route. Another way still. A very old way and one that, just to think of it, put a scare in him. Damn it to hell, again.

There was nothing so useless as a splendid education squandered because of a dumb-tongue Indian packer who was too stupid to follow the white man's stage road.

Unless it was, as the old saying went, tits on a boar pig. Wings on a garden mole. Buttons on a pocket gopher. Or maybe hobbles on a stuffed horse.

But Bubba wouldn't quit.

He looked from under his juniper's shade to where he could see the noon-halt horse droppings of the retreating outlaws, where they had watered at Mesquite Well. The well was not only the sole water short of Paint Creek but a camp of more importance than that. It was here that the Comanche Road set out for New Mexico. Here where it veered suddenly northwest from the run of the Overland Stage Road. And it was from here that Bubba McCalister could see the tracks of the renegades turning off to follow the Indian trail.

The well and its ancient campsite was not fifty paces from where the ranch boy rested under his lone juniper.

Bubba knew better than to lay out alone in such a storied place. He had gone in carefully to refill his old canteen with the good water from the rock tanks of the well, yes. But he hadn't lingered on the campsite. He had done what any white boy twenty miles from home and without a horse to ride or a weapon that would work to fire would do. He had drawn off those fifty paces and hidden under a scrub tree. Any arriving Comanches from New Mexico, or returning renegades from West Texas, would not catch Bubba McCalister snoozing in their ancient, or recent, camping place.

Well, all right then, now what?

Bubba's feet were in bad shape. Going so far at such

a pace had rubbed raw and blistered his ranch boy's horn-callused soles. Too, he had carried his grub sack, water tin, and above all, weightwise, the old Walker Colt. With its thick belt, powder horn, bullet pouch, and percussion cap pocket, plus the hog-leg holster of heavy steerhide, the rusted weapon would sag a Toledo scale to past six pounds. When you didn't weigh but ninety-eight pounds yourself and multiplied that six pounds by the twenty miles you had come by that sultry four o'clock afternoon "decision halt," you found Redeemer weighing about sixty pounds, not six.

And you didn't have lead ball number one in the bullet pouch. Nor black-powder flake *la primera* in the charging horn. Nor yet a single percussion cap to make it all go off.

Well, there was your first decision.

Throw old Redeemer away.

Lighten the load.

Take along only food and water and, when you'd decided that, you had made the second decision already.

You were going to fight on.

You would retake the trail of the murderers of your true friend Cap Marston. You would cling like a bulldog to the tracks of the evil men who had torn the clothes off mama and Sissy. You would get up and go on from here if you left blood in every one of your footprints away from Mesquite Well. Those foul and filthy men had your mother and your golden-haired big sister captive. They intended fearful things for them. The big, heavy-voice niggerman had told you that, talking down the well to you. And you knew from the way he made that talk that it was the gospel. That was why you were going to get up and go on after them. Till your feet fell off or your guts spilled out or you ran dry of good water and went to babbling crazy and walking in circles, like old Cap had said people always did, lost in a sun-and-sand country without sweet water, or from drinking at alkali holes when the mind went twisted, along with the crooked walking.

Bubba gathered weary body for the rising up.

One thing, by God and Dear Jesus, was sure.

Bubba would not quit.

Yet, even as the boy started onward from Mesquite Well, it was evident he could not go far. At the outset, something had compelled him to keep the Walker Colt. He carried it bare now of accoutrements, holding it over bowed shoulder, by the long barrel. He didn't curse its weight but seemed to have accepted the weapon as a part, inseparable, of his vengeance. There was more in it than the hope he might find fresh powder and ball and percussion cap up the trail. He kept thinking of the inscription he had read on the barrel, *Be not afraid* and *call on me*, and, doing so, he would shift the great gun to the other shoulder and stumble forward.

But the will wavered. The flesh and blood of Bubba's tortured feet could not endure. It was finally the sheer refusal of nerve and muscle to be commanded to do further damage to the wounded members that stopped him. Where he went down in collapse, he was but little over a mile out from Mesquite Well. It used all he had left within him to roll in under a nearby shelf of outcrop rock. There he lay gasping in pain, racked by the shakings of exhaustion.

It was then that he heard the soft thudding of unshod pony hooves approaching from the west.

Again, the out-prairie knowledge of the ranch youth worked to shield Bubba McCalister from his dangerous environment. As he had lain cautiously out from the old Indian camp at Mesquite Well, so had he traveled away from that oasis out in the brush and fifty feet parallel to the Comanche Road. This, as against following the track of Fragg's troop along the roadway itself. Thus it was that the Indian packer Gabby, backtracking to look for pursuit, missed the redheaded boy holed up but a pebble's toss from his pony's loping passage.

Bubba watched the red man ride the mile back to the water hole. Saw him mount a rocky promontory to scan the campsite from above. Squinted hard to follow him on down into the Mesquite grove of the well itself, where he briefly surveyed the site from horseback, then turned from his inspection and came back along the Comanche Road, westerly, going faster than he had coming in. Bubba's breathing eased.

It was plain the mute horseman had satisfied himself the camp was clean and no danger threatened him and his companions from the rear. Bubba shivered, wondering how "satisfied" the plug-ugly buck would have been had he spied young Randolph Barnes McCalister taking his rest halt out in the open, at the water hole. Or had he spotted his bootprints in the soft dirt about the outcrop which held the "well" that gave the camp its name?

But Bubba was born the day *before* yesterday.

He had taken his boots off and sock-footed it up over the outcrop to get at the water and then back to his lay-out juniper. And not even a South Plains Indian could read "sock sign" from on horseback. That was why Bubba was alive and watching Fragg's Indian packer dwindle to a welcome dot and disappear over the curve of the land, way yonder, going where the Pecos flowed.

The scare by the Indian provided the ranch boy with another lifesaver. It reminded him forcefully that he was all done for that day. What he had to do now was make it back to Mesquite Well for the night. It broke a sob from him to think what losing that night would mean to mama and Sissy. Bubba had made the utter effort that he had to keep up with their captors so that he might, by some miracle of fortitude and luck, come to their camp with that same day's darkness. Doing so, he had prayed God would guide him into and out of the renegade camp, rescuing mama and Sissy from the brutes before they could finish what they had started at the homeplace. Failing their rescue, admittedly a forlorn gamble, he had hoped at least to steal powder, cap, and ball enough to load full the cylinder of Redeemer and kill as many of them as he could from out of the night and shooting by the light of their own fire.

Now the terror of that coming night must find mama and Sissy alone.

Bubba and Redeemer would be far, far away.

Still, there would be a next day and a day after that for vengeance, if Bubba rested now, going back to the well for the bathing and soothing that could restore his battered feet. If, instead, he went on forward, he could die all noble and courageous but wouldn't be any help to his mother and sister. Likely, in fact, he would never see them again. Nor might anybody but the buzzards find his own body for months.

Water was the reason.

Water was the last determiner in that fierce southwest land. Only God knew how far it was to the next water on the Comanche Road. But the Indians would try to space the springs or tanks at least a pony ride apart—thirty to forty miles—and so would the buffalo herds that used the trail before the Indians did. That meant that maybe water could also be fifty miles between. Or even sixty. With a good horse or even a wolf-bait like the Indian packer rode, the Comanche Trail was no doubt passable. As a matter of Bubba's remembered fact, it was so passable to horse traffic that it was labeled "practical for wagons" on the 1859 up-to-date map in the Red Hawk school-house. That was from Captain Marcy's original survey. And old Cap Marcy, he *knew*. If he lettered down on his field charts "passable to wheeled conveyance," you could bet your Murphy or your brand-new Studebaker Brothers rig on getting through. So, sure, with a horse or even a wagon and stout team, help could yet be got to mama and Sissy in time and that night. But afoot? And those feet already blistered and bled to a mush? There was no chance, none at all.

Bubba would have to go back to the water.

Even if he had to crawl partways.

There, he could rest and pray the night away, asking the Lord to let the morning sun see him restored enough to follow the devils on foot. It was the last card in the deck away from "total hopeless," and Bubba knew it. But he knew something else, too: he would never quit.

He made the mile back to Mesquite Well by 5 P.M.

As he had foreseen, the last few hundred yards of it

were made on hands and knees. But he got there. He lasted to find again his salt-juniper hiding place and to fall, face-flat and barely conscious, beneath it.

It was perhaps ten minutes later that the mustangs came.

The old mare brought them into the water sneaking like kit foxes up a shallow defile in the rimrock that held the pothole tank called Mesquite Well. Bubba lay flatter yet to his earth beneath the juniper. He had heard no sound. One instant there was nothing at the well, and next moment there were wild horses all about its sunken basin. The boy risked raising his head. He must see the beautiful creatures.

The sight stayed in his mind and heart.

There were half a dozen foals. This being June, they had been on the ground for a spell. They could stay with the band in nearly any circumstance of peril, yet they still went at the flanks of their dams as if drawn there by magnets. The little devils had whisk-broom tails, short round bodies, long-boned, trim-hoofed legs, and, most striking of all to Bubba about their Spanish Arab heritage, the short dished faces and great dark eyes and small elegant ears that marked the true mustang wherever found.

There were additionally four or five barren or aging mares, the lead or bell mare—a mare always led wild horse bands—and then the nervous stallion, some twenty animals in all.

The old mare was up on the rocks now, above the tank, watching out over the surrounding country. The stallion was circling the drinking band, watching the old mare up above. He drank next to last of the band. Then he went up on the rock, relieving the old mare, who then slid down to the tank and slaked her thirst sparingly. When this was done, she gave a soft chuckling sound to the stallion, a sharper alerting whicker to the other mares and their foals. A young mare tried to ignore the signal and slip back to the tank for another muzzle-suck of the cold sweet water. The old mare leaped after her and bit her rump and shoulder, turning her back like a sheep dog cutting woolies away from going over a drop-off. The young mare squealed and kicked but she got back into her place, *más pronto*, and next blink of Bubba's straining eyes the band had circled up over the rimrock and were streaming off through the juniper and salt-sage breaks, to the west.

Something seemed to have alarmed them, the boy was thinking. The old mare had been so cross with the young mare. She had also brought the band into the water in a nervous, quick way. And now the stallion, still on the overlook above the well, confirmed Bubba's thought. Whatever had been bothering the band had been behind it, as that was the direction both the old lead mare and the edgy studhorse had been mostly looking.

Now the stud, with a last stomp and snort, uttered one sharp, defiant whistle and vanished off the rimrock to reappear three jumps later and sixty feet beyond the water hole, running flat to catch his moving band.

Bubba shook his head and dug at his ears, for he could have sworn he had heard another mustang's whistle answering the stud's, off to the rear where the stud had been so anxious to look.

Another stallion following the band? A rogue stud looking to steal the first one's mares? Or to fight the other stallion for them?

Again Bubba shook his head. No, the mares wouldn't have behaved so uneasy in that case. They generally loved to stand around and have studs fight over them. So it wasn't a rival stallion. Or, if it was, he had the sickest whistle of any he-mustang Bubba McCalister had ever listened to. This indeed and inevitably proved to be the case. For now, up out of the brush to the rearward and the southeast of the water hole, shambled the damnedest-looking "wild horse" that ever prairie boy or man had seen or imagined to see, even in West Texas.

# 31

Bubba's first impulse was to run out and throw arms about the neck of this ugliest of all possible horses. He saw in this ready-saddled mount the one slim chance God had granted him to catch up to mama and Sissy.

But the Paint Creek boy had been around horses all his life and knew their peculiarities. No matter how broken down or spavined they might look, they were all of them a little *loco en la cabeza*. You had to watch them careful as rattlers in a sack. They would go out from under you or come down on top of you or just plain up and run off from you for no damned reason you had ever given them. That was if it was your own personal horse, and one you knew like a brother. Coming to strange horses, ones you'd never been on nor even threw a blanket over, well, Christ Jesus, it was Katie bar the door.

So Bubba hung like a field mouse in under his juniper clump, trying desperately to figure out how best to go at the horse. The latter, being upwind of the hidden boy, did not scent his presence. He came on shambling directly past Bubba, going to the water. In passage, he clanked and banged and clinked along noisy as a gypsy tinker's cart. For the first time, Bubba noted why this was. And then he understood just *how* good God had been to send him this particular huge bone pile of a mustang plow horse.

It was his rigging, surely the strangest ever seen.

The ancient wreck of a high-horn Mexican saddle was made with the biggest square skirtings possible to cut. And every inch of these vast skirts was adorned by hook, snap, or strap, holding an oddment of gear to surpass belief. A bull's-eye lantern. Two flat-side army canteens. One genuine Matagordo machete. Coil of stranded steel trip wire. Bundle of bias-cut piggin' strings, strong enough to bind captive a longhorn herd bull. Set of ankle irons, hand manacles, and one dog-collar neck chain, all old enough to be Spanish made. Wire cutters. Shoeing nippers, nails, spare shoes, a tiny smithy's bellows. Six loops of blasting-powder fuse, the new shiny kind with two huge corked horns of what had to be the powder the fuse would blow. Even a mean-looking No. 5 set-pan wolf trap, with teeth like a sand-bank crocodile. And then a bullet mold, lead fluxing pot, reloading tongs, a whole miscellany of metal-crafted things that, for the moment of their passing by, puzzled Bubba sorely.

And then it came to him.

It was the wolf trap that sprang the answer.

What he was looking at clanking past on the old splay-foot plug was one complete, blood-rusted set of West Texas manhunting tools.

Bubba McCalister not only had a horse to ride, he had an armory of war supplies.

His heart, his stubborn spirit, the first fire of real hope, soared within him. There was a chance now. Of a sudden it did not seem a forlorn nor daft thing that a thirteen-year-old boy thought he was going to catch a wolf pack of depraved drifters and take his vengeance on them. If he were in time to keep the devils away from his mother and sister, only the Lord had the say of that part. But Bubba would get up to the men. By *God*, he would do that. With or without the Lord.

His hands tightened into fists, knuckle-white. The narrow jaw shot out and set itself determined as a dog salmon fighting fast water. The freckled, homely face got that look of wildness on it that the townsfolk talked about—the one they called the crazy McCalister look.

"*Lon, Jim Junior,*" he whispered fiercely, "*gimme your prayers. Mama, Sissy, don't be afeared no more.*"

With that, he seized up and reholstered The Redeemer, slung the old weapon's rig once more cross-body, Mexican-bandoleer-style, burst silently out from under the juniper clump in full charge of the manhunter's horse.

The horse, which now had its pendulous lips sucking at the cool green waters of Mesquite Well, heard the thud of the boy's running feet but only laid back one hairy

166

ear and kept on drinking. A slant of rock ran up the offside of the old horse, about wither-high, and Bubba sprinted up this natural mounting ramp and took a flying leap from it to the beckoning, empty saddle. His aim was good and the jump a beauty, landing him fair astride the seat and exactly center, fore and aft, of pommel and cantle.

But the old horse resented it.

He raised his head and just sort of sidestepped gently to the left, made a funny small hump in his swayed spine bones, but quick as a nudged snake about it, and dumped Bubba off into the rock-tank water of Mesquite Well.

By the time the ranch boy surfaced, the old horse had his muzzle re-buried in the water and was going on with his drink as if nothing had jumped into his saddle from the wrong side, and uninvited. Bubba was mad but thankful to the Lord that the horse hadn't run off, and scared to all hell that he still might.

But he didn't.

When the boy scrambled out of the water, the horse swung his broad rump around, presenting the proper left side, to Bubba. At the same time, he bobbed his head and whickered in his throat as if to say, *Look now, boy, you want to start over again and do it right this time, I'm your horse.*

Bubba could scarce believe it but did not linger.

He had to jump for the horn to haul himself and the holstered Colt up to where he could get a boot tip in the left stirrup bow and so make it on up into the saddle. He would have to worry about shortening those long stirrups at their first rest halt. Also, about recharging Cap's old gun with the powder and ball sure to be found somewhere on the war-rigged saddle. He could likewise fret about the former rider of the war horse long-gone down the trail. For now, for this sundown and its night to follow, Bubba McCalister had the most fateful, dangerous way of his life to go with this old horse.

He leaned up along the ponderous gelding's thick neck,

horse-talking him fervently, low-voicing the words directly
into the back-turned, attentive ear. In reaching to pat the
shaggy jaw, he noted a name studded with copper rivets
into the cheek strap of the bridle and he laughed despite
his intensity, because he figured it was just about the
right name for the old rough-coat wreck of a horse beneath him. But then the voice went soft and fierce and
the boy said, "All right, old wolf bait, let's go far away
from here!"

He gathered rein. Set foot in stirrup leather above
oaken bow. Straightened to full four foot eleven, and
yelled at the manhunter horse, "*Heee-yaahhhHHH!!*"

With the stirrup stand and the range cowboy's whoop,
away from Mesquite Well and swift to the west along the
Comanche Road went Bubba McCalister and the gallant
old mustang Percheron called Kickapoo.

# 32

Cursing his luck, trooper Creech stumbled out of the
dry camp at Kiowa Peak to take his turn—the first of the
night—at sentry.

God knew, Creech grumbled to himself, that there
was no decent need for anybody to go on watch. They
had made wondrous good time the whole of that long day
and never a sign of pursuit. What the hell was Fragg
afraid of?

Indians, the captain had said. They must always
remember that the Pioche posse could be outdistanced—
even, if need be, pitch-fought with fair chance of victory
for the Fifth Alabama. But this was Comanche country
they were heading into, and they were taking the
Comanche high road. Guard must be posted and hard-
kept. Elsewise, their bones might molder forever amongst
these nameless rocks.

"Bull chips," Creech muttered. The captain knew better

than that. So did Creech. The real thing was that Fragg was trying to get all their minds off of the women. More bull chips. Nobody was fooling Ralph Waldo Creech. Not about guerrilla rules on captives and camp booty. Fragg was wanting to save it all for himself.

Creech stumbled and cursed again.

He looked around.

This ought to be far enough from the fire. And there were good rocks all around. Nice high ground. And the way the rocks were set, a man could put his back to a good smooth one without being seen from camp. If somebody had to stand first watch, he might as well "sit" it, instead. Maybe catch forty winks and no harm done.

Creech laughed at his little joke about sitting first watch, made himself comfortable against a boulder backrest still warm with the day's sun heat. Almost at once his eyelids began to droop. He thought a bit of the women and Fragg's idea to "stretch their services" as camp wives by making up a lottery and all drawing for "first night in the wagon," two lucky winners to be drawn for each night camp after that.

Well, Fragg was right about not using the women too hard. You didn't want to drive their minds to the idea of killing themselves. Any good horse guerrilla knew that a woman, once decided to kill herself, would find the way to do it. So Fragg was solid with his idea to get the most out of the two women. And the men—double-weary from the long driving of the Pioche posse short of Paint Creek ranch and then the hard forced march all the past day away from the ranch—had seen the reasoning of their leader and agreed to it. The lottery, proposed, was now going forward.

Creech had come out to stand his guard, assured his name would be in the hat and fairly drawn for, along with the others.

Old Fragg knew his men. That picture he had sketched for them of just the lucky two winners being in the wagon all night with just the two women was enough to put drool on a dead man.

Creech stirred and dug at himself, muttering and grunting like some boar pig rubbing on a stump tree. There was a trickle of small stone from the hillside just above him and he heard it and even saw the little spill of pebbles move down, but he couldn't get his mind away from the women. What did it matter anyway? There wasn't anything up there on the hillside. Just a marmot or a rock rat or maybe a kit fox snuck in to spy on the camp, drawn by the firelight and the smells of cooking food. Creech, giving himself over to the thought of his lottery prospects, grinned, muttered some coarse obscenity, shut his eyes, eased against his backrest rock, and was stone-sound asleep in thirty seconds.

From the rocks above the sentry post, Bubba McCalister slid cautiously but quickly down upon the sleeping guard. The boy had with him one of the large horns of blasting powder from the armory on Kickapoo's saddle skirts, and a long stick that closer view revealed to be a ramrod for black powder percussion rifles of the make and nature of the old Confederate Forces cavalry carbine borne by trooper Creech.

Carefully retrieving the sentry's weapon from its leaning place beside the sleeping Creech, the boy filled its barrel full of the coarse powder from the horn and rammed the deadly load home with a heavy-patch wad, tamping it firmly with the hickory rod. Next he seated a lead ball atop the wad and, in turn, tamped it tight against the wad. He then as carefully replaced the powder-packed weapon to the snoring guerrilla's hand, exactly as it had been before his borrowing. With that, he went scuttling back up to his overlook of rocks. Selecting a handful of good-sized pebbles, he aimed them, with an arching, accurate throw, to clear Creech's backrest rock and thump and splatter down about the head and shoulders of the sleeper.

Poor Creech roused up groggily and in time to receive another thumping shower of small rock from above. Now he scrambled unsteadily to foot, seizing up his rifle-carbine and peering with last-moment alarm up the slope.

In that instant, Bubba McCalister deliberately showed himself to the renegade sentry, jumping up from the higher rocks as if he believed himself to be discovered.

"Hey, thar, halt!" Creech cried out hoarsely and, when the figure did not halt, raised his carbine and fired.

The ignition of the blocked barrelful of blasting powder thundered forth upon the peakside. The obstructed barrel burst full in the face and upper body of trooper Creech. When his comrades, rushing forth from the camp, reached his position moments later, the stunned call of the first to arrive echoed in the sudden dead stillness.

"Here's a arm," said Israel Girty, stumbling over the grisly object. "It be a right arm, and it be Creech's, certain sure. You kin tell by the hair on it. Creech, whar be ye?"

"Christ Jesus," croaked another voice.

And then a third voice, awed, into the unanswering darkness: "Creech? Creech—!"

# 33

In the camp of the Fifth Alabama Horse there was a spreading confusion.

When Creech's gun blew up out on the peakside, his number had just been drawn from the hat. The other winner was trooper Fowlis. Indeed, Girty had been selected to go out and fetch the good news to Creech and to relieve him at guard. Fowlis was already over at the tailgate of the wagon waiting the joyous return of his fellow trooper and the then-following word from Captain Fragg to "go aboard." The word didn't come in that camp.

Instead, while what remained of Creech was being put under a pile of rock, a council of war was called for fireside. The Indian packer Gabby and the black forager Scipio were betimes sent out to scout the camp's perimeters for any track sign of an intruder, or intruders. They returned to report no visible sign of human visitation. Fragg, denying trooper Hoad's request to put a marker on his partner's final resting place, hurried the company back to camp and council.

First, Fragg told them, it must be judged whether Creech had actually seen somebody, or something, up on the peakside or was "shadder shooting," a reaction of stress all too familiar to raiding guerrillas. It bothered the captain that Creech had yelled out just before blowing himself apart, but again they all had to remember the fierce-long retreat they had been running since the botch of the Pioche Bank robbery. The condition of all of them was on the edge of breakdown. Fragg's own verdict followed that Creech had fired at some unreal creature of his utter exhaustion—hence his alarmed cry of "Hey, thar!"—but that a troop in their position could not trust that belief either in whole or in part.

If any man of them, the guerrilla leader concluded, had an idea of what was a wise course, let him come forward with it now.

"Captain," said a worried trooper Hoad, "I ain't no idees on that, but you ain't explained how come old Creech's carbine done made such hellish bust, yonder."

"No need for that to fret anybody," Fragg said. "If each of us had a dollar for every soldier that's blown himself up by forgetting he already had a charge in his rifle, and putting in a second atop the first, we would all of us be rich as old Jake Astor got unloading them beaver-hat peltries on Johnny Bull. Now you know that, Crawdad, and so do the rest of you. We got *real* problems here, men. We'd best not be wasting our brains on dumb-butt soldiers tamping down double charges."

There was uneasy agreement, but another interruption stalled the military decision.

"By God, cap'n," trooper Ollie Fowlis reminded the company, "you ain't explained something else that ain't so dumb-butt. Who's gonna git old Ralph Waldo's place in the wagon? Now that's what I call a real *real* problem!"

The men at once surged in on Fragg with demands that

Creech's ticket be "redrawed" and the one to go with Fowlis "inter the meat wagon fer the fust cut of the tenderloin" be named before anything else.

Fragg wisely agreed but insisted on having an answer to his tactical question first: Was there any one of them who had an idea about the camp's next move? Ought they to just mount double guard for the night, hoping it wasn't redskins that had drawn Creech's fire, or maybe even an advance scout of the Pioche posse, which the Indian had told them was coming hard up the rise east of the Paint Creek ranch? Or should they pack up and move on to a farther dark camp, jaded and whipped as they were? "After all," the pale-eyed captain said, "there's no winners 'mongst a heap of dead soldiers. Holding a ticket for first night in the wagon won't raise up no corpses. Question again: Do we stay here telling ourselves there ain't nothing out there?" He pointed into the surrounding blackness, intense now just before moonrise. "Or do we force on, keep moving, guessing that there *is* somebody got us under watch?"

"Cap'n," Sergeant Levi Tranch said, "we ain't nothing left to travel on. Man and horse, we're whupt."

"Wait a minute," a deep voice said. "Maybe we ain't."

The vast shadow of Scipio Africanus loomed closer to the fire. The packer, Gabby, was still with him.

"Goddammit," Tranch snapped, "I don't need no nigger chicken thieves telling me when my men and horses are wore out."

"That's so, cap'n," chimed in Corporal Pike. "The nigger ain't no vote here."

Braxton Fragg knew better and said so. "*This* nigger has," he rasped. "He's the best forager I've seen in my days a-horse, and we'll hear him out. Nigger," he said, turning back to Scipio, "talk hard."

Scipio proceeded to tell him that the Indian packer had told him, Scipio, that the Comanche never stopped here at Kiowa Peak, except for one reason—to massacre other Indians, or white-eyed fools, who were stupid enough *to* stop here. It was a deliberate bait camp, the packer said, set up by the Comanche just to lure parties to stop there. It was open ground surrounded by rocks that had superior elevation for firing down into the tipis or wagons pitched or parked there. It was Gabby's final word to Scipio that it wasn't safe here. First, because of what Gabby had just told him of the Comanche ambushes here in the past. Second, because in Gabby's Indian opinion *there had been somebody out there.*

This last brought the company to sharpened attention.

"Is the Indian saying it was the Comanche drew Creech's fire?" Fragg demanded.

"No," Scipio answered, "he said it wasn't Comanche."

"The posse, then. Is that it?"

"No, not the posse, neither."

Fragg shot the pale eyes at the black forager, and said, gravel-rough, "Who, then?"

Scipio Africanus shrugged, showed the pink palms of his huge hands. "He don't know, or he ain't saying, one. Just keeps gargling and making the hand sign for 'somebody there.'"

Fragg studied the surrounding night. He looked at his huddled men. And at the parked wagon. Then lastly back to Scipio and the gargoyle-ugly Indian packer.

He nodded toward the latter and said to Scipio, "And what does the bastard suggest we do about it?"

Scipio hurriedly told him that Gabby had said there was sweet water and a better camp but five miles on. It was called Yamparika Tank and was the place the Comanche themselves used, being secret to them and taboo to other Indian bands. A white man or Mexican, the best of either in trail wisdom, would drive right past it and never guess it was there. Gabby could take them to it by the Comanche way in one hour.

Fragg looked at Scipio as he finished, and said, quickly, "And what do you think?"

"Lord, Lord, cap'n," Scipio answered, digging at brow with apologetic knuckle, "I don't know nothing."

"That"—Fragg nodded decisively—"is good enough for me. Tranch," he snapped, rising to his feet from the fire, "get the column in order. We're moving out."

## 34

As Fragg's men gathered to the fire, and Scipio and the Indian packer came in with their report of scouting the peakside where Creech had died, a half-sized shadow detached itself from the rocks beyond the parked wagon.

There was no careless spill of pebbles this time, no on-purpose showing of self to draw fire. The shadow kept the wagon between itself and the arguing council. It swifted in nervous as a bobcat coming up on a pack of bickering prairie wolves. It made the far, dark side of the wagon safely. Sliding from front wheel to rear, it held there, listening intently to Scipio's translation of what the packer Gabby had told him. Then, as Fragg commenced to question the big black man, the shadow went again to the front wheel, mounted to the driver's box, and went into the wagon by the front puckerhole.

Inside, the apparition was greeted by a stifled gasp from Sissy McCalister. A desperate hand shot out in the darkness, found and covered Sissy's mouth.

"Blast it, Charlotte May, it's me, Bubba!"

"Bubba—!" He had released the hand, now clamped it back, frightened and rough.

"Will you hesh up! Here, leave me cut you loose."

He did so and at once the girl threw her arms about him and commenced to shudder and sob. He grabbed her by the hair, shook her mean as he dared. She quieted.

"Is mama all right?" he asked.

"Yes, just dead tuckered. Mama, it's Bubba, come to take us home. Mama?"

There was no response save labored breathing from Mary McCalister, and Bubba said, "Leave her slumber. Is she bound same as you?"

"She's double tied; she give them trouble."

"They been at you since the ranch?"

"Fragg tried me at noon halt, on the sneak from the others. Mama like to kilt him, even tied. Bubba, her mind is fighting to come clear. She knew me for a minute. Said my name and tried turrible hard to say something else, but I couldn't make it out. It were something about you."

Bubba nodded. His throat ached and the tears were not far away. It was all he could do to control the fears and confusions inside him. His heart panged him to think of his afflicted mother and the wondrous courage of her spirit that could force up through her prisoned mind and order her rope-bound body to lash out in defense of Sissy. He thought, too, of the loyalty in her to think of him and say his name in such a parlous condition. The tears almost won then, but they didn't. Bubba tightened his grip on the knife, passed the weapon to Sissy.

"Cut her loose," he ordered. "I got to go spy out the rear canvas. Make out what they're doing, yonder."

Sissy took the blade, hesitating. "We going to run for it when I get mama free?" she asked.

Bubba, who had started off, turned and rasped, "We are iffen you get to sawing 'stead of jawing. Dammit, Charlotte May, do it! And squinch back out'n my way so's I can clamber over mama, here."

Sissy obeyed but the restlessly sleeping woman turned on her side just as Bubba started over her. His sharp-boned knee struck her full in the ribs and she roused up mutteringly. Bubba cursed himself to Charlotte May for his awkwardness but before she might reply to him both of them were startled to hear another voice say clear and calm and strong, but to no one in particular:

"Randolph Barnes will be here. I know he will show up. I tried to tell Charlotte May he would come but then it rained and the bluebonnets was so pretty . . ."

"Oh, dear Lord, mama." Sissy's voice broke with the strain. "You see, Bubba, what'd I tell you? Mama's going to be all right. She's showing flashes, sure."

Bubba didn't answer. He moved swiftly to find his mother's face in the pitchy dark. His hands caressed her cheek, the fingers finding and resting lightly on her lips. He was not sure, not sure at all.

"It's me, mama, your boy Bubba. Come to take you and Sissy home to Paint Crick."

"Paint Crick? Where it rains. And the rooster, the rooster . . ." Mary McCalister started up, voice rising, escaping Bubba's fingers. The boy smothered the words with a crude bear hug.

"Mama, listen, don't try to say nothing more. We got to be precious still. Quiet as hay-bale mice, mama. You hear? There's heavy trouble all about us." He leaned in the night and kissed her, easing his hold. "Mama, you understand me?"

For the moment the boy's heart had leaped with hope, even as his throat tightened with the unwept tears of his hurt to hear mama struggling so hard to find her mind. But Mary McCalister had lapsed back into the darkness that engulfed her. She hadn't been talking to anybody, only the empty night. She commenced to hum the tuneless air of her derangement, and Bubba's fingers, still at her lips, could feel the lifting corners of the mindless smile's return.

At the same time the singsong humming grew dangerously louder. Bubba clamped his hand fiercely on her mouth and called to Sissy.

"Quieten her down, Charlotte May, she's gone agin. Jesus, mama be still. You'll get us all three kilt!"

Sissy slipped to his side in the stifling dark and relieved him, calming mama sufficiently to permit her brother to continue his original journey to the wagon's rear puckerhole. There, he saw that the arguing at the enemy camp fire had halted. Fragg was talking to the black man again, hard and quick now, coming to it for certain.

"Bubba," he heard Sissy call worriedly behind him, "these here ropes ain't cutting."

"Saw harder," he answered her. "Meeting's shortening up, yonder. Fragg's decided his move. How's mama?"

177

"Lost agin. Staring vacant as old house winders. Oh, Bubba." Sissy was near to giving up, Bubba could sense. He came away from the rear of the wagon, joining her, putting a skinny freckled arm about his sister's shoulders, braving it out for both of them.

"Gimme the blade," he said. "I'll get mama loose. You go watch out the tailgate. We're gonna make it away, you hear? There ain't no way we ain't."

The girl started toward the tailgate, obeying him. She said nothing and his hoarse whisper followed her.

"Charlotte May, I done my damnedest to get here in time. Honest to Jesus."

Sissy stopped crawling, called softly back. "Randolph Barnes, you *was* just in time. That vile Fowlis come to the wagon only now. Said him and Creech had won them a lottery to be the night in the wagon with mama and me. Then we hearn this frightful bang out on the mountain and that Fowlis turnt puny as collard-green water and run off to go with the others to see what that there bang were."

"What it were," Bubba said, "were old Creech. I stuffed his rifle barrel with blasting powder."

"Bubba, you never!"

"Well, cripes, Charlotte May! I had to draw the others off somehow. Elstwise, I wouldn't be here. Now you go on to the back like I toldt you. Peel a sharp eye!"

When she had reached the rear canvas, he called to her, "They still at the fire?" And when she answered him that they were, he jumped the whisper at her.

"I got a horse stashed yonder, back trail. Great big bastard. Carry you and mama double, easy. There cain't nobody track nor catch you, onct away on this here animal. Damn these sons-of-bitching ropes, they cut like barn-loft cable.'"

There was a moment then while Bubba sawed and cursed at mama's bonds, then Sissy tensed.

"Jesus, Bubba, here they come!"

"Oh, Christ, I ain't got mama free." He leaped to the wagon's rear, saw what his sister saw, understood what it meant that he must do.

178

"All right," he said, "they're going to break this here camp right now. It means we leave mama behind and me and you go for it alone."

"I won't leave mama."

"Charlotte May, we got to leave her. It's the only way we can ever hope to save her later down the trail."

"I cain't do it, Bubba."

He knew on the instant that she could not, and knew from that that he must flee to save himself, selfish and cowardly as that might look to be. But the big niggerman had been forever right. And he, Bubba, was still the only living thing that could rescue mama and Sissy. He had to stay free in order yet to get them free somehow. He must do the ugly thing of seeming to desert them, no human way around that, but he could surely leave them something of hope, no matter.

"Charlotte May," he said, "you know I got the ear of a kit fox, so believe this fast: I hearn the drift of yonder talk at the fire. The niggerman was telling the others of a old taboo Comanch' camp with good water but five mile on. That has got to be where they will head with you and mama. And, Sissy," he whispered intently, "I'll foller them and set mama and you free, God's witness, and don't never fear I will fail you."

With the brave words, or in spite of them, he passed her the knife.

"But in case I don't get there," he finished grimly.

Sissy took the knife, threw her arms about him. "You never failed nobody," she said. Then, sobbing: "Oh, hurry, Bubba, they'll catch you yet. Hear that?"

Outside the wagon, the rough voices of nearing men arose. Horses snorted as trailing reins were gathered. Bubba's time was flat gone. Words were empty as socket holes in a buffalo skull. The boy seized up his sister's hand, gave it an eloquent, clumsy squeeze.

"Guard mama," was all he said.

And was gone, scrambling dead-scared, out the front puckerhole of the government surveyor's wagon.

# 35

The moon came up in an hour, luminous and misty at first rising, then, gaining sky, bathing the roughlands with near-day brightness. The light was in nick time to permit Bubba McCalister, fearfully trailing the wagon that held his mother and sister, to swing wide of the guerrilla column and come ahead of it into the rocks of Yamparika Tank. There, with scant minutes in which to work, he found a brushy draw above the tank itself and prepared to leave Kickapoo.

Tethering the old horse, Bubba tested the wind.

It was moving cross-draw, neither to nor from the tank and the camping ground beyond it, but parallel. The ranch boy thanked both his God and the Yamparika father spirit, Ka-dih. Kickapoo would not get scent of the guerrilla horses, nor they of him. That could mean live or die, right there. But it still left Bubba with the next and mainly deadly risk—to get down from the draw and up close enough to where the killers would park the wagon so that he could get to it.

He had already chosen his weapon.

His frontier boy's mind stayed with what was familiar to it. Moreover, in a simplistic way which no grown man would have been fool enough to believe, Bubba McCalister still thought he could save his mother and sister. He would do it "one devil at a time." As this was a wolf pack of bad men that he pursued, so too would Bubba remember what he had seen the lobo wolves do time and again to the great bands of buffalo out in the Comanche grass. That was to isolate one buffalo from the herd. To cut out that individual, or lead him astray, or misdirect him in such manner as to have him alone, even if but for a moment. To get in behind this one animal and cut a hamstring required only a second or three. And, once down, that animal was as good as dead.

As dead as trooper Creech was.

And as the next of these devils to try and get in the wagon with mama and Sissy would be.

Bubba unhooked the great wolf trap from Kickapoo's saddle skirt. He muffled its shark-toothed jaws and short stake chain within the old sheriff's empty grub sack. Shouldering the awkward burden, he went swiftly downward to Yamparika Tank. There, he had no more than gotten into scant cover of some old dried reeds than sounds of curses, shod-hoof clankings, and the groan of iron-rimmed wagon wheels squealing upward over sharp rock roadway grated into the tank's moonlit stillnesses.

Bubba had guessed well.

There appeared to be one best place to park a wagon at Yamparika Tank, and that place was flanked by the dry reeds in which the Paint Creek boy lay scarce daring to breathe. Scipio Africanus brought the government mules skillfully to this place, as the mounted troopers of the Fifth Alabama Horse crowded up into the small meadow of the tank behind him. And Bubba went rolling out from his reed covert, with his deadly burdened sack, just as Scipio was at his loudest talk with the mules and maximum noises of setting hand brake to wagon wheels for the park.

It was risk two of the young night for Bubba.

But had he waited for the wagon to stop rolling and hence making noise, his own roll-in under the now parked and braked vehicle would never have passed the sharp ears of such guerrilla raiders as these.

But now he was under the wagon with the wolf trap wedged beneath the canvas possumbelly slung there to carry firewood over this treeless plain. The belly, hanging down, was what made Bubba's gamble good, hiding him where ordinarily he would have been revealed by the wagon's high bed. But the belly made its own dangers, too. The first thing the niggerman would do after unhooking his team would be to get supper for the men—the supper interrupted by the accident to their sentry at

Kiowa Peak—and getting that supper would require fire-wood. And right soon. Like in maybe five minutes. And that wood must come out of the possumbelly.

Bubba winced, made himself smaller still.

Over across the way, he could see the troopers rigging their picket line. They ran it from the sentinel cotton-wood at tank's side to the thicket of red willow, camou-flaging the trail leading to the tank from the Comanche Road below. What a great secret place, Bubba thought. No wonder the Indians made such grand raiders and retreaters. What chance had white men trapping them? About as much chance as Bubba had trapping these rebel vermin, that's what. But the boy's jaw tightened.

He reached in the dark and dragged the sack to him. Easing the vicious trap from its greasy lair, he thought again of its fearful design and workings.

Thirteen-inch main jaws—big, nearly, as a bear trap. What was called a double-trigger trap. Made with two sets of two jaws each. When the victim stepped on the trap's pan, it sprung the first set. These were smooth and small. But their seizing of the victim's ankle made him jerk to get free. And that jerk triggered the second, "killer" set of jaws. The big main set. Studded with interlocking tempered-steel teeth. Snapped by a spring so powerful it had to be set using a pry bar. Bubba sweated cold, just considering that trap.

It was no wolf trap such as he had first guessed.

This trap was designed somewhere across the water and long ago to catch, and maim past recovery, human beings. Slaves or serfs or whatever of poachers or poor folk that might be hunting food where they weren't let to do so, on the lands of dukes and earls and such, and so made to pay for their trespass that most could never walk again. And that was what the terrible-jawed trap had been doing hanging from its hook on the saddle skirt of the old sheriff's manhunting horse: waiting to be set and sprung on human prey.

For a long-held breath the ranch boy wavered.

Then he remembered where he was and why he was there.

He thought again of the way he had seen mama and Sissy cornered and dresses torn to nakedness in their own house. He heard once more the boom of The Redeemer and the vile curse of Captain Fragg to take his life. Then he wasn't wavering anymore. He swiftly removed the blocking stick, but ah! so carefully, from the previously set trap. Thank God the jaws stayed open. Praise Jesus the cocking triggers held their deadly set. All that remained was to lay the cocked trap flat, set-pan up, and : . .

Suddenly, the niggerman was there, arms reaching under the wagon right above Bubba's body, to bring wood out of the possumbelly. Then reaching in again to retrieve a last fat chunk that slipped from his grasp and hit Bubba on the back of his hat and bounced two feet.

But he didn't see the boy.

And now he went with his armload of wood over to the ancient fire spot of the Comanche, made in the Indian fashion in the exact center of the tiny meadow flat of Yamparika Tank.

The fire was soon set, the iron boiling pot hung on its hook over the blaze, some cornmeal and jerky thrown into it, with water from the tank to make an outlaw stew. Lean pickings, but these were desperate men in desperate trouble, and on the hard run out of Texas.

Bubba got ready. He knew from talking with Sissy back at Kiowa Peak what would come after the jerky and cornmeal had been gulped down. They would be picking that other man to go in the wagon in place of Creech.

But he was wrong.

There was a clay jug of Taos Lightning being passed by Captain Fragg around the fire to his loyal men, to restore them after the long day and double drive to reach this lonely tank and overnight safety. As the raw whiskey hit the empty bellies of the pack, thoughts of boiled cornmeal and rain-molded jerky diminished, indeed, vanished. "Goddammit, captain," growled Hound Dog Fowlis, "I say get out the hat and be done with it. I hunger to have them women!"

"Aarrr!" snarled the pack, as one. "Get the hat!"

"Stand down!" rasped Fragg, rearing to his feet. "I will not have insubordination here."

The men quieted only enough to stop talking but keep growling. Fragg eyed them. He made a move. His hands appeared suddenly filled with the Navy Colts. Motioning to them with the guns, he said, "All right, Fowlis. What were you saying?"

"Begging the captain's pardon sir." Fowlis now joined Fragg, afoot. The others came up off their haunches with him. "But we been talking on the run up here. We're spooked somewhat, as you can understand." He threw in a gesture at saluting. "It's just that we don't aim to wait no more. The whiskey's talking."

"You'd best hear this, captain." It was Sergeant Tranch, edging up to side his commander. Corporal Pike joined him, flanking the guerrilla leader from the other side. Both men had their rifles at the ready. Fragg noted the rifles were pointing at him, not the men.

"What is the whiskey saying, Fowlis?" he asked of the surly trooper. He glanced at Tranch, then Pike. "My trusted noncoms appear to be ready to listen to it, rather than to me." With a lightning double sweep backward of his arms, he struck both Tranch and Pike full across their faces with the barrels of the .36 Colt Navies. The men staggered back, grabbing at their wounds and, in the process, dropping their rifles.

Fragg kicked them out of reach without looking down. "Talk," he said to trooper Fowlis.

The latter, made rash by passion, ignoring the brutality of the officer, nodded and spoke. It was the new vote of the men, he said, that this time the hat would be drawn from until empty. Each man would get fifteen minutes in the wagon in the order his name came out of the hat or until the women stopped moving, one.

"Excepting for the nigger, natural," said Walleye Pike.

"Natural," Fowlis concluded, "and I go first on account of me winning back yonder. Ain't that so, boys?"

He turned to his comrades and they, joined now by both Tranch and Pike, nodded in scowling unison. "Aarrr!"

Fragg computed the guerrilla arithmetic confronting him. To the fatigue of his troops he added the whiskey plus the lure of the camp wives, subtracted from that sum his own weariness and need to hold his command together long enough to get over the Pecos. He holstered the twin Colts. Indicated Fowlis with a bony finger.

"The whiskey wins," he said. Reaching into his Confederate officer's longcoat, he produced a stem-winder watch, held its face to the light of the fire. "You got fourteen minutes. You wasted one augering."

Fowlis let out a whoop and the gang crowded after him as he made for the wagon.

Beneath the wagon, Bubba McCalister went white-gill pale. There was no time to scoop a pit in the sand for the trap, to bury it in place under the tailgate of the vehicle. No time to cross-hold the chain stake between two wheel spokes. Here came the legs of all the men, with those of the lucky Fowlis in the fore, squarely toward the tailgate and poor dear mama and Sissy. There was no time for anything at all, save for what the wild-eyed ranch boy then did on pure instinct.

As the group reached the wagon, its members stood back to permit their comrade his just due of room to step up over the tailgate. All their eyes were peering atop craning necks to see into the wagon, past Fowlis, and so to share with him a foretaste of what was awaiting every one of them.

Fowlis reached blindly behind him, waving an empty hand toward his old partner, Israel Girty.

"Gimme yore blade, Pig Dirt." He grinned. "I'll need to cut them loose for their turns at me, har! har!"

Girty handed him his knife, whacking its haft into the extended palm. Fowlis grasped the haft, planted his left foot for the little spring that would place his right on the lowered tailgate.

But in the moment of that left foot's reaching for its planting, Bubba McCalister shoved the cocked man-trap out from under the wagon, the set-pan full beneath the reaching foot of the lottery winner.

Fowlis gave a startled grunt of surprise as he stepped

on the pan and trigger one released the trap's smooth jaws to seize his leg just above the ankle. In reflex, he pulled away. And trigger two released the fearsome steel teeth of the thirteen-inch jaws.

Fowlis screamed burstingly.

He ran three leaping, crazed steps, the loose trap chain and its iron stake whipping about him in his frenzy.

Then the stake lodged accidentally between ground-rock outcrops and threw him to the full length of the chain. The locked teeth of the man-trap raked down his leg, calf to foot, to the bone, burying themselves finally in the ankle knobs.

# 36

"Secure the camp, secure the camp!"

Fragg's gravel-voiced order carried over the mill of the men about the screaming Fowlis. The troopers broke away to go leaping in every direction to cut off the retreat of the attacker. The common thought that ran with them was that the death of their comrade Ralph Creech, back at Kiowa Peak, had been no accident. Whoever had set this fiendish trap for poor Ollie Fowlis had also killed Creech. The two incidents were pups of the same litter. The damn dumb Siwash packer had known it all along: there *was* somebody out there.

Fragg did not follow his men toward the camp's perimeters but ran straight for the tailgate of the wagon. He had seen that the "trapper" must be in the vehicle itself. He could not have had time to hide himself any other place. The men would make sure of possible error, sealing off the small meadow from its surrounding rocks. But Braxton Fragg *knew* where the game had gone to ground. And he made the lowered tailgate with a single bound. Waving drawn pistol, he dove through the rear puckerhole, shouting, "Don't move! Hold where you be!" at whatever enemy might be cowering within.

He was correct in one assumption.

There was an enemy waiting for him within the wagon. But this enemy was not cowering. Neither was she holding where she was upon command.

Scipio Africanus, standing yet at the supper fire, thinking in truth of running for it himself, of taking this chance to get away free for good, was the sole renegade witness close enough to hear Fragg's muffled outcry from within the wagon. He was thus the only member of the pack to see his commander stagger back out of the wagon. Fragg's right arm had been slashed open, elbow to shoulder cap. The bloodied right hand was empty of its Navy Colt, the left-hand clutching to staunch the wound.

In the same instant, Scipio saw the ranch girl, knife in hand, bombard out the front puckerhole of the wagon. She leaped desperately outward from the high driver's box, fell heavily, regained her feet, and ran off, quartering and dodging like a kicked-out cottontail rabbit.

"Run!" the black man shouted unthinkingly. "Run!"

Sissy, still carrying the knife Bubba had left with her to use when she must, spurred now by the black forager's yell, eluded the dives of two of the men to catch her, made it into the first of the rocks. There, she ran squarely into the arms of Sergeant Levi Tranch, appearing out of nowhere to cut her off.

Tranch spun her about, twisted the knife out of her hand, threw her bodily downward into the meadow. The two henchmen seized her up from there, dragged her back toward the wagon, Tranch following. She managed to back-kick one of the men in the groin and severely bite the other when he tried to spin her back straight again. Tranch knocked her to the ground, put a knee in her chest, gagged her with his foul neckerchief, kicked her back up on to her feet.

Fragg, meanwhile, was ordering Scipio, the company surgeon now that his master, Henry Canfield, was dead, to see to the intractable pain of trooper Fowlis, but only after, and as, the big Negro finished bandaging Fragg's own superficial knife slash. Now, seeing his men had recaptured the girl, he ordered them to bring her to the supper fire, where he had had Scipio carry Fowlis for examination.

"Well," he snapped at the black man, as Tranch and his men came up with Sissy. "What do you see there?"

Scipio, turning from his brief scanning of what had been the left leg of Private Oliver Fowlis, grimaced.

"Bone's broke to shatters," he said. "You push it back in and splint it up, you going to get the gas rot in it. You don't, it'll be the blood fever sets in." He looked up at Fragg. "Got to amputate."

Fragg scowled, shook his head. "We do that, we got to carry him," he said.

Scipio nodded. "Carry or bury," he said.

For Fowlis, the pain was supreme. He could not abide it. "Help me!" he cried out. "For God's sake, help me!"

Fragg pulled his left-hand gun, shot him in the head. "He's helped," he said to the others.

They all drew instinctively away from him but nodded to the reality of what he had done.

"Now," Fragg said, "next order of business for this inquiry: Who cut the girl loose?"

The abruptness of his question returned them to a semblance of troop order. They drew back in. But all they could do was frown and mutter and shake heads.

All but Walleye Pike.

"The nigger," he said suddenly. "Cain't be no other but him."

"Mebbe it were whoever set the trap," Hoad offered.

"No," Fragg ruled icily. "Pike's right. Grab him!"

Scipio tried to break and run for it but Tranch hit him from one side, and Israel Girty from the other, with swung rifle butts to head and neck. He went down, and the company swarmed him before he might recover.

"Whatcher going to do with him, cap'n?" Pike asked eagerly.

"I don't know." The pale eyes were blinking furiously and there appeared little chance the guerrilla leader would not think of something, but Pike was before him.

"Cap'n," he said, "you recollect that uppity free nigger up north to Manassas what had hid out his mistress on us and wouldn't say whar? You call back how we put him spread of that corn-wagon wheel, and whupt up the team? Har, har!"

Fragg wheeled about. "Sergeant Tranch," he said, "put the nigger to the off-rear wheel. Hoad, fetch the mules."

Tranch took the order, relayed it to the men, stayed a moment with Fragg as the troopers dragged Scipio toward the government wagon. "What you going to do about the trapper?" he said to Fragg. "Oughtn't we to keep after him? I mean, keep digging about the camp here. In them willers yonder. And over past the tank. All in them first rocks. This feller's kilt two on us a'ready, cap'n. The nigger will keep, won't he?"

"Well." Fragg scowled. "All right. Send the Indian out to cut for sign clear about us, here."

"Too late." Levi Tranch shrugged. "The Injun hopped on his nag and got the hell scarce of us the minute Fowlis let out his first yelp."

"All right, the Indian will wait," Fragg ruled. "The nigger won't. He been traitoring on us since Corpus Christi. I want him on that wheel, Tranch. Now!"

The sergeant trotted off, coming to the wagon in time to hit Scipio again, re-stunning the powerful Negro as he managed to break stumblingly free of his captors. It was but the work of a minute, then, to bind the black man to the large rear wheel, spread-eagled, with his head, hands, and feet protruding beyond the iron of the rim. The members would thus be repeatedly smashed against the ground with each revolution of the wheel.

It was a prospect, as the laboring Hoad came up on the run with the reluctant team of Missouri mules, that not even brave Scipio might endure in silence. "Jesus' Name, Tranch," he said, "you ain't going to do this to old Skip. Cain't you see the cap'n's mind has blowed itself loose?"

"All I can see," Tranch answered, "is that he will blow mine loose iffen I don't do his orders."

"Pig Dirt, Crawdad"—Scipio appealed to Girty and Hoad—"ain't neither on you going to give old Skip a chanct?"

"Whyn't you try me?" guffawed Walleye Pike, helping Hoad back the mule team into position for hooking up.

From somewhere Scipio Africanus found the dignity to shame his tormentor. "Pike," he said, "God ain't going to take me and leave you. Not never. He will send a sign to old Skip."

"Sure!" Pike chortled. "And bears won't make dirt in the trail no more. Nor turkey buzzards eat dead meat. Nor a strange dog get his rear end sniffed. Har, har!"

But Scipio Africanus was right.

In twisting his head to gain last desperate views of the world he seemed about to depart, he caught an eyecorner glimpse of something familiar. It was a pair of eyes looking back at him. And he had seen the same pair before, looking back at him from somewhere else, from the old hay-burner stove in Cap Marston's bunkhouse room at the Paint Creek ranch. Scipio gasped.

Great God in the Land of Beulah!

It was the redhead kid again, only now not in the bunkhouse stove but the firewood possumbelly slung under the government surveyors' wagon.

Lord God, but wasn't that a sign for any nigger so close to Glory as old Skip?

"I got the sign!" the big Negro yelled out suddenly, startling his binders. "I knowed it, I knowed it!"

"You hooked them mules all four tugs, Hoad?" Levi Tranch stepped back from the wheel. "We got the nigger fast to the wheel. Let's go, hurry it on."

"One more trace to snap," Crawdad signaled. "Whoa, damn ye!" He finished buckling the tug, crawled to the driver's box, reached for the rim-iron brake. "All set here; I got 'em in hand. Whoa up, steady, easy—"

Levi Tranch turned to relay the call to Captain Fragg, still standing at the fire, staring at the dead Fowlis, the left-hand Navy Colt yet hanging at his side. He roused from his stare, answered Tranch—"Coming, sergeant"—and started toward the wagon.

Beneath that vehicle, Bubba McCalister made the choice of his own life against that of a niggerman. Bubba could see the instrument of his deliverance of the one-time slave. It was the knife of trooper Girty, given to trooper Fowlis just before the latter took his fatal step into the four-jawed trap, and dropped by Fowlis when the steel teeth closed upon him.

The knife still lay in the dirt below the tailgate.

By a chance wink of moonlight on its burnished blade, the Lord had sent Scipio's prayer to Bubba. No one but the boy himself would ever know if he did not answer that prayer. No one else had yet seen the knife, no one had yet remembered its being dropped. Of them all, surely the mean-looking niggerman would be the last to know of Bubba's courage or cowardice.

The ranch boy saw Fragg approaching. He heard the curses of Private Hoad trying to hold the spooked-up mules. Tranch and Pike and Girty stood but six feet from where Bubba lay safe-hid in the possumbelly. The boy's legs and stomach went weak.

Then he saw something else. It was the well shaft back home at Paint Creek ranch. And he heard again the voice of the niggerman growling down that well shaft at him. Saying he knew Bubba was down there. Knew he was yet alive. And was leaving him that way just because it was in his heart to do so. That big black man had saved Bubba's life.

What did the Book say about that?

A life for a life?

Fragg was up to the men at the rear wheel now. He peered quickly at Scipio's bonds, stepped back, raising his hand to signal Pike. It was in that moment before eternity that Scipio Africanus felt the hard slash of a razored blade sever the ropes at his right and left hands, at the wheel's top. And as Scipio grasped the iron rims to hold himself in position on the crucifix of the wheel, so obscuring God's answer to his prayer, he felt also the bonds of his feet being slashed free.

"Roll 'em out!" Fragg shouted to teamster Crawdad Hoad, even as Scipio's cut-away ropes were falling free.

*"Hee-yahh!"* screeched Hoad at the mules, and laid the whip to them.

And the wagon lurched forward, grinding the rim where Scipio's head had been into the sharp rocks and trampled dirt of the Comanche campground. But Scipio and his redheaded rescuer were free of the wagon now. They were rolling out from under it on its far side, away from the dumbfounded troops of Captain Fragg. Away from them and with Scipio racing forward to swarm up onto the back of the nearside mule. Doing that, and then reaching back down to scoop up the swift-running Bubba McCalister from the ground and hurl him like a sack of sweaty wheat onto the withers of the offside mule. And, all the while, on the box, Crawdad Hoad was sawing at the jaws of both mules with the lines, dragging and fighting back to get the team halted. Or at least to get them slowed. And to do it quick enough that Captain Fragg and his comrades could get to their picketed horses for the pursuit.

But now the nigger and the ghost of the redheaded kid from the ranch were guiding the team, defying Hoad to do anything with the lines. And Hoad dropped them and went for his belt gun, a .44-calibre Union Cavalry Remington.

He fired once at the boy, once at the nigger, missing both times as the wagon swayed and pitched wildly behind the running mules. Then the second ghost of the night from the cursed Paint Creek ranch materialized. She came out of the front puckerhole, behind Crawdad Hoad. In her hands, the wrists still tightly bound, was the right-hand Navy Colt of Braxton Fragg, slashed from his hold by Sissy, gathered up now by the ghost. In her eyes blazed a clear light that had not been there since the night Tabebekat had died in south gully, two long years before. And she put the muzzle of the Navy Colt against the tensing spine of the guerrilla teamster, as the latter sought desperately to steady his aim at Bubba and Scipio.

"Damn you, damn you, damn you," Mary McCalister said in a low, calm voice.

And with each of the first consciously directed words she had uttered in twenty-five months, she triggered a point-blank shot into the spasming vertebras of Private Archimedes "Crawdad" Hoad.

"My God, it's mama!" Bubba shouted to Scipio. "Sissy must've got her partways loose."

"Gather the lines, boy!" Scipio yelled back at him. "Get them up to your mama. Grab Crawdad's gun. C'mon, I need your mule. There's one more passenger to board!"

As he spoke, he swung his mule to the left, just avoiding a pileup in the rocks that walled the meadow. The wagon swayed, almost went over. Then it righted as Scipio got his team straightened out from the turn and headed dead-back across the meadow toward where Fragg and his remaining three men were getting their mounts free of the picket line and swinging to saddle aboard them. Bubba believed for one open-mouthed instant that the big black man had gone daft. He seemed heading right at Fragg and the others, all deadly shots and heavily armed and wheeling their horses now to come at the careening wagon. But in the last second, as Bubba got the lines gathered and made it to the driver's box along the bucking wagon tongue between mules, he saw what the black man had seen, first flash.

It was Sissy.

Though Tranch had gagged her and Girty knotted her hands loosely behind her, they had not bound her feet. And Sissy was second only to brother Bubba for marvelous speed afoot. She was coming now right at the careening wagon, darting and veering in her cottontail style as Fragg and the others were firing at her.

Bubba got the re-gathered reins in his teeth, freeing his hands so that he could grasp his mother's extended grip and so be brought to the seat beside her.

"Pass me Crawdad's gun, mama!" he shouted joyously.

And she laughed the old, wonderful, bright laugh and shouted back to him, "I'll trade you it for them reins, Randolph Barnes," and she pried the gun from Hoad's dead hand and they made the exchange and Bubba took desperate brace on the swaying wagon's front stay and fired blastingly away.

He didn't hit anybody but his shots ricocheted wildly off the rocks, forcing Fragg and his three riders to veer their horses and so lose ground. In the moment thus gained, Scipio was able to steer the mules on an angle that brought them into a dead heat with Sissy running alongside, on Scipio's side. The latter scooped her up and dumped her on Bubba's vacated mule, and the escape was on, full tilt, for the meadow exit.

They made the opening with a wagon length to spare over their pursuers, who could not then fire into them because of the thick shield of the yellow willows.

But the track down the narrow defile was so closed in that no horseman could pass the wagon. Neither could the fugitives take an equal speed to individual horsemen in such steep going. The result was that, once through the willow thicket, Scipio could see that the guerrillas must ride into the tailgate in another few jumps. Then they would need but to abandon mounts and board the wagon from its rear, ending it all.

The big black man understood that both Fragg's and Hoad's revolvers must be empty, or the redhead boy would be using them to fire back at Fragg's pack.

They had nothing but the two knives, Girty's and the redhead boy's, to fend off four human wolves, each of whom came on the lunging downward leap with six-gun in hand and carbine in boot beneath leg. Scipio put his feet in the mule harness and stood tall to look back over the top of the plunging wagon. He saw trooper Girty leading the charging van—Private Israel "Pig Dirt" Girty, fellow raper to skinny trooper Oliver Fowlis—and Scipio Africanus reached back to remember a debt owing to his dead master, Henry Canfield, and to Scipio's mother, and to his own ravished young sister, Florene, and to all helpless women who had known the evil of such men as Girty and Fowlis.

On the driver's box, clinging to the reins, Bubba was

startled now to see the wild black man leap up astride the mules, Roman rider–style, a foot in the back of each, but twisting to face the yelping guerrillas. There, he threw back his head to utter such a chilling scream as the ranch boy had never heard from mortal throat. Then instantly he was bounding back along the wagon tongue, toward Bubba and the careening driver's seat.

The boy believed the rolling-eyed Negro meant only to join the others in the wagon—he had already ordered mama and Sissy into it and to lie flat there on the hammering bed boards—so that he and Bubba might stand to the last between the women and Fragg's howling pack.

In a way he was right.

Scipio, reaching the driver's seat, seized up the heavy, flopping body of the dead trooper Hoad. He lifted it like a sack of rags far above his head and, with another of the blood-turning shrieks, hurled the corpse down beneath the driving, iron-shod heels of the mules, back under the wagon.

Girty had in fact made good his first handhold on the iron of the tailgate and was preparing to leave his saddle for the wagon when the cartwheeling catapult of Hoad's gross body bounded out from beneath the wagon, full into the legs and forechest of Girty's horse.

The animal went down, croup over wither.

Girty flew from its saddle, turned half over in the air, crunched back first into the opened tailgate, and hung there for the fraction of a second as his horse, completing its somersault, crashed into the tailgate. Horse, rider, shatter of tailgate timber—all went to earth in a crunching flurry of hide, bone, and hideous human screaming. Into this shapeless tangle, helpless to swerve and miss it within the crevice of the Indian trail down from Yamparika Tank, thundered the three horses of Fragg, Tranch, and Pike.

The pileup was of tremendous wrenching force.

Girty was dead. If Fragg and Tranch and Pike were dead with him, the fugitives could not know. Nor could they guess as to the crippling of their horses in the crashing together. All they might do was to whip on the loyal team of big Missouri mules. This they did, reaching the Comanche Road in safety. Here, they turned hard eastward and were headed for home.

After that, there remained nothing but to pray for one more miracle.

When low-voiced Mary McCalister, peering with wan-faced Sissy from the front puckerhole, suggested as much, black Scipio shook his head. "Too late, lady," was all he said.

They all looked back.

They all saw what Scipio had seen.

Three horsemen.

Three horsemen issuing from the black shadows of the defile behind them.

Three horsemen coming on.

Riding in the moonlight swift as night wind where there was no night wind.

Fragg and Tranch and Pike.

# 37

The moon rode clear of the ragged upthrust of rock that shielded Yamparika Tank. Beneath its paper-white glare, the contest for who would live and who die was joined. It seemed to Scipio Africanus that those lives in his care must be the ones forfeited. Lashing up the weary mules, exhorting them with all his skills, he yet glanced back at the gaining horsemen and knew what the end must be. In his mind no other answer glimmered.

They had no ammunition for the Colts of Fragg and Hoad. There was no gunpowder, no weapons of any kind, in the surveyors' wagon. Even its camp axe had been removed by Scipio to split firewood back at the tank. They had nothing but the two knives, Girty's dropped by

Fowlis and the redheaded boy's own blade. And these had already been passed back to the two women crouched in the wagon behind him and the boy. This time, they would have to use them on themselves, Scipio believed.

"Redhead boy," he said to the youth beside him, "you any notion whereat me and you might come upon some artillery to wheel up and blow apart them devils chasing us?"

"By God right I have!" Bubba surprised him. "And if you will swerve the wagon my way in the bottom of yonder dip, I will go and get it for you."

"What you saying, boy?"

"It's the old sheriff's horse. I got him stashed not two minutes up that little ravine you see running inter the rocks from yonder dip."

"We ain't *one* minute," Scipio said. "Look ahint you." Bubba looked, paling at how close the guerrillas were, and Scipio added, "Besides, what good's the old horse?"

"It ain't him. It's old Cap's Texas Ranger gun. She's ahanging on the saddle horn, loaded all six around!"

"That thing! More apt to blow *us* up than them."

"It's a killer!" Bubba shouted. "Cap said!"

"You're daft, boy. You got the guts of a back-home bobcat, but you're looney. You cain't jump off this wagon and get up to that old horse and cotch back up to us ahead of Fragg and them. Lord Jesus, boy, there just ain't time!"

"There'd be time, goddammit, iffen you'd just think of something to delay them!" Bubba yelled. "Come on! You're supposed to be such a great battlefield forager and all!"

"Redhead chile," Scipio said with sudden intensity, "you brung the word. It's called the Guerrilla Good-bye, and we *can* give 'em one more hooraw with it. See'd it work in the war whens they'd blow and burn a barn or house with no gunpowder. We got coal oil yonder, hull big can of it. I can make us a bomb out'n that. Rather, you can do it, boy, if you'll foller whats I tells you. Listen clost to me."

The pursuers were again firing with their saddle carbines, saving their revolvers for the closing in on the faltering mules and swaying wagon. The heavy slugs from the short rifles were splintering wood, ripping canvas, ringing off metal top stays. The sudden fusillade drowned the words of Scipio's instruction to the ranch boy, but it could be seen by Bubba's bobbing head and close attitude that he was getting the information on coal oil combustion for guerrilla war-work.

When Scipio had finished, he took the four reins in one huge black fist, put the other arm about the thin shoulders of the white boy. "Wisht I could do it, chile, but ain't no way you could holdt these mules to keep the wagon upright. God's sake, be keerful!"

Bubba squeezed the black man's hand and was gone back through the puckerhole to join mama and Sissy.

There, he could see straight-line out the rear pucker-hole and got a cold chill in his belly doing it.

It seemed he could have reached out from the tailgate and touched the noses of any one of the three horses hammering after the wagon. "Goda'mighty!" he gasped. "I'd call that close enought!"

"Oh, Bubba, Bubba!" Sissy cried, and threw her arms about him.

He cast her off roughly and told her and mama what they had to do—find material to make a twisted wick for sticking in the neck of the uncorked coal oil can. There was a scurry to do so but nothing came to hand in the darkness of the wagon's tossing bed.

"Dammit, mama," Bubba cried out, "gimme *something*—!"

Mary McCalister reached beneath the shreds of her dress and they heard the cloth rip to her wrenching hand and she took the torn petticoat and ripped it again and yet again. With the three long swaths of cloth she braided a wick at unbelievable speed. It came out shorter than Bubba would have liked but it had to do, and he plugged it into the can after saturating it with oil. "Rope, rope!" Bubba cried. "Gimme the longest piece of them bindings you cut off yourselves!"

A hand reached him the rope in the darkness and he fastened one end to the bail of the coal oil can and gave the other end to Sissy McCalister.

"Charlotte May," he said, "I'm going over the side of the wagon and get into the possumbelly underneath. When I'm in, I'm going to give you a rebel yell up. Then down you lower the damn can by the rope on it, so's I can reach it from the belly and haul it into thar with me. You got that, now?"

"Bubba, you can't do that. You'll fall under the wagon. Just light it and throw it like the niggerman said."

"I don't give a damn what he said," Bubba raged. "I got a better way to do it. Mister Skip," he bawled up at the cursing driver, "lean in hyar!"

Scipio put one eye and one ear to the front puckerhole and Bubba informed him that he was going to try to get the coal oil bomb into the possumbelly and light it to blow just as the mules took the wagon down into the ravine dip, now approaching its last yards away along the Comanche Road. "Oh, Jesus, redhead boy," Scipio began, "you cain't do thet! It ain't a chanct. Leave me have the can up hyar—heave it clean over the wagon."

"No!" Bubba screeched back. "It'll make ten times the bang fired off in the possumbelly."

"Christ Jesus, yes, boy, and you'll blow up the wagon and all of us with it." A long black arm snaked back through the puckerhole, pawing at the air. "Gimme that there can!"

"Sissy," Bubba said, ducking under Scipio's searching grasp, "you got the rope? Lower it away when I yell."

With that, he was gone beneath the lower edge of the wagon-top canvas, slipping over the side of the wagon, hanging on by hand strength and kicking his feet under the wagon until he hooked the possumbelly with them, and then acrobating his way on into the belly by more handhold strength. From there, he yelled up for Charlotte May to lower the can, and next instant there was the can bumping down into view on the rope.

Four times Bubba grabbed for the rope and missed. On the fifth stab he snared it and reeled in the sloshing can.

This he secured deep in the wood behind him and dug into his pants pocket for the three sulfur matches Scipio had given him—the last three matches in the world so far as Bubba was concerned.

Strike one just fizzled and went out.

Strike two stayed alight but Bubba jammed it too excitedly into the wetted wick, drowning it.

Bubba sent a round oath up to heaven, and went for the third match.

It scraped beautifully on a fine dry cedar chunk in the belly, took handsome spark and flare, set immediate and high fire to Mary McCalister's petticoat-braid wick.

"Burn, you beauty!" Bubba shrieked, and writhed out of the possumbelly pursued by smoke and oily flame. Outside the belly he clung to its sling-canvas, pulling himself forward to reach its twin ropes, where they joined in single strand at the crossbar from which the hammock of the possumbelly was suspended, in front.

Gripping the knife he had taken back from Sissy, he readied the final effort. As he drew back knife arm to strike the rope, he felt the wagon plunge into the ravine dip of the Comanche Road and saw, looking back past the now furiously smoking possumbelly, the rearing horses of Fragg and Tranch and Pike leaping to follow the wagon down into the road's depression.

Bubba slashed with the knife.

His luck held and his strength was good and the rope that held the belly was frayed anyway, and the entire belly full of cut firewood chunks gave way and spilled back under the wagon into the bottom of the ravine. In the precise second the wagon cleared the bottom and was up the far side of the ravine, the horses of Fragg and his henchmen were bombarding into the flying kindling and Scipio's coal oil guerrilla bomb blew up with a cannon flare and thump that lit the prairie a hundred yards about.

Battlefield panic ensued among the mounts of the pursuers lost in the roiling black smoke and shattered cordwood at the bottom of the ravine.

Tranch's horse went down and fell on its rider. Pike's

mount pitched its rider off in falling, stomped him severely in regaining its feet. Fragg's animal did not fall but went to bucking and sun-fishing through the shards of wood and smoke-black rocks. By the time the three men had recovered their mounts and themselves, the mule wagon was a quarter mile gone down the Comanche Road, rolling bravely but at a slowing gallop. Nowhere—in ravine, on surrounding moon-bright prairie, or up or down the ancient Indian road—was there sign of human attacker, or sapper, to explain the military havoc of the coal oil bomb.

"Mount up," mumbled Braxton Fragg, between split and bleeding lips. "I want the nigger alive. This was his doing."

"Let me and Tranch crotch-split him," Pike begged, wiping soot and rock grime from weeping eyes. "Get a rope, each, on his opposite feet and whip our horses apart."

"Goddamn you, Pike, get to your horse!"

Walleye pulled himself to saddle. "The nigger's mine," he snarled.

"Fine," grated Sergeant Levi Tranch, wheeling his mount with an ugly laugh. "Since the captain has already spoke for the girl, that leaves me the woman. Yo!"

"Ride out," growled Fragg, taking the lead.

They galloped three abreast and in silence a little ways, and Tranch, showing the last glimmer of sanity among them, said suddenly to Fragg, "Captain, maybe we'd ought to think about giving it up. We're all that's left of us. We could still make it over the Pecos."

Braxton Fragg bared his crooked, malformed teeth. "I've taught you better than that, sergeant," he said. "Never leave anybody alive to your rear that can witness against you. If you've forgot that posse out of Pioche, I assure you they ain't forgot you. Forward, *hohHH!*"

Fragg slashed at his horse with his rifle barrel. Pike and Tranch spurred to gain up to him. The three horses shrank the moonlight remaining between them and the mule wagon, along the old Comanche Road.

Braxton Fragg pulled out his big stem-winder watch. He angled it to catch the glare of the moon. "Two minutes," he estimated, watching the ever-failing wagon ahead. "Pike and me will go in over the tailgate; Tranch, you head the mules. Look sharp now. They may still have a round or two left."

"I got a better idee, captain," Tranch said. "And nobody gets shot. Lookit yonder. Off to the right, thar—"

# 38

It seemed all but over then.

What Tranch saw yonder was an old skeleton of an emigrant wagon ribbing up out of the blown sand that embedded it. The single one of its remaining bones that attracted the professional eye of the guerrilla sergeant was the wagon tongue, still intact and rearing up stark as some Comanche taboo-pole.

Fragg read the tongue's usefulness to them as instantly as his sergeant. He instructed the latter to "go and get it," and Tranch, shaking out his lariat on the diverging gallop, obeyed.

Dabbing a loop over the spar, he snared it from the sand and went veering back to the Indian road with the oaken tongue bounding at rope's end behind him. As he went, however, he was reeling in the rope and bringing the timber to "gaff," as it were, seizing it like some cumbersome lance when he had gotten it to him. So armed, he charged at an angle to rejoin his comrades, now closing on the wagon. They held in their mounts to permit him to come up and pass them. It was then apparent that to be an irregular cavalryman of the great war between North and South meant knowing how to do many things never taught in regular manuals of battle.

Tranch spurred his horse even with the right rear wheel of the careening wagon. "*YaahhHH!*" he yelled, and drove the wagon tongue, jammed spearwise, through the wheel spokes to lodge in the running-gear strut of the axle, beneath the wagon's bed. The wheel locked and the wagon slewed, teetered, and went over. It fell to the left, taking the mules with it. The latter, surviving as mules will, managed to scramble back up, still in harness. But their driver, thrown off the seat and over the heads of his struggling team, lit too heavily on packed earth. He lay there as if shattered of every bone in his black body. Then, even with wheels still spinning from the tip-over and the dust still rising, Mary McCalister and Sissy crawled from the collapsed canvas, worse only for a scrape or contusion of no concern. The two women were no more than clear of the wreck, and standing huddled together beside it, than the three horsemen slid their mounts to neighing halts so near as to shower the two with rocks and dirt chunks.

The three left saddle as one rider, and came for the helpless women.

Mary McCalister it was who had the remaining knife. Clear of eye and fired of same in the McCalister way, the ranchwoman bared her white teeth, tossed the blade to her daughter, and literally sprang upon Fragg, diverting him from Sissy.

Tranch in his turn seized upon Mary McCalister to drag her from Fragg. This delay permitted Sissy to swing the knife. She cut Tranch superficially but with a sear of raw pain across the great muscles above the kidneys. He straightened and threw a vicious back-arm blow that knocked the slight girl sprawling. His boot found her knife wrist, grinding it into the ground, and Tranch had the blade away from her.

In the same moment, Fragg had overpowered Mary McCalister, slamming her against the overturned wagon, the side of his bony face bleeding profusely where her strong teeth had torn into it. The ranchwoman's hands were red with the same blood and her mouth dripped it, as her groping fingers went to her mouth and came away with something picked therefrom. Fragg saw the object and his own hand went to the side of his head and he whimpered snarlingly, as a wounded animal would, and they both knew what it was she held in her hand. It was Fragg's left ear.

Tranch came up to aid the mutilated guerrilla leader, dragging Sissy by the long hair, brutally, as angry with her, nearly, as was Fragg with the girl's mother. He threw her against the wagon, as Fragg had done with Mary McCalister, and Sissy slid down to the ground, crouching there with her mother, their arms protectively sheltering one another.

"Goddamn the luck," came Pike's coarse complaint from beyond the overturned vehicle. "The nigger is knocked out colder than a dead sheep. He's mebbe even stone-slab done for. The traitoring bastard has cheat me of my fair evens with him!"

"Shoot him," Fragg said. "Be done with it."

"First I got to take something off him," Pike called cheerily. "You know how to scalp a nigger, cap'n? You takes his hair low down, and leaves the handle on it. Har, har!"

"Bind both these women," Fragg said to Tranch. "I'll cut the mules out of harness. We will put the women on them and ride. We'll make your Pecos River yet, sergeant. And with our booty on our baggage animals, right and fit and military proper." Fragg's eyes glared, and Tranch saluted hurriedly.

"Yes sir, captain," he said, and began working to free his lasso rope from where it was still tied to the jammed wagon tongue in the rear wheel. To Mary McCalister, who made a sign of stirring, he rasped warningly, "Don't try nothing more. He'll kill you outright."

"Mama, mama, for God's sake, what'll we do?" Sissy sobbed.

"We'll see it through," Mary McCalister answered, and gathered whatever shred of fighting strength she had remaining to her wearied body.

"Mama," whispered Sissy, "I want you to know something; I'm glad to God that you got all right again."

"Honey," the ranchwoman said, taking the girl's hand, "we're all going to be all right. We are, we are—"

The voice faded and Tranch, returning with the rope in time to hear it trailing off thus, muttered something that sounded like "Crazy, crazy as hell," and reached to seize and haul Sissy roughly to her feet for binding.

But Mary McCalister was not crazy, and never would be again.

Into the moment's pause, from startlingly near down the moonlit track of the Comanche Road, a high-pitched rebel yell echoed in defiance. It was blended with the fierce sound of a wild mustang's whistling. The three renegades came running together to stand before Mary and Charlotte May McCalister and to stare off down the Comanche Road.

"What," breathed Sergeant Levi Tranch, "in the name of God a'mighty is that?!"

Neither Tulliver Pike nor Braxton Fragg answered him, but the ranchwoman did.

"That," Mary McCalister said, coming to her feet to stand tall against the wagon, "is my boy, Bubba."

# 39

The man on foot is forever aces down to the mounted attacker. Bubba brought old Kickapoo thundering in upon the dismounted guerrillas. The boy did not swerve or slow. Too late the trio tried to run.

Fragg, quickest and most savage of the pack, did elude Bubba's charge enough to get his remaining left-hand Navy Colt out and fire twice. Pike shot once and ran off. Tranch, between the other two and the wagon, was not so lucky. Kickapoo's huge shoulder struck him a terrible blow and knocked him into the wagon and bouncing off of it, still on his feet. Bubba shot him two times with old Redeemer, downing him as with a sledge.

Fragg, however, had gotten to his horse and mounted up. He came in behind Bubba now, who was just turning Kickapoo for his return charge. Bubba laid up along Kickapoo's thick neck and Fragg's second two shots thudded into the heavy muscle of the Percheron mustang as, next leap, the big horse smashed joltingly into Fragg's lesser mount. The shock of the collision sent the guerrilla leader flying off to land on the roll in soft earth, unharmed. Bubba, thinking him stunned, slid off Kickapoo and ran forward to finish his enemy afoot.

In this instant, two things occurred.

Tranch, not yet dead, recovered his senses and strength just as Bubba slid off Kickapoo and ran past the downed sergeant, to come at and finish Fragg. Tranch put his two elbows in the dirt, steadied and swung his Colt between the shoulder blades of the ranch boy. As the sights centered the lad, the trigger finger tightened.

But old Kickapoo saw the man on the ground move behind Bubba. And he flung up jughead and whistled the mustang warning whistle, sharp and blasting, to the boy who had come back for him and ridden him down out of the Yamparika rocks in the best race the aging and grateful horse had run since colthood.

Whirling about and jumping to one side in response to the shrill sound, Bubba felt the hot wind from Levi Tranch's bullet burn past his temple. In his own turn, Bubba fired once with Redeemer held before him in the double-handed hold and bent-knee crouch that old Cap Marston had taught him, of the Texas Ranger style. The heavy .44-calibre slug took Tranch where neck base came to collarbone hollow, in front. It went the long way through heart vessels, intestines, and bladder, deflecting from the hip blade and exiting the groin.

Levi Tranch was dead, propped up on his elbows in the rock and dirt of the Comanche Road.

Bubba knew it and was turning to face Fragg again when the latter fired his two remaining shots from the Colt Navy. The first bullet struck the boy in the flesh of his right side, spinning him two times around and like a spiked top. This spinning ruined Fragg's second shot, which struck low and wide, knocking off the heel of the ranch youth's left boot, and that was all for Captain Braxton Bonaparte Fragg.

Bubba McCalister, blood coursing his wounded side, walked into the guerrilla leader with The Redeemer before him in the two-handed hold and fired once—Fragg shocked down to knees on ground—twice—Fragg blasted backward from his knees and halfways again up onto his wavering feet—and the third time—Fragg screaming and seizing himself in the front, crumpling to earth again, gut-shot from twenty inches. Then, no other sound, nor movement even, except for the reflex blinking and final wide-open set of the glazing, wolf-pale eyes.

# 40

Corporal Pike, in the moment that he ran to put the fallen wagon between himself and the blasting of guns that ended in eternal silence for his comrades Sergeant Tranch and Captain Braxton Fragg, knew he was the last man. And knew what that meant.

He must keep running. Must get to a horse, any horse, be up on it and be gone. The nearest mount was Tranch's, held from leaving the field by the dead sergeant's lariat. A man needed but to swing up, knife-slash the rope, and be away on the flying gallop.

Pike, never slowing his pace, had to leap over the body of the black forager to return around the wagon to the tied mount. Scipio, just then rallying his senses, threw up a blocking arm as the guerrilla vaulted over him. He succeeded only in knocking Pike off stride, but that proved the necessary fraction of time. It permitted Scipio to gain his feet and run unsteadily the other way about the vehicle and come to where old Kickapoo was already grazing quietly away. In this fashion, the black forager was able to find an emptied saddle on the battlefield as quickly as did the fleeing corporal.

The pursuit lined out, with old Kickapoo galloping gamely but rough. He had been twice hit by bullets and had run a hard course before that to get Bubba caught up to his family. It seemed to the anxious watchers from the wagon now that Scipio and the Percheron mustang were losing one jump for every three Pike's fleet animal made. The last they could make out through the distance of moon's light were the dark figures of both horses disappearing down into the ravine of the coal oil and cordwood bomb.

Strain as they might, not even Bubba's famed "antelope's eyesight" could see either horseman re-emerge on the far side of the ravine.

But the boy could hear, and mama and Sissy heard it too, the sudden booming of Pike's remaining revolver shots—five of them—from down in the ravine, muffled and ominous.

It made a sadness for them all.

But they understood they could not change it, nor in any way have saved the big black man from his fate. They had all three of them come too hard a way, and too long, without rest, to force another step onward that night. Human flesh wouldn't bear more torture, nor would that of their animals. In the morning, mama said, they could sort it all out and make the best of what was left to them. Sissy agreed. Bubba nodded in his turn.

He went out and caught up Fragg's and Pike's horses, unhooked the mules, tied all to the wagon. Neither body nor its saddlebags yielded up any ball or powder or cap to recharge the several weapons recovered. Bubba noted that and worried over it, until search of his own pockets brought out three caps and one ball and two fair pinches of coarse black powder for The Redeemer.

He loaded the single chamber of the cylinder, capped it, and felt worlds better about any return old Pike might make in the coming moon-dark, before dawn.

He and Mary McCalister and Sissy dragged a stack of surveyor blankets out of the wagon and made a snug bed against its upturned bottom. Bubba condescended to sit a minute, Sissy and him on either side of mama, and let his mother have an arm about their shoulders, the while they all prayed to the Lord and thanked him for their safe deliverances.

After the "Amen," mama wept a little, softly and inside herself, and Bubba thought he would sit on long enough for her to quiet, then he would take up Redeemer and go sleep on top of the wagon, "standing watch" over his loved ones. The next thing he knew, the sun was shining in his squinted eyes and it was the morning of the first day of July, 18 and 63, the greatest day of the grandest summer that ever could be.

What started it off so great was that about five minutes after they'd all woke up and were scouting around for squaw-wood scraps to feed the breakfast fire, they heard, far off down the Comanche Road, a wondrous deep voice singing a sort of poignant but yet pretty tune:

> *"Way down yonder in the fields of cotton,*
> *Far away but not forgotten,*
> *Look away, look away,*
> *Look away, Dixie land—"*

With the song, up out of the yonder ravine in the Indian trail, rode Scipio Africanus on the limping old war-horse Kickapoo, still singing away. And that was wondrous enough by itself, but the black man was not by himself. He had something following after him. It was all done up in the Spanish slave chains from the old sheriff's saddle skirt. Wrist and ankle irons were on, and a long chain run up from them to the iron collar and passed through it and tied onto the free end of Sergeant Tranch's lasso rope. The other end of which rope, naturally enough, was tight-held in a mightily powerful big black hand. And that was the way Corporal Tulliver "Walleye" Pike was taken in the field by the renowned forager, Scipio Africanus, and led in dog-collar chains to face some other vengeance than Scipio's.

Bubba charged out to meet them, eager to know how the burly ex-slave had survived all those pistol shots.

"Matter of being black." The big Negro grinned. "Old Pike, he just kept shooting at them black places wheres old Skip weren't. What's boiling for breakfast, white boy?"

They laughed together. Scipio took Bubba up to ride with him on Kickapoo back to the wagon and the womenfolk. Mama and Sissy knuckled at some warm tears shed to prove to "old Skip" that they cared for him, black or any color, and there was more laughing and it was some summer morning in July, all right.

To top it off, they even had company for breakfast.

It was the Pioche posse, a little late but welcome all the same. After a bad mutter upon seeing Scipio there, the story of his hero work from Mary McCalister, plus the old sheriff talking private with Carlos Ortmann, earned the black forager temporary freedom under field parole to Charley Skiles. The reunion of Lonsford McCalister with his family was reward enough for most of the Pioche manhunters. Only banker Hardeman grumbled on about settling for the single prisoner, Tulliver Pike. "Not much of a bird," he scowled, fingering his shotgun. "Cheaper to flush him here."

"None of that, A. J. He'll go back for fair trial." The old sheriff reached in his pocket and pulled out the star of his office and leaned from his livery-stable horse and pinned it firm on young Will Hatch, and said to him, "Ain't that so, sheriff?"

Hatch took it mightily sober, saying he wasn't sure he deserved the second chance.

"Don't worry about that," Carlos Ortmann reassured him. "We'll let you know if you're standing short."

There was a wave of friendly murmurs to that and somebody said, "Well, let's get that wagon back on its wheels and rolling. I got to get home to Pioche; ain't nobody going to feed my bulldog whilst I'm away."

"Nor mine," said another.

"Likewise," echoed a third, and the men fell to the work and soon enough had it done and were gone back down the old trail toward their home country. Walleye jangled along behind them still in his Spanish chains and mounted on the hardest-gaited horse they could find for him. Of the group, only the old sheriff lingered by the righted wagon after his fellows were gone.

"Best not let them get too far a start on you, Mister Skiles," Bubba said. "Old Kick has had a hard night and took two hits in the neck."

Charley Skiles shook his head. "Not going their way," he said.

Lonnie McCalister looked at him. "What way you going?" he asked.

The craggy old lawman looked at them one by one, lastly at dark-haired, indomitable Mary McCalister.

"Your way," he answered Lon. "If you'll have me."

"We're going home." Lon frowned, a little puzzled.

"So is Mister Skiles," said Mary McCalister.

She looked past her eldest son, nodding to Charley Skiles. They said nothing, nor had to. Both had been too long lonesome in their separate worlds. Lon felt it now. They all did. And felt the warmer for it.

The old sheriff turned again to Lon McCalister.

"Well, son," he said, "what are we waiting for? Let's go home."

Lon's dark face lightened, the weariness fled.

"Hee-yahhHH!" yelled Scipio Africanus, to the big Missouri mules, and the wagon began to move.

"Home, oh, mama!" cried Charlotte May.

"Yes, dear God, yes," whispered Mary McCalister.

And, after a moment of sitting there on his borrowed horse watching the others start away, it was the last McCalister's turn.

"I will be damned," said Randolph Barnes McCalister.

And gave his horse a kick in the ribs and sent him off on the gallop after the Paint Creek cavalcade.

# EPILOGUE

•

At the time of the events recounted in *Summer of the Gun*, nothing further was known of the McCalisters beyond the violent ending of Braxton Fragg and the family's setting out for the return journey to Paint Creek ranch. Three eventual sources—the respected *Letters from Long Ago*, Mary Starr McCalister; the rambling self-told *Monk Beckham, Frontier Stager*; and the touching *Memories of a Free Man: My Story*, privately published in Los Angeles when Scipio was ninety-three years old—provide the following, generally accepted conclusion to a story that did not quite end on its last page.

Upon reaching the homeplace, they gave Christian burial to Dr. Henry Canfield and old Cap Marston. The ranch house was cleansed and set straight to occupy but an uneasiness lingered about it. That night none of them cared to sleep there. The women retired to Cap's bunkhouse, the menfolk bedded in the horse shed. Only the children rested well.

With first light, Mary McCalister had made the breakfast coffee and her dark-hours decision with it. The homeplace was too inhabited by hauntings that could not be laid to rest. It was a time for moving on.

The children vowed they would never leave Paint Creek and papa's dream. But brother Lon said their father had never intended his dream to make a prison of Paint Creek for them and, moreover, would surely want them to stay by mama no matter what. As that last was forever true, the children yielded and Mary McCalister, looking off west, told them of *her* dream.

She had seen a thousand wagons rumble past along the Overland Road, trekking to where the sun went down, she said, and she could not recall a solitary one of them ever coming back. She believed those wagons had found the Beulah Land out yonder in far California and that the family should follow them there.

Scipio Africanus, who, like the Sheriff of Pioche, had pondered much and spoken little since the return, volunteered that California was the very place Mister Henry had said was the Promised Land. There was even an old forty-niner gold-rush song about it that he and Major Canfield would sing along the way, when spirits were low or faith despairful. It was a joysome tune the black man remembered. The name of it was *On the Road to California*, and he sung them a little of it:

> "*On the road to Californy
> It were a long and a tejus journey
> For acrost the Rocky Montaynes
> Crystal springs and flowing fontaynes.*"

The words, the air itself, something in Scipio's grand deep baritone, aroused his listeners. The decision was taken. They would do as mama visioned.

With that, they all took the California fever and worked like field hands to prepare the departure. By noon mealtime they had the worldly goods sorted to load and Lon reckoned the moment had come to look the old sheriff square in faded blue eye and ask him right out didn't he think that, facing such a considerable distance of trail and for the sakes of the younger children, he had ought to make an honest woman of their mother, not to mention an honest man of himself.

The sheriff got his cheroot smoke backward up his nose and Mary McCalister gasped and grabbed her notable bodice and turned red as rooster comb.

But Lon held them to it and Charley Skiles, liking vastly what he saw of his ready-made new family, rose boyishly to foot, and just flat out asked Mary McCalister if she would have him.

That was a Wednesday. It was agreed the ceremony would take place the immediate Saturday morning. Stage driver Monk Beckham was intercepted and asked to bear the good news into Red Hawk. He was to notify the preacher and invite all who wanted to come. For any preferring to make the long drive the day before, arrangement would be made to put them up at the ranch Friday night. Stager Beckham includes a footnote that the only thing that brought retiring Mary McCalister around to such a public celebration was that she could thus find use for the mail-order anniversary present her children had gotten for her way back when the war started. Which gift turned out to be the wedding dress she had never had for her first marriage.

"It were a thing of surpassing beauteous wonder," Beckham recalls. "Veil, trail, and the hull damned regale."

Next day, Thursday, the government wagon and span of fat mules recaptured from the guerrillas were driven into town. There, the vehicle was crammed to its top-stay sockets with supplies for the journey. The ranch was reached again late Friday. At this time the selected household belongings were stowed aboard, the most prominent item mama's old brass spindle double bed. All was then believed ready. Some concern was registered that no one from Red Hawk had arrived for the night. Mary McCalister thought their real friends would still show up, perhaps as a surprise next day.

Saturday dawned memorably bright, hot, clear.

The family's confidence rose with the sun. At least some of Red Hawk would be there, and for sure the reverend from the First Southern Baptist Church.

Nine A.M. wedding hour came and went. One guest arrived, the Siwash mute, Gabby. It was never established how the gargoyle-faced wanderer knew of the occasion. He simply appeared, pridefully hand-signing to Scipio that he bore a wedding present. It was the gift of himself as faithful Indian guide through the perils of Comancheria and Apacheland, ahead. Scipio advised

214

surrender. There was nothing that would drive off a faithful Indian guide, once he had smelled free food for the summer.

Nine thirty, and a second guest materialized from out the salt sage, northerly and moving fast: Mexican Jack. Jack had with him a poignant-special gift for the bride. It was the old McCalister ranch wagon drawn by its original rat-tailed team of Sam Houston and Sugarplum. The sentimental man of the *monte* had borrowed the rig from the Red Hawk Livery Barn in the dead of the just-past midnight. He was in fact still looking back when he drove into the Paint Creek ranchyard.

While Bubba hugged the old horses and they happily nuzzled and head-bumped the boy in return, Jack informed the nervous company there was a proviso; he and his celebrated flock of Mexican poultry went with the wagon. Trail boss Lonsford McCalister made instant strong hint that the hot place would scum over with rim ice before Mexican Jack rode their train to California. But Bubba turned indignant. After all, he owed his own start in the chicken business to good old Jack. What was more, since when wasn't a perfectly honest, hardworking Mezzicun horse thief to be given the same shake as a lazy-tail Siwash redskin guide? Cornered square, Lon threw in; Jack could go. The wedding awaited only the invited guests and the hired preacher from Red Hawk.

The guests came in a bunch at ten o'clock.

They came in a bunch because they consisted of the full load of regular stage fares on the morning run for New Mexico. His passengers were some agitated, Monk Beckham was to report, but what could a man do? The townsfolk had voted to snub the wedding entire, and the damned bluenose preacher had hid out on him. Monk had had to leave the Overland Road and drive the coach the nine miles up through the blind brush to Paint Creek ranch so that it could never be spread about that nobody came to the wedding of Miz Sunny Jim McCalister and the Sheriff, by God, of Pioche County, Texas.

Still there was no preacher.

Again according to the irascible eyewitness Monk Beckham, this put a crimp in the affair only until the sassypants girl (Charlotte May) remembered how well the big niggerman had read over Jim Junior. "So the Book was once more brung forward and old Skip found some wedding-part words in it that sounded like the proper ones, and proceeded to reel them off serious and certain as if he had on a round collar and took pay for it, regular.

"When he come to the end, Miz Mary and old Charley Skiles they said their lawsome I do's and it were a knot tied good as any."

The echo of Monk's sentiment and the last farewell to Paint Creek ranch is found in the letters of Mary McCalister. It is in an early note dated Mesquite Wells, the first night out. In its way, like Scipio's wedding-part words, it tied as good a knot as any to the Paint Creek days and to their particular hero, Randolph Barnes McCalister.

Wrote Mary Starr McCalister:

*When the service was done, Mr. Skiles thought to pay the stage driver for his help. Mr. Beckham took insult at the proffer. He ordered his stage fares aboard and wheeled that old Abbott & Downing off through the screwbean mesquite and away over the buffler grass, mad as a spit-on sowbug.*

*As long as we could put ear to what he said, he was calling on the Lord to witness against us. It remains in doubt that the Lord heard his case favorable. I never before in my life knowed they was so many cusswords in the West Texas language.*

*Well, pretty quick after that we was set to leave ourownselfs. Brother Lon had our two wagons in line and the teams hooked up. Bubba was taking a last look at the ties on his chicken crate, the one that heldt his rooster and three hens, and that Cap Marston carpentered up for him so long ago in Red Hawk.*

*Of a suddent, one of the three hens got loose and run off on him. It was the one called One-Eyed Juarez Sally. Bubba had to shag her down and snare her with his hat, all the while cussing her to make you cover*

216

your ears. It was when the boy went to pull the dumb thing out of the hat to squeeze her back into the crate that it happent. She just up and squinchered, squat-down, give a brawky cakkel, and done it right there in his hat.

Old Bubba he peered into that hat fearing he knowed the worst again. But he was utter wrong this time.

His eyes saucered up big as barn owls and he commenced yelping like a runover sheepdog, only joyful, and went on the full-out gallop over to where his sister was at, aholding out the hat for her to see the treasure that was in it.

"Gawd Amighty, Charlotte May," he cried the final triumph. "She's did it at last!"

And sure enough she had.

There was an egg in Bubba's hat.

WILL HENRY was born and grew up in Missouri. Upon leaving school, he traveled and worked throughout the Western states, acquiring the personal experiences reflected later in the realism of his books. Currently living in California, he writes for motion pictures and continues his research into frontier lore and legend, which is the basis of his unique blend of history and fiction. Several of his novels have won top awards, including the Wrangler Trophy of the National Cowboy Hall of Fame, the first Levi Strauss Golden Saddleman, and five Western Writers of America Spurs. Mr. Henry is a recognized authority on America's frontier past.